DECODING **DOT** GREY

NICOLA DAVISON

NIMBUS
PUBLISHING
— NIMBUS.CA —

RECYCLED
Paper made from
recycled material
FSC® C021322

Nimbus Publishing Limited
3660 Strawberry Hill St, Halifax, NS, B3K 5A9
(902) 455-4286 nimbus.ca

Printed and bound in Canada

Editor: Penelope Jackson
Editor for the press: Whitney Moran
Cover design: Jenn Embree

NB1572

This story is a work of fiction. Names characters, incidents, and places, including organizations and institutions, are used fictitiously.

Library and Archives Canada Cataloguing in Publication

Title: Decoding Dot Grey / Nicola Davison.
Names: Davison, Nicola, 1970- author.
Identifiers: Canadiana (print) 20210377968 | Canadiana (ebook) 20210377976 |
    ISBN 9781774710562 (softcover) | ISBN 9781774710579 (EPUB)
Classification: LCC PS8607.A9575 D43 2022 | DDC jC813/.6—dc23

Nimbus Publishing acknowledges the financial support for its publishing activities from the Government of Canada, the Canada Council for the Arts, and from the Province of Nova Scotia. We are pleased to work in partnership with the Province of Nova Scotia to develop and promote our creative industries for the benefit of all Nova Scotians.

ADVANCE PRAISE FOR *DECODING DOT GREY*

"*Decoding Dot Grey*, Nicola Davison's deft portrayal of a young woman juggling the joys, sorrows, and messy complications of new adulthood, hits all the right notes. With a cast of charming, memorable characters, and a vividly realized menagerie of rescue animals, *Decoding Dot Grey* strikes a confident balance between humour and heartfelt sentiment, but it's Dot herself, a true original—whip-smart, wryly observant, and deeply compassionate—who will stay with you long after you've turned the last page."
–**Tom Ryan**, award-winning author of *Keep This To Yourself* and *I Hope You're Listening*

"While Dot Grey is one of the most unique and compelling characters readers will come across, in her, author Nicola Davison has crafted a truly relatable protagonist. An engaging and emotional story built around Dot's relationships with family, friends, and animals—Toby the crow will steal your heart!"
–**Lisa Harrington**, author of *The Goodbye Girls* and *The Big Dig*

PRAISE FOR *IN THE WAKE*

Winner, 2019 Margaret and John Savage First Book Award (Fiction)
Winner, Miramichi Reader's Very Best Book Award for Fiction
Finalist, 2019 Dartmouth Book Award

"*In the Wake* is a subtle, heartfelt meditation on intimacy and the many ways we can lose those we love. Behind the seemingly tranquil backdrop of quotidian, seaside lives, a storm is building. As the novel moves towards its dramatic conclusion, Davison sensitively explores how grief and mental illness reverberate through families and across generations."
–**Sarah Faber**, award-winning author of *All is Beauty Now*

"Memory's siren pull is as comforting and treacherous as the ocean in Nicola Davison's gorgeous debut novel. With striking acuity, *In the Wake* reveals how people's deepest desires are charged with danger, the bonds between those who love the most often fraught with self-deception. Nothing is ever quite as it appears to Davison's mothers of sons, who cling to their own visions of the past and present in this beautiful rendering of nouveau Nova Scotia."
–**Carol Bruneau**, award-winning author of *Brighten the Corner Where You Are* and *A Circle on the Surface*

"*In the Wake* gathers like a storm wave, throwing the characters forward. Nicola's writing is a lighthouse catching moments of sorrow and joy. Here, mental health is not a hashtag, but broken glass under wounded feet. This novel can deepen you."
–**Jon Tattrie**, award-winning author of seven books, including the novels *Black Snow* and *Limerence*

"*In the Wake* is a novel that contains a mild, but ever-present strain of suspense and an undertone of distrust amongst its protagonists, which makes for the type of novel that keeps you reading until the final page."
–*The Miramichi Reader*

"Nicola Davison nicely matches the quotidian of chores and outings and errands with slowly breaching crisis.... The rapidly changing point-of-view...allow[s] for steadily building tension within and around scenes. Their voices chime off against each other nicely, and build to a crescendo of Atlantic storm."
–*The Telegram* (**Newfoundland**)

For Jen & Frank Eppell
and all the dogs, cats, birds, rabbits, and horses
who enriched my childhood.

ONE

September 1997

oⓒo

WHEN THE CAR HITS HIM, HE'S MID-LAUGH, WHIRLING THROUGH the air, chasing someone for the sport of it. I'm one vehicle behind, my heart hammering at the lack of brake lights. Downy feathers swirl upward as the car rolls on, the driver not even slowing to check what he hit.

People. Unaware of or indifferent to their trail of destruction. Just cruising by carcasses on the highway.

Jamming on my brakes, I put on my flashers and ignore the bleating horns. I grab a towel from the back seat. He's at the curb, trying to right himself, dark eyes mirroring the September sky.

I'll just get him out of the street to the nearby grass. He opens his beak, intent on biting me. But I have plenty of practice avoiding teeth and claws, so I swoop in, firmly snugging him to me.

No one is at the nearby playground with kids back in school. A good thing, as I can't stand the pushy questions of small people, their need to touch everything. I crouch under a massive maple and loosen the towel. Again he tries to get up, but he's lopsided, left wing hanging. Above, branches flutter, his cronies watch, cawing and rattling their throats like a riled biker gang.

He lifts his right wing and springs with his legs. I wince for him as he tumbles.

A chorus of angry caws as I descend on him a second time with the towel. No good deed goes unpunished.

"I know," I say, bundling him into the kennel in my back seat, "bloody cars. Same thing happened to my mum."

He's silent as we head for the shelter, spent from the pain and the discovery that he's grounded. My fingers tap the steering wheel, *SOS*, as we wait at a red light, but I'm not asking to be rescued. It just helps to quiet the storm. Something she taught me, a way to occupy the mind and the muscles, a way to reach out when words can't. Even though it does no good now—trying to reach her—my hands carry on.

THE SHELTER SQUATS BESIDE AN INDUSTRIAL PARK. A HOUSE THAT grew awkwardly into its new purpose, first one wing then the other, it's brick on the sides and wooden in the middle, like a hopeless airplane. Above the door are large wooden letters, *ARS*, for Animal Rescue Shelter, just one letter off from spelling *arse*, inspiring the occasional prank phone call from bored adolescents. The windows are too small on the sides and too big in the front. If I had my way, we'd block them off so people couldn't peer in at us when the "closed" sign is displayed, as it is right now. Three cars are in the parking lot, waiting for the sign to turn. People hover with sad stories. Trouble is, it's easier, faster, to say yes to them than no. It's how I ended up with four of my pets.

Rachel's car is out front, although judging from the floral steering wheel cover, I'd guess the car belongs to her mother. She doesn't have classes at the college on Tuesdays. Quickly, so as not to attract attention, I take out the crate and squeeze alongside the building. Within it, the crow staggers. I can feel his fear right through the plastic. He's never been without his blanket of sky.

At the back, three concrete steps lead to an ugly metal door. Rachel has it propped open, using a rubber boot filled with gravel.

I'm the doorstop inventor, having experienced being stuck on the wrong side of the door with a shivering dachshund. Inside, whines echo off the walls. *Who will she walk next?*

I put the cage down outside, hoping Rachel doesn't come charging out the door with a bouncing dog before I can explain. The crow reaches out through the bars with his beak.

The dog room has twelve kennels. Concrete everything, divided by chain link. The smell of urine underlines everything no matter what chemical you use. There's a drain in the floor so we can hose things down, because we need to, every day. It's not their fault. They have to wait through the night for us to come and take them out. Some are too young to know. Some are too old *not* to know. Either way, we have shit in the mornings.

Rachel is dealing with a particularly liquid case at the moment while Thor, a goofy pit bull, tugs at the back of her lab coat. She's hosing down a wall, directing the worst of it toward the floor drain. It's best to move the resident dog to an empty kennel or tie them to the metal ring near the door while we clean, instead of how Rachel is doing it, half-arsed, chewing a large wad of gum.

Now that I'm on my own, gum is not on the grocery list. I won't spend money on something you chew but don't eat. Also, I keep my mouth closed—an underrated skill—and wash my face after the kennel cleanings are done, glasses too. Just as I have that thought, a stream of water dislodges a chunk of poo, ricocheting off the wall and spraying Rachel square in the face.

"Dot," she says, spitting the gum on the floor. Maybe she hopes I'll take over, like last week.

"Sorry, I have an emergency." I step into a shallow tray of bleach and water, then onto a damp towel, meant to keep us from tracking germs between rooms. "Don't let the dogs near the crate out there."

In the centre of what was the original house is a line of washing machines that only stop when we reload. Not the commercial variety, but donated by people who no longer want this shade of beige in their home. I turn them off before going out to get the crow. The last thing he needs is clanging machines to greet him. The bleachy air is bad enough.

Before heading out, I exchange my jacket and shoes for a lab coat and rubber boots. Our shelter garb; it's easily shed if we get splattered or smeared. It covers most of my clothes, but I always leave my hat on. Crocheted by Mum a few years ago, it keeps my hair from flying everywhere. Even though I lash it into a braid, the feathery bits claw at my face if left unrestrained. I'm not sure how I lived without the hat. Warmth, shade, camouflage. With my glasses—"Havana" tortoiseshell frames (no tortoise was hurt in the production of them, I checked)—I'm unrecognizable from my younger self. People don't comment on my chalky skin or the shape of my nose. And no one says, *Aren't you the girl from that commercial?*

My father, the self-proclaimed Sleep King of Atlantic Canada. When the kids put together that I was the daughter of Mattrust TM, the bullying got worse. I was already a target with my motor tics, disrupting reading time by tapping the words out. They called me rusty, they treated me like a mat, made up insipid rhymes. If only Dad had given it some thought before registering the name. Even now, he'll argue it with anyone who'll listen, "It's meant to be mattress trust, Mattrust. Get it? Trust in one's mattress?" If only I'd been around to consult. But I was still waiting in the fallopian tube. A bona fide dot. Many a night I've drifted off to sleep thinking of better company names. Alliteration would have been a good choice. Even its previous name, The Mattress Store, would have been fine.

If it weren't for the commercials, my royal lineage might have remained a secret. In one of them, I was coerced into starring as The Sleeping Girl; my only acting role. *Who sleeps with their glasses on?* The kids laughed, holding me down at the top of the slide, where the teachers couldn't see. I'd just gotten glasses, and Dad argued that I couldn't see without them. Anyway, kids don't like it when you're a small-time star. Try to stand out and you get stuffed into a garbage can, alongside banana peels and egg salad sandwiches. Then they harass you for the way you smell.

Every commercial began with Dad lying on his side, a close-up of his face, sagging a bit on the pillow. "How did you sleep last night?" Then he'd have a wonderful nugget of information about what a lack of sleep will do to a person. The kids liked to imitate his English accent, badly, finishing off with the Queen's wave before abandoning me, hair knotted to the monkey bars. The camera would pan out to a showroom filled with high-quality mattresses at an affordable price. Layaway available! Pun fully intended. Right in the middle of them all, Dad on his back, arms behind his head. It would end with me, eyes closed (very convincingly) underneath my purple-framed spectacles.

Now, with the tops of my glasses hidden by my hat, people say *nice hat* or *nice glasses*. It's the art of disguise. Watch any spy film and you'll see how a hat can transform a person. No one says, *Hey, it's the Shortsighted Sleeping Girl!*

A bedspread droops from the shelter's clothesline, featuring the Spice Girls aggressively smiling out from stitched polyester. Posh has been shredded by teeth, but the rest of the group is intact. It's an appropriate flag for us. I pick up the cage and head back in before Rachel can come out with one of the dogs.

The kitchen was *renovated.* In other words, the stove was yanked out and the remaining hole plugged with a grooming table, enabling us to have coffee while we search for fleas on small dogs and/or cats. Placing the crow's crate on the table, I peek inside. He's in a broad stance, like a sailor on a bucking ship. I apologize to him for the bumpy ride before going in to grab the first-aid book, a massive tome that falls open with a satisfying thump. I've read it many times while gulping lunch. I've even taken it home once or twice. Most of the cat and dog chapters are committed to memory. I can close my eyes and see full sections, the ladder of vertebrae and nerves, illustrated and annotated, how to perform CPR on a dog and bottle-feed puppies.

The bird section is less familiar. I know I need to bandage the wing. Scanning the diagram, I find the bones: humerus, ulna, radius, digit. I'll have to feel along them to figure out what's broken. First, I gather the supplies and cut them all to size.

"What the—?" says Rachel, closing the kitchen door behind her.

"Bloody car." I cut the last piece of tape and stick it to the edge of the table. "Right in front of me."

"Shouldn't you wait for the vet?"

"She's in tomorrow. Hold the bandage for me?"

"We're supposed to open..." She trails off as I reach into the crate. Wrapping my hands around his wings to keep him from flapping, I pull him toward me carefully, hoping he won't sense my worry.

I gather up the good wing in the palm of my hand and cup his feet in my fingers.

"Seems calm," Rachel says as I feel along the wing. Nothing is noticeably broken, but there's a wound.

We work quietly, talking in low voices, different from the ones we use for cats and dogs. He follows our movements with his beak but doesn't try to peck either of us. I do an X wrap, binding the wing firmly against his body.

"Not bad," says Rachel, exhaling. "I've never done this."

"Me either."

"Seriously?"

"Not on a bird." I tuck him back in the crate. I'd helped with a kitten's leg a few months back, and there was that Lab with a broken tail.

"I thought you'd, like, worked at the vet's or something."

"Just here." Most of the time, Judy guided me, having worked at the emergency vet clinic before. She'd coached me through proper restraining for procedures.

"When did you start here?"

"When I was twelve. So, six years now, I guess."

Rachel has been here a few months. At first, I thought she was a goth, with her pale skin and black hair, but when she told me she was in her first year of Fine Arts it all slid into place. Black everything. Studying us like we're part of a project to be brought to life in oil or acrylic. Mum did the same thing.

From the front comes an insistent knocking. We lock eyes. None of us enjoys the front desk. If possible, we'd all work with the animals, not answering a phone or speaking to the public ever again.

"It was me yesterday," I say.

Defeated, she removes her splattered lab coat and grabs a fresh one.

"So, can you go downtown yet?" Downtown, meaning out drinking. That's where most of the pubs and bars are, within stumbling distance of the universities.

"Nope." I know she's nineteen. Judy had me file the job applications.

"That's too bad."

She leaves the door open behind her and flips on the lights. A man in a trucker hat stands on the other side of the glass, arms crossed. I don't wait to find out his story but slip past Rachel with the crow.

Beyond the room that houses cats and smaller creatures, there's an office and a meeting room where we eat lunch. The table is littered with donations. People clear out basements and attics then plonk it all at our door in garbage bags, even if it's raining. *Beggars can't be choosers.* Some things come in handy. Luckily, an oversized birdcage has been sitting in the corner for months. Digging through a box, I unearth a perch and a set of bowls.

There's a short-lived scuffle as I transfer him. It could be a positive sign that he's feeling feisty. Once inside, he pulls himself up and turns away. I'm used to that. He's not regretting that dive in front of the car, but I'm the one who strapped his wing and locked him up.

I tap three times on the table. He tilts his head, so I repeat it. He blinks twice.

"I'll get you a snack in a bit."

They say I was born tapping. Mum could feel it in the womb, knocking against her rib cage. As a baby, I'd rap my tray, commenting on the cuisine. I knew how to ask for more. More milk. More banana. More applesauce. More Mum. I didn't talk for ages, but I could blink messages to her. Or so the story goes.

Judy finds me in the cat room before lunch. When I started at the shelter, Judy wasn't the manager. It was a woman named Birdie, who looked nothing like a bird. I never did get if it was her real name or a nickname. Anyway, according to Judy, she didn't run a tight ship. Birdie always smelled skunky. It must have been how she coped. One morning she was gone—mental health leave, I was told in a whisper—and never returned. Judy marched in, white lab coat, scarlet lipstick, tall rubber boots and took stock of us. What was a then-thirteen-year-old-girl doing in the back, unsupervised? We've come a long way, me and Judy. I now make sure there are no unsupervised thirteen-year-olds in the back.

She has two addictions: caffeine and rabbits. Don't get her started on people buying bunnies at Easter. Her bronze hair is, as always, in pigtails. She likes to drape them over her shoulders like a pair of silky ears. It might be a tad youthful a hairstyle for her, but I like it. It makes me think of the tune, *Do your ears hang low, do they wobble to and fro*...She frowns at me. Was I humming it?

"I suppose," she says, standing back far enough that she doesn't get a nose full of cat litter dust, "that you didn't hear him from back here?"

"Who?"

"The crow. I couldn't hear a damn thing on the phone."

"Sorry."

"So, I went in there to reason with him." *Reasoning* is Judy's term for her low growl that, she says, communicates across species.

"And do you know what he'd done? Opened his cage door—don't ask how—and ransacked my lunch."

"Sorry."

"How many times have I told you that this is not a wildlife shelter? We have enough animals as it is." She gestures around the room at the sullen cats. "Although, I'm kind of impressed. Crafty bugger. Anyway, you're doing a lunch run." She pulls a five from her pocket. "Turkey soup in the bread bowl? Not the lima bean." She makes a face. "No soup for you." She waits for me to laugh. I don't. "*Seinfeld*? Right. You don't have a TV."

I shrug. I'm aware of *Friends, Seinfeld, Frasier*...We had cable at home. But I don't have a TV or a phone and in my car it's just AM radio. Pop culture is a language I don't speak.

Fetching lunch gives me a chance to get outside. I pass Rachel on the front step sneaking a smoke. She blows a circle in my direction and tips the filter my way.

"No thanks."

"You don't approve?" She raises an eyebrow.

I shrug. I just don't like to burn the small amount of money I make. "Want anything from the cafe?"

"No money," she says.

Rusty—my nicknamesake and ticket to freedom—gives a puff of blue smoke when I start the engine. Every time I put gas in the tank, I add oil. They disappear at equal rates. Dad taught me to check the oil at every fill-up. All of his cars have been second-, possibly third-hand. He doesn't appreciate depreciation—*bloody waste of money*—which is what a car does the moment you drive it off the lot.

As if he knows I'm thinking of him, my pager buzzes. He's sent another code that I have to look up. After parking at the cafe, I pull the sheet from my bag. Knowing my affinity for Morse, he thought I'd enjoy beeper codes, so he printed me off a page. Most of them are saucy dating shorthand, including *I want your sex, Hello Baby, Boobless* and *Get in line*. He tried to blot those out with a thick black marker, but if you hold it up to the light, it's all there.

Nineteen means *hug*. I wince and shove both back in my bag.

When I get back, there's a young couple at the front. She holds a braided leather leash with a brass clip, clicking the latch like it's the switch for speeding up time. They watch me, bumping my way in with a tray of drinks, paper bag rammed under one arm, keys between my teeth. *No, really, I'm fine, no need to hold the door.*

"Here he comes," says the man. Nails click the floor as Rachel approaches with the beagle straining at his collar, tail beating the walls.

The woman covers her mouth to keep a lid on her joy. It muffles the dog's new name, which could be anything from Esther to Buster. Both drop to their knees and do everything wrong, according to the trainer. Hugs and squeals. Today the beagle is a rock star. Rachel hovers, sheaf of papers in hand, ready to tell them about boosting vaccines and neutering as I hobble through to the boardroom. I'd stick to reminding them to keep him on leash. Hounds are scent junkies. What can they do but follow their noses until they don't remember where they live? If they're lucky, someone finds them before a pack of coyotes or a distracted driver. Sometimes they come right back here.

We eat in the boardroom with the crow gurgling at us.

"Dot, this is no place for a wild bird," Judy says between slurps. She says it's too loud for him or he's too loud for it, switching the argument around just enough to confuse me. "You've got enough on your plate," she says, not meaning the one I have in front of me, empty but for a few bagel crumbs.

She wipes her hands and heads into her office, returning with something for me. "Call her." She slides a business card across the table, one of those floppy ones that someone did on a home printer, edges perforated where it was ripped from the page. How committed are you to your cause when you print off ten cards at a time? It reads *Wings of the Wild, freelance rescuer, donations welcome*. Does she mean to donate wings or money?

There's no answer and no machine when I call the rehab place, which seems dodgy. A machine with an outgoing message—how hard can that be? Freelancers.

Surely, the crow can stay a night and meet Dr. Trainer tomorrow. I sit next to him, doling out bits of Judy's complimentary soup crackers. Whenever there's a pause in food delivery he sidles closer and knocks the bars with his beak. I could be mistaken, but I think he's tapping six. So, I wait. He blinks and repeats. Six means *I'm ready*. I tap back, using the same cadence. He watches my fingers on the table then repeats. Charmed, I hand him a larger piece.

Judy figures he detached his perch and used it as a tool to open the latch on the cage. After that, he must have worked out how to undo the zipper on her bag.

"Tobermory, from the Wombles, that's you," I tell him. "Toby, for short."

When I was eleven we visited my grandparents in England. Their house resembled ours if it had been shrunk in the wash. I was allowed to watch the BBC. The Wombles are little creatures living under Wimbledon stadium, scavenging from humans,

making good use of bad rubbish. After that visit, my grandparents
sent us Womble things in the mail at every holiday.

"Tobermory is the handy one," I tell him, "like you. Not that
you have hands—"

Rachel walks in and gives me one of those gotcha smiles, as
if she doesn't talk to the cats when she thinks I'm not listening. I
clear my throat and stand to brush crumbs from my lap.

"I'm calling him Toby."

"Nice." She digs in her bag and pulls out a plastic container.
"Can you watch the front while I eat? Judy's on the phone."

Someone has to be near the front to guide people when they
come in, like a grumpy flight attendant. *You'll find the dogs ready for
adoption to your right, cats to your left, please wash your hands over
here...*Also, it's a good idea to make sure they don't do something
rash, like try to set everyone free or leave kennels unlatched so
that cats can wander about, taunting their neighbours, or make a
break for the parking lot. Almost anything is possible with people.
You have to keep an eye on them from a safe distance.

Really, I can see everything from the boardroom window, but
that would mean talking to Rachel, so I head for the kitchen and
update the whiteboard with today's tasks.

Judy comes in with her crumpled napkin, tossing it in the
garbage can from halfway across the room, missing. I pick it up
and pop it in for her without comment. The shelter is not staffed
with people who would succeed at team sports. She tells me we
can move Thor, the goofy pit bull, up front later. He's ready for
adoption. She reaches for the clipboard and flips to his record. "You
want help with vaccinating him?"

"Maybe with the Bordetella." You have to spray it up their nostrils, and if you're not quick about it, it can end up in your own nose.
She nods, opening the fridge where we keep tiny bottles of vaccines
lined up like soldiers. "You left your dad on hold the other day."

She'd picked up the phone to dial out and the line was occupied by a man humming "Hey Jude" by the Beatles.

"That must have been unsettling." Her name being Judy. Also, I've experienced his musical attempts.

"Actually, we had a good chat."

Because I started here so young, my parents kept tabs on me, calling, dropping in. Less and less over the years, but still a little more familiar than I'd like. After all, I'm now a full-time employee. I have my own place and a car.

"He worries about you."

Mortifying. I hope he didn't cry.

"I'm fine."

"Right." Her eyes flit away. "Anyway, you can call him. Use the phone in my office, shut the door if you want privacy." Like Dad, Judy doesn't like my lack of phone.

"Thanks, maybe after. I'm on the front desk."

"Right, well the offer stands."

But someone comes through the front door at that moment. A wild haired woman with a hopeful smile, in search of a cat to complete her life. So, naturally, I'm too busy to think of calls.

AT THE END OF THE DAY RACHEL FINDS ME DRAPING A SHEET OVER Toby's cage. She takes the other side, helps me tuck it under so that it won't fall off or be pulled into the cage by a bored bird.

"So," she says, "what do you do for fun?"

"Fun?"

"Yeah, like when you're not working."

"I don't know." I grab my coat and slip into it. "Read. Relax."

"Read books?"

I consider what else I might read. Magazines? Sales flyers?

"Books, yes. Novels. Stuff about dogs, cats, birds." I gesture at the cage.

She squints at me. Fun, I am not. At school when others went outside to gossip and smoke, I'd find somewhere to read or finish my homework. It freed up time to spend at the shelter.

"Cool. You do have a certain librarian vibe."

It might be a compliment. I dig through my bag for my keys, wondering what she wants.

"You heading out?" She's eyeing the car keys.

"Yes, and I have to lock up behind us. Judy's gone..." Part-timers can't lock up.

"Shit, right. Hang on. I need to call Ted. He's supposed to pick me up."

I plop down on a chair and listen to her side of the conversation filtering in from the office. Apparently, he won't be here for a bit. He forgot. She'll have to wait. I pretend to know none of this when she returns.

"Don't suppose you want to hang out?" she says. "Get a beer?"

"Can't," I say, thankful I'm too young for *downtown*.

"Right. Well, don't worry about me, I can wait outside. It's warm enough."

"You sure?"

She shrugs. So, I drive away, leaving her slumped against the outside wall, smoke jetting from her nostrils.

TWO

TWELVE DOGS BARKING IN A CONCRETE ROOM AT SEVEN IN THE morning. Jack, a Lab mix, wags furiously as I unlatch his door. Overnight he's chewed his blanket to bits. It's just scraps now, useless for comfort. None of the dogs wear collars—shelter policy; we use a slip-on leash, one-size-fits-all. Sometimes, I have to sit with the shy ones and remind them that I'm not their previous owner before slipping the noose over their heads. Jack pushes his nose through the loop and drags me to the door.

I spot Earl's truck pulling in just as I'm finishing Jack's walk—a quick circuit of a sickly patch of grass, crunchy from its regular soaking of urine. Earl's early. Officially, he starts at eight. After volunteering for years as a cat-napper, he became an employee last year. A little top-up for the pension. On weekends he still comes in, scoops up a needy cat, and falls asleep in the rocking chair in the back. Every one of his sweaters is plucked to a fuzzy mass across the chest.

"Dot, you're bright and early," he says, pouring a mug of coffee.

"I don't know about bright."

"Nobody left on the step this morning?"

I shake my head and look for my cup on the shelf. Desperation must make people do it; leave a dog tied to the handrail, or a sealed cardboard box of kittens, or a carrier containing an ancient cat panting inside. Sometimes there's a note. Our security video is grainy. I get to see them pulling up. They feign casualness, or they look everywhere like there might be a sniper on the nearby roofs (not a bad idea), and then they do it. Some dogs howl as the car drives off. One dog cried himself hoarse then never barked again.

"Thank God." Earl pulls a carton of coffee cream from a plastic bag. If it wasn't for him, we'd all be drinking black coffee (and only until the beans ran out). "Enough grief on a Wednesday."

It's euthanasia day. A devious word, so soft, like a fond memory; *my youth in Asia*. Dr. Trainer comes in and we go through the list. If she doesn't bring her assistant, I do the restraining.

"You feel okay to help out?" Earl's eyelids droop at the bottom. His moustache hides his top lip so you can't see his smile unless he really cracks a grin.

"It's fine."

I don't know how ending a life can be on a list. But it is. So I do my best to make it peaceful. Earl sips his coffee and reviews the number of animals in each room. When he tosses the coin, I call heads but it's tails, so he'll carry on cleaning while I take the front desk.

"You ought to go in the boardroom and meet Toby."

Without a word, he shuffles off. I hear Toby's beak clanging the bars from here. When Earl returns, he's grinning.

"We're rescuing crows now?"

"Don't let Judy hear you say that." I fill him in on Toby's sandwich theft.

"Smart birds, crows."

People are waiting outside when I turn on the lights up front. They've already armed themselves against me, worked on their story.

The phone starts before I can unlock the doors. The first call is Dad. I put him on hold. The second and third are lost cats. I jot them down. Another person has a moose in their backyard. I give them the number for Natural Resources. The worst calls often start out with, *Got a quick question for ya.*

There's a woman with a cat carrier, her coat straining at the belly. As I open the door she turns sideways to come in.

"Oops. Keep forgetting I'm bigger that way," she says. "All of a sudden I'm a friggin' house." She puts the carrier down and winces, one hand bracing the midsection. "This here's Nippy. The doctor says I can't scoop out the tray cause of that thing pregnant people can't breathe...taxo-whatever—"

"Toxoplasmosis. What about—"

"And Mack says he ain't doin' it neither."

"I see."

"Plus he's shreddin' every fuckin' chair in the place."

I dig out the form and put her and Nippy on the end of the counter while I talk to the next one.

"Hello, miss." This one is a well-dressed man with a full head of white hair. "I'm sorry. I can see you've got your hands full, but I called and spoke to Julie."

"Judy."

"Excuse me. Judy. We did try a number of her suggestions, but we have to move next week and I fear this is our last resort. It's a terrible shame, but the new building won't allow pets—"

"You're moving into an apartment?"

"My wife, she's reached a stage...I have to move her to a facility where they won't allow pets."

The dog, a senior himself, sits at the man's side, shuddering whenever there's a bark from the dog room.

"I can give you a list of pet-friendly buildings—"

"We've already signed the papers. And no one can take Oliver." At the mention of his name, the dog stands. Perhaps it's time for them to go back outside on that walk?

The pregnant woman clears her throat and puts down the pen with a clack.

"Just a moment," I tell him, moving to her end of the counter. I scan the form to make sure all the boxes are checked and take Nippy's cat carrier into the back for Earl. When I return, she's heading out the door, sideways again, nary a backwards glance.

"Oliver." I crouch in front of him, putting my hand out for him to sniff. He glances up at the man before reaching to explore the scent of my sleeve.

"Surely he won't last long here," says the man. "I mean, someone will give him a good home?"

Oliver licks the back of my hand once, as if to signal that I'm adequate.

"We'll need you to fill out the paperwork," I hand him a pen and turn to Oliver. I lead him to the back in search of Earl, past the kitchen, past the laundry and to the edge of the cat room. Oliver hesitates, but the owner doesn't change his mind and call out.

DR. TRAINER ARRIVES TOTING A LARGE LEATHER BAG. THOUGH IT WEIGHS the same as a well-fed bulldog, she carries it like it's full of feathers.

"Grey Dot." She enjoys my name, uttering it like she's a James Bond villain.

"Dr. Sneaker," I say, straight-faced.

"What have we today?"

"Not much," says Judy, soundlessly appearing beside me. "But we do have a wild bird in the boardroom."

"In a cage," I say. "His name is Toby."

Judy shoots me a look. "Dot bandaged him, but I'm hoping you can take a look before he goes to the wildlife rescue."

His door is now secured with a small padlock. Someone has added a hanging toy. I suspect Earl.

"Well, look at you," says Dr. Trainer, tilting her head to mirror Toby. "Bright-eyed."

Judy unlocks the door and stands back. She's told me many times that she's better with fur than feathers. The vet gets him out of the cage with minimum fuss and I help her unwrap the bandage.

"I hate to do this," she says, unravelling the second layer. "Not a bad wrapping job, Dot." High praise indeed.

No one speaks as she examines the wing, extending it so she can feel along the hidden bones.

"Well, good news. It's minor, right here." She shows us. "I think what you've done is the best thing for it." She pokes her bag with her toe. "Let's give this wound a clean while we have it undone." She looks at me. "The right side has the gauze."

The bag's top opens wide so you can see everything easily. It's what I imagine James Herriot had, rushing into barns to save calves in the middle of the night. I dig inside, gathering everything.

"There's a blue bandage in there. Grab that too and we'll get him snugged up after."

Though my job was passable, the speed and precision of hers is something else. She places him back in the cage and digs something out of her pocket.

"You look good in blue," she tells him. Toby knocks six times, eyeing me. Dr. Trainer pushes something through the bars. "Apricot," she says. "Give him about six weeks and he might be okay to go."

"Okay."

"You did try Audrey?" says Judy, catching my eye. That was the name of the rehab person.

"No answer."

"She's away," says Dr. Trainer, glancing over at Judy, "a family thing. Someone else is watching her place. So they might not want to take in new cases right now." Then, to me, she says, "But all he needs is a quiet place to recover," and pops an apricot in her mouth.

BEFORE GETTING THE BIRD CAGE OUT OF THE CAR, I HAVE A GOOD look at the upstairs windows. The lights are on but the curtains are drawn, so I pull Toby out of the back seat and head into my abode. I flip the lights on and the crickets go silent. For the moment, I settle Toby on my only piece of furniture, the bed.

Magoo—that's not my landlord's real name, but if you met him you'd call him that too—said, *Absolutely no dogs* when he swung open the door to my underground home. I waited for him to continue, but he didn't mention gerbils, guinea pigs, hairless rats, reptiles, a fluctuating population of crickets, or, now that I think of it, injured crows. I don't think Magoo hears us. Even with his hearing aids, I have to speak up, almost shouting. Usually, I have to repeat myself before I can be sure he's understood. I suspect he leaves them out most of the time, turning up the TV to compensate. As a result, I've become familiar with the characters on *Coronation Street*. He must tape them so he can watch any time of day, the sad trumpet in the opening sequence working its way through the thin ceiling every half hour in the evening.

All eyes are on me as I shuffle the stacks of cages around to find a good spot for Toby. The cages form a condo complex. I make a gap just big enough for Toby and drape a towel over one side so he can't intimidate the rest of the brood.

After feeding everyone I let Toby explore the bathroom. I brush my teeth, staring at a concrete wall. Magoo said he'd put a mirror in when he showed me the place, but he must have forgotten. I've decided to embrace the lack of reflection. It's not like I have to see my face; I don't wear makeup. So now, with the exception of the mirrors I use for driving safely, I avoid them completely. Mum would have liked the idea. Had she thought of it, we'd have done it as one of our challenges, kind of like the month we ate all our meals blindfolded. Anything that required utensils was either tedious or dangerous, i.e., piping hot spaghetti.

Before Toby can fall into the toilet bowl, I carry him back to the cage. He watches as I slip out of my overalls and climb into bed with my T-shirt on.

"Night, everyone."

I push the button for my white noise CD. It muffles Magoo's multiple voyages to the bathroom and his wall shaking snores. Who knew you could buy a compact disc of traffic noise? Atlantic Canada's Sleep King did.

At home, my bedroom was closest to the highway. A four-lane road swooped past us at one hundred kilometres an hour. A highway is not all that different from the ocean's rumble and swish. In summer, I'd open my window a crack and try to identify the sounds as I drifted off to sleep. Tour bus. Logging truck. Diesel Jeep with tousle-haired driver heading to a beach.

Between our house and the road is a tall orange street light preceded by road signs cautioning drivers to slow down for the turn. Not everyone sees the signs, adjusting their heat knob or flicking doughnut crumbs from their lap. Some take the turn too fast and, voila, there's our house like a mirage in the peachy light. The lucky ones hit the shoulder and come to a stop in the scrubby vegetation on the slope below. On foggy nights Mum was often awake. If a car went off the road, she'd put on her boots and go out. Most could drive away, some couldn't.

I didn't wake up the night the Old English sheepdog came. It was a station wagon that hit a tree. The driver was embedded in the steering wheel, something I do my best not to visualize. The dog was trapped in the back, saved from being hurled out the windshield by one of those dividers. The driver must have adored his dog; impeccably groomed, not a tangle in his generous coat of fur, a cashmere blanket woven through the bars to cushion the edges.

Mum reached into the shattered front of the car and released the lock for the back gate, cutting her hand in the process.

Archie (according to the brass bone swinging from his leather collar) came home with her and was panting in the kitchen when I came down for breakfast. Dad was hunched over, bandaging Mum's hand at the kitchen table.

"Dot, we're not keeping him," he said, instead of good morning.

He didn't have to tell me. Mum's allergies were not news. Although, there was the briefest flutter of hope when I saw Archie. Maybe she'd secretly been cured—it happens—and chose a dramatic gesture to announce we could have the fluffiest of dogs.

Mum said she had to go out, but I should stay with him. Already her throat was closing and we didn't want another emergency on our hands. Later, Dad said she'd needed to be alone after what she saw. Either way, she could barely breathe when she looked at Archie.

That day I was allowed to stay home from school because he'd whine and leap around if I left the room. Someone came from a rescue group, one that only takes sheepdogs. She picked him up that evening. Archie would not be going to a concrete building with a drain in the floor, but a foster until he could find his *forever home*. He didn't want to leave; he put his paw on my chest when the woman clipped the leash to his collar. I think he was feeling my heart tap the same way I'd been feeling his.

"How did you know to do that?" she said, watching me massage his ears. I shrugged. She said something about reflexology and endorphins, words that I looked up later. "You're good with animals," she said and wiped at her eye.

The following weekend I started walking dogs at the shelter. A month after that I was part of the regular weekend crew, thanks to Birdie's lackadaisical hiring practises.

It was the street light that brought Archie, too briefly, into my life, and the street light that took Mum away. Dad asked her to leave it that night, picking up the phone to call 911. It was raining and they were just getting into bed. She went anyway, trudging along the shoulder of the road to reach them. A second car, the driver spotting the wreckage of the first, pulled over, slamming into her. She flew briefly, I remember that being said, not high and not far, but when she landed, it was on her head. We hoped she'd wake up eventually, but it didn't happen. It still hasn't. We carry on in the waking world without her now.

Traffic Trance plays on a loop until the morning alarm. I curl in the dark trying to unsee things by tapping the alphabet onto my wrist in Morse. But I'm still awake at Z.

THREE

ο◯ο

ONCE A MONTH, JUDY GOES OVER THE ORDERING WITH ME, figuring out where we are with supplies. We're hanging over a binder when Rachel comes in.

"Missed my first class," she says, shedding her coat. She's in her Art Student clothes; they look like rags but she's loathe to get them dirty—probably because they wouldn't survive a washing machine—so she heads for the bathroom. "Mum had to shake me awake, she thought I was, like, *comatose.*" She mimes a drooping face for us. When the bathroom door clicks, Judy pauses and looks hard at me.

"Does she know about your mother?"

I shake my head. I prefer not to talk about it.

"Okay, up to you." Rachel wasn't her first choice of employee, but Judy was low on applicants for midweek shifts. Most college students work evenings and weekends, going for jobs with tips.

On Friday afternoons, we're flooded with volunteers. The cat room has a circle of *cuddlers.* They drag chairs in and make high-pitched noises. Judy reminds me that it's good for them—the cats, not the humans—but it requires more work to monitor the people than the animals. There's always one escape.

"You're not a people person," Judy says, as if it's a revelation. I wouldn't classify any of us as *people* people. But it's true I always try to dodge any tasks involving the public.

"You should head home early today," Judy says, meaning at the end of my shift instead of after dark.

"The freezer people are coming," I say.

"I can do that, or Rachel." Rachel appears in my periphery, sagging.

The freezer is where the bodies go. We fill it up. I try not to watch as they're lifted out, rigid inside plastic bags.

"Up to you," says Judy and, in a quieter voice, "it would give you time to visit her, though."

She turns for the office, leaving me to wonder about her chat with Dad. Did he ask her to poke me about my lack of visits to Mum?

I fire up the kettle. For my break, I'll sit with Bodie, the skittish spaniel. If I had a little cottage away from everyone, I'd bring him home. I imagine us sitting on the porch, looking up at a canopy of trees. Rachel ruins this, leaning her back against the counter so I can't avoid eye contact.

"What are you up to this weekend?" she says.

I can hear Earl on the phone jotting down the details of a lost cat.

"Laundry."

"The whole weekend?"

"I have to visit my grandfather." I don't tell her he's a ten-minute drive from here, in a locked ward, and that I barely last an hour with him.

"You ought to come out with me and Ted sometime. He's got friends." She raises her eyebrows, waiting. I tap the counter, *n-o*. She stares at my fingers. "They're all film geeks, but Kevin's okay. I hate being the only girl. Anyway, after this place, you need to have some fun."

Why must fun always involve groups of people? Or any people? Even friends can be cruel.

The front door clangs open. It's a guy with shaggy brown hair and an oversized red beard. He looks too young for the beard, as if he's picked it up a costume shop. His plaid shirt is tucked into a pair of snug jeans.

Rachel brightens and elbows me in the ribs. I dunk my tea bag and make no comment.

Earl is still on the phone. He glances back at us, his eyes saying *would ya mind, kinda busy here...*I point to my mug to indicate that my break has only just begun. So, Rachel strides over to help, wearing a large smile.

IN THE DOG ROOM, BODIE IS THE ONLY ONE IN HIS KENNEL. A group of volunteers has taken the rest out for a walk. He sits behind his warning sign, tail sweeping the floor. Yesterday, a volunteer went to put him on a leash and he grabbed her arm. He didn't break the skin, but he's now off-limits to everyone but staff.

I take my tea inside and sit leaning against the wall. The best thing to do is let him make the first move. I just ignore him, feigning boredom, yawning until he shuffles forward and puts his chin on my leg. Bodie has only just closed his eyes when Rachel finds me, beckoning the bearded guy to follow her. He glances around like he's trespassing.

"This is Dot." As if I'm an exhibit that has been discussed.

"Hi," I say, not standing, unwilling to disturb Bodie.

Rachel gives me an intense smile and says she's assured him that I'm the one to talk to about signing up to be a volunteer.

A lengthy silence follows, except for the sound of dogs barking outside. Finally, he takes his cue, introducing himself as Joe. The tops of his cheeks flush like he's flustered by the pronunciation of his own name. I sense a fellow social outcast, so I try to smile when I ask what he'd like to do here, hoping he'll confess to a love of deep cleaning and talking to the public.

"Um, I don't know exactly, but I'm good with dogs." He crouches and waggles a finger through the bars, but he's chosen to demonstrate his gift with the wrong dog. Bodie doesn't budge, but he doesn't growl either. That's promising.

"How about cleaning?" I say. Behind him, Rachel gives me a thumbs up and retreats, doing a little dance in the footbath on her way out.

Cleaning? He loves it. Not his exact words. And he actually prefers the weekdays so that he can still take weekend shifts at a restaurant downtown.

"What a good boy," Joe says, his voice growing cartoonish in his attempt to befriend Bodie. For his efforts he gets a twitch of the tail; Bodie's hackles stiffen too, sending mixed messages.

"Don't take it personally." I point to the warning sign on the door. I fill Joe in on the job and he nods along, undeterred by the prospect of chiselling poop from walls. "If you go back up front, Rachel can give you the form to fill out." I point to the door he came through. "I'm just going to finish up my break."

"Oh, sorry." He closes his eyes and shakes his head like it's an Etch A Sketch with a bad drawing. I watch him go, shoulders around his ears. Bodie lifts his head, tail fluttering as if he might have changed his mind about Joe.

Twenty minutes later, Rachel finds me in the boardroom.

"That didn't take long." She sinks into a chair opposite me.

"What didn't?"

"Talking to Joe."

I look up from the application forms. Someone has to call the adoption references. If I do it just after lunch on weekdays I get mostly answering machines. That way, I just leave a detailed message and they can call back and ask for Judy if there are any concerns.

"Not much to say, until he starts." I flip to the next page. Finally, we have an applicant for Patches, a cat that's been here for three months.

"He got all tongue-tied when he saw you." Her tone is teasing. "You have a boyfriend?" I squeeze my eyes shut, but she's still there when I reopen them.

I should lie. This is the kind of things girls did to me in school, pretending like we were friends then mimicking my hands when they thought I wasn't looking.

"No, no boyfriend. And Joe was just shy."

The front door clangs. Earl has gone for the day, so the front desk is all by itself. She sighs as she leaves.

Sex never seems far from Rachel's mind. While we were folding bleached-out blankets, she told me all about the boyfriend unsolicited, and the thing she does with her toes. I'm not a prude, I'm just underwhelmed by it.

When I was fifteen, Mum signed me up for a week at art camp. It was a compromise. Dad thought I needed to experience a typical Canadian summer; i.e., canoes and eating amidst heavy clouds of mosquitoes. Mum insisted it be mentally stimulating.

Upon arrival, I begged them not to leave me, discreetly tapping *home* on Mum's arm. Bunk beds in a cabin with a bunch of strangers. The horror. They were sending me to prison.

The first night I got up to pee and discovered I was alone in the cabin. All the bunks were lump-less and snore-free. In the morning, my roomies were back, looking tired and itchy. *Tried to wake you but you were dead to the world.* I'd worn earplugs, missing the sound of the highway. They'd gone skinny dipping with the boys from the opposite side of camp after the counsellor did the check-in.

On night two, out of pure curiosity, I snuck out with them but stayed on shore. On night three, a boy sat next to me and offered a drink of warm beer. I gave it a swig.

"You don't swim?" said the owner of the beer.

"I do."

He crossed his legs and flipped back a strand of long hair. "I'm Hubert." It sounded soft, the way he said it, *hue bare*.

I handed the beer back. "Dot."

"Short for?"

"A bigger circle," I said, a Grey family quip.

He smiled, "Dorothy, right?"

"Oui." That was a mistake, because I do a pretty convincing French accent despite only knowing a few phrases. He rattled off several excited sentences in French, much faster than my teacher of *français* in school.

"It's okay," he said, "I speak excellent, good *anglais*."

Someone did a bellyflop from the dock. Hue Bare said he couldn't swim, even though he loved the water. But he wanted to hold on to his fear, to examine it with his work. He was the first person I'd met at the camp who actually wanted to make art. I told him about Mum's paintings, inspired by her one psychedelic experience when she saw the world revealed in code.

"Each one has a layered message hidden in Morse underneath."

"Cool." He breathed the word. "What are the messages?"

"Dunno, she hides them away as soon as the paint's dry."

On night four, he brought me my own beer and kissed me. His hair was longer than mine, it fell around my face like a shredded wool blanket. He pulled back and peered into my high-density, anti-scratch lenses.

"We don't have to do anything," he said.

Maybe that's why we did all the things we did, because it was non-mandatory. On night five, he brought his sleeping bag and unzipped it for us. We walked away from the lake and found a clearing on a rise of land where we drank his last beer. I told him I was a virgin. He told me he was not and that he would teach me all he knew. I neglected to mention my research.

All of it was in books, plus, I'd watched porn with Mum. Dad was irate, arriving home from work to find us on the couch with popcorn. "What mother rents a sex tape for her child?" But what if I watched it with the wrong people? Namely, anyone my own age.

"Most women are not turned on by this," she said, looking away from a man ejaculating onto a woman's face. "It's okay to say no. You have a right to pleasure."

Dad disagreed with her about my early sex education, but Mum was insistent. There was no stork that delivered babies and no fucking G-spot.

Hue Bare seemed scandalized.

"I thought you were a virgin." He was wide-eyed, but there was no denying he enjoyed what I did with my knuckle.

"I read."

He laid back and put an arm behind his head.

"But did you...?"

"No, I didn't." I was thinking about the noises women made in porn.

"Tomorrow, you will."

It was to be the last night. He asked me to make myself *smooth*. I barely had anything to shave at the time but decided it was worth it. A week later when the stubble rubbed against my underwear I thought otherwise.

He certainly tried. And it was a pleasant enough sensation, in the beginning. When it didn't yield the results he'd planned, he tried faster, harder, and from a different direction. Things were starting to get raw, so I faked it with the sounds I'd heard from the videos. He collapsed beside me, his knees by my face.

"My turn now, baby."

And then he wanted the stuff that all the porn guys wanted. But I was tired and wondering if it would be safe to rub After Bite on my genitals.

He didn't say goodbye to me the next day while parents loaded dirty laundry into trunks. He moved past me like I was a stranger.

"Look," says Rachel, marching back in. She puts a piece of paper in front of me and taps a line near the bottom of the page. "Joe asked for your shifts." I can barely read his chicken scratch. "See?"

"Right." I pull the page closer and read. He lived just over the bridge. No phone number. "Yes, that's because I told him we need more people during the week."

"Oh." She deflates. "Anyway, he starts Monday."

AT THE END OF THE DAY, JUDY FINDS ME PROPPED IN BODIE'S KENNEL.

"Didn't I tell you to leave early?"

I give him a treat and reach for his paw. "I'm not really here," I say. "And I made a promise to someone." I clip a nail before he pulls his foot away again.

"Ignoring reality doesn't change things, Dot." She frowns, scratching at the back of her neck.

"Still." I don't need to say the rest of it. I think of it as our ping-pong talk. She says it's futile, I say they deserve the best right up to the end, she says it's not all on me, I say it's my decision. Then she goes back to the futility of it all.

Crouching down to my eye level, she varies it. "It's draining you." I can tell by her face she doesn't just mean cuddling animals on death row. "Your dad is up front."

Shit.

"SPECK." HE COMES AT ME WITH HIS ARMS OUT EVEN THOUGH WE'RE at my workplace. "I've been worried."

The hugs are a recent development. Before the accident, Dad was the joker, the ruffler-of-hair, the tweaker-of-cheeks, but never the hugger. And when he did hug me, say on a birthday, he was all soft. Now his shoulders are sharp.

"I'm okay," I say, looking at Rachel's back at the front desk.

"Come with me tonight."

He pulls back, but clasps my shoulders, like when I was little and he wanted to make sure I was understanding. I manage to make eye contact. But I don't speak, I just shake my head.

"I won't force you." He releases my shoulders. "I just don't want you to regret this later." His arms hang, long and useless. Have they stretched? Maybe it's the fluorescents. Damn lights. I want to close the door between us and the front desk, but I feel stuck.

"Did you get my messages?"

I nod. Maybe he sees me glance behind him at Rachel and finally realizes he has brought this into my haven. "Okay, I'm heading out. But please just let me know you're okay. A quick 88 on the pager." Mum's code for *love and kisses*. Hugs and now this.

We stand, looking at each other, him with the broomstick arms and me all clenched up, fists in pockets.

"Oh, almost slipped my mind." He fishes a folded paper from his pocket. He's left the feeder strips from the dot matrix intact, knowing how I like to pull them off. "You've. Got. Mail," he says in his robot voice.

"You don't have to print them," I say, taking it from him. He has yet to embrace the idea of emails saving trees.

"Then you'd never see them." As if letters from my pen pals require a timely response. "It's from Yu Yan." She did an exchange at my school in grade eleven. We formed a book club of two.

"She's back in China?" I glance at the top paragraph.

"No, she's on the west coast, in her first year." So, he does read them.

The computer sits in the corner of the dining room gathering dust now that I'm not there. Mum hated the screech of it dialling up the internet, *metal nails on a cosmic chalkboard.* But, I caught her playing solitaire on it once.

Dad shuffles off. "Thanks," he says to Rachel because that's what we do. She glances up and says, "take care," then goes back to pretending she's been absorbed in updating the cat book.

Before heading out, I duck into the bathroom with my bag because I need to smuggle some toilet paper home. My keys are in the ignition, radio on, and I'm almost free when Rachel knocks on the driver's side window. Before I can roll it down she's climbed into my back seat uninvited, sitting on top of layers of crinkly things.

"I thought you were familiar," she says. "You were in those commercials. So your dad is the Sleep King. What does that make you?" *As if I haven't heard this one before.*

"Not a princess." It was only a matter of time, I suppose. Here we go with the teasing. God, I wish I'd been there for the whole branding thing. Think of your offspring, not just coil springs, I would have said.

Instead, Rachel tells me about her dad's business as a portrait photographer. He'd travel around to schools in the fall. Every time he got a new backdrop for the business, she'd be his model. So, when the strip of sample photos went out to the schools, there was a smiling Rachel in front of the standards—fake forest, bookshelves, smudgy pastels—to the trendy neon laser beams. The class photos weren't as bad as the sports ones. All the local teams got an annual flyer. He had her pose with a tennis racket, a baseball bat—neither of which she held correctly—and the most infamous of them all, the bowling balls. This didn't strike me as particularly problematic.

"It's that he had me hold two of them. At chest height. I don't know why. Maybe to show I was strong..."

After that, every boy from grade six upwards asked her to hold his heavy balls.

"So there, you might have seen me before too," she says. "Want to get something to eat?" I meet her eyes in the rear-view mirror.

"I'm a vegetarian."

"Me too!"

I can't think of any more excuses without being fully honest. Am I the only one who is happier with my own thoughts? But there's not much in the fridge at home.

We drive separately, even though it's just a few minutes away. I insist.

"I can't stay long," I say, looking at the menu.

"We could get it to go and take it back to your place."

"I'm okay to eat here."

So we take our tray to a table for two by the door. I get the seat that looks at the door, which allows me to avoid looking at her the whole time, but it means she has to choose between me and the green wall at my back.

Rachel talks about her high school job at the local Dairy Queen with her best friend. But she quit when her friend went off to school in Montreal. "And I figured if I was making minimum wage, I should work somewhere that I care about, you know?"

"Yeah."

"Plus, the smell of sizzling beef..." She shudders.

"Say no more. So you're in second year at college?"

"Actually, first. I had to do some upgrading. I failed English," she mumbles into a napkin. "Anyway, second time's a charm. What do you want to do?" She waves a forkful of tofu at me. "After this? Be a vet?"

"I don't know." Like her, I'd have to do some upgrading, and I hate that I'm supposed to know the answer to that question. "What kind of artist do you want to be?"

She finishes chewing a bite of food first, then lets out a long breath.

"The deal is, my parents will pay for first year as long as I live at home, then I have to figure out the rest. Dad wanted me to go get a business degree. Me!" She points at her tangled hair, like that's enough to disqualify her. "Anyway, I'm doing a series of charcoal drawings right now, my crit's coming up soon. But for my performance piece I'm weaving a nest using stuff I find on the waterfront. Like garbage that's washed up, you know?" All I can think of are plastic bottle caps and cigarette butts. I wonder how that could be coaxed into a nest.

"What's a performance piece?"

"It's like a mix of visual work and dramatic performance." She squints like she can see it on the wall.

"Okay, and the nest?"

"It's going to be huge." She stretches her arms out to show me, nearly whacking someone squeezing through the door. "It'll be hung somehow and I'll be, like, inside. It sounds weird when I say it out loud."

"No, it's...resourceful."

She smiles, an alfalfa sprout sprouting from the corner of her mouth.

"Earl says your mum's a painter."

"Mm-hmm." What else did Earl say?

"Cool. What's her work like?"

I close my eyes and think of the paintings lined up behind my woolly walls. Each one wrapped in thick brown paper. I can't look at them, but I know they're there.

"Hard to describe."

"Oil, acrylic?"

"Everything, I think. It's layered. Kind of impressionistic."

They're heavy with paint. The first coat is a message, but she'd paint over that with a wash of colour that represented the mood. The topmost layer is the subject, but it's a red herring.

The only thing that connects them are the circles subtly woven over the subjects and the surrounding landscape. She said the viewer doesn't get it unless they spend time looking at it from several angles. It should communicate with people on different levels. But she made me promise not to tell anyone. They had to make the discovery on their own. Of course, without knowing about the deeper meaning, the galleries just saw her as a scenic painter and were polite in their refusal.

"You don't want to talk about her," Rachel says, watching me pick at my front teeth. Earl must have spilled the beans about the car accident too. Otherwise, I doubt she'd be burning with questions. I don't want to talk *about* Mum, I want to talk *to* her and have her answer me.

"I want...to be useful."

This seems to satisfy her; she nods, chewing.

"I get that."

RACHEL FOLLOWS ME HOME, CLAIMING I'M NOT FAR FROM THE VIDEO store where the boyfriend works and she just wants to use my place to get changed. Upstairs is flickering with pale light. Magoo will be in his armchair with his TV dinner, or so I imagine. Rachel stays behind her wheel while I unlock the door, and I see my abode through the eyes of a stranger. How to stop her from coming in... Too late, she's tapping at the door. When she goes to take off her shoes I say no, maybe too sharply. She wobbles a bit and looks at the bare concrete floor.

"I haven't had a chance to vacuum." As if I own such a machine.

"It's okay." Her face softens. "Hey, Toby."

He answers, with six clangs.

Rachel doesn't take off her big black coat.

"What's with the blankets?" She's staring at my woolly walls.

"They do it in castles, hang tapestries on the stone walls." I saw it on a show called *Ancient Abodes* and thought it would suit my abode nicely. "It helps insulate things." There's nowhere to sit but my bed, so she perches on the edge as I make the formal introductions: Abbott and Costello (the gerbils), Waldo (the gecko), Bungo (the guinea pig), and Ori.

"You have a rat!" Apparently, she's a fan. She reaches out a finger to touch Ori's skin. "How long have you had him?"

"A year and a half?" Ori was rescued by Mum. The only one I got to keep.

"You know a rat's lifespan is—"

"Painfully short."

"I had one when I was little." She holds both hands out and I let her take him. "They tried to talk me into a hamster, but I wanted a rat." She holds him at eye level and lets him tickle her face. "Is that something crawling over there?"

In the shadows, a sowbug lumbers along as if it weighs a metric ton.

"It's okay." There are bugs that bug me and those that seem harmless. I've made my peace with these ones. I read somewhere they're related to lobsters. I hope Rachel's not a screamer. She says nothing but I notice she's scratching. A lot.

"You're lucky you found a lease that allows pets." Ori stands on his hind legs, requesting permission to scale her arm. Rachel's hair is loose around her neck, always a big draw. "Ted had to leave his cat with his parents."

I don't have a lease, but there's no need to go into that with Rachel. Those landlords wanted references and post-dated checks and more rent than I could afford. With Ori safely hidden by hair, I open Toby's cage door so he can hunt down the sowbug.

"Ted'll be off in ten minutes." Rachel looks at her watch.

Ted. I can't help but think of him as coated in squashed brown fur with button eyes. I'm hoping I don't have to meet him after her sharing the toe sex thing with me.

"Mind if I change in your bathroom?"

Toby insists on going in with her, pecking at the door before she can close it. I listen to her wrestle into pants and talk in what must be her bird voice while I tuck Ori under his blanklets.

From above comes the sound of pipes sloshing. Every day around this time, Magoo's meal remnants, mostly vegetables, end up in my bathtub. If anyone needs a dog, it's him. Usually, I wait for it to drain so that I can rinse it away.

She emerges in a cropped black sweater and jeans holding up an eye pencil like a question mark. Some people won't be seen without certain armour. For Rachel, it's the eyeliner. Judy is all about lipstick. Mum permed her hair; she thought it gave her height.

"What happened to your mirror?"

"There never was one. Rear-view mirror?" She nods and shrugs into her coat.

"There's stuff in your tub." She points at Toby, who's busily gobbling up the leftovers from the drain.

"Did you help him get in there?"

"No, he did it by himself." I'm impressed by his agility and resourcefulness, but Rachel looks a little queasy as she heads out.

Yawning, I lock the door behind her. I notice she's scratching as she walks to her car.

Can I get away without cleaning the terrarium tonight? Waldo belongs to a guy I intercepted in the shelter parking lot. He didn't really want to do it. That was clear by the tears splashing onto the glass. But no one in his life could be trusted to care for a lizard. No one.

With Waldo came his food supply, crickets. At first, it was kind of fun having the chirping at night, but then I realized I was hearing their swan song. It's one thing to euthanize an animal, but it's another to watch something be eaten alive. It's different with the sowbugs; they're wild. They've enjoyed their time roaming the depths of moist places. Only the risk-takers who decide to cross the vastness of my floor fall prey to the peckish crow. It's natural selection. After all, their main population is thriving somewhere beneath me.

My pager trills from the bowels of my bag.

Dad: *077*

On my bedside box is the page of codes he gave me: *077* is Sunday. Instantly, I'm heavier. It's a reminder to visit Grand. This way, I can't claim forgetfulness, unlike Grand, who lives in a terrifying blend of the present and World War Two.

It used to be me and Mum visiting on Sundays. She could jog his memory with names from her childhood while I hid behind a book in the corner. Every once in a while, he'd register my presence and ask what I was doing. If he remembered me, we'd play his favourite game, blinking Morse messages at me: *cookies* or *Smarties* or *toffee* (ill-advised with his dental situation). When I decoded it—and I always did—he'd tell me to go down to the shop and get us something. Then he'd bully Mum into handing over the cash.

Now, our games are rare. I'm a familiar stranger who may or may not be friendly. Each time, he shows me every framed photo on his windowsill as if it's our first meeting. It's hard to stay put, like I have crickets in my legs. Nevertheless, on Sundays I go, because 1) I said I would; 2) I know she'd want me to; and 3) there aren't many things I can do for her now.

FOUR

☙❦❧

O N SATURDAYS, DAD IS AT THE STORE, SO I GO TO THE FAMILY abode, do my laundry, and try not to look around. Her glasses are still in the bathroom, her robe on the hook. I've tried tucking it into her closet but it reappears in the exact pose: left arm inside out, pocket with a piece of limp tissue peeking over the top. *Nothing has changed, says the robe. She will return, re-robe, and bring life back to my 100% cotton world.*

Upstairs, it's dim. He's not opened the curtains, which makes the house seem like it's hiding something, like a pair of sunglasses covering swollen eyes. I want to go to each window and fling the drapes wide. They do that in movies, striding into the bedroom of the self-pitying person and saying, *Right then, enough of this,* and sunlight slices across the pale face on the pillow. But I've grown used to muted light and he's not here for me to make my grand gesture. And he would say it was *Dot calling the kettle black.* It wouldn't be the first time he's said that.

In the fridge is a brown paper bag with an oily stain. A stamp at the top reads, *The Voracious Vegetarian.* On the other side is scribbled, *You're welcome.* He thinks I don't cook. He's correct. I still resent the assumption.

Maybe Dad has noticed the contents of his fridge diminish whenever I do my laundry. It's probably stuff he doesn't eat anyway.

I try to picture him smothering a cracker with natural peanut butter, but even in my imagination he goes to the cupboard and returns with the sugar bowl to sprinkle a tablespoon on top.

In the bag are Monster Muffins, Serious Samosas, and Flawless Falafels. I find a pad of sticky notes and draw a face. I give her a hat, a pair of glasses, rosy cheeks, and some freckles, but no mouth. Everyone has a standard doodle; this is mine. I stick it in the newly vacated spot in the fridge, instead of a *Thanks, Dad.*

The carpet has a greyish hue. I don't think the vacuum has been out for a spin in many months. Would it hurt too much if I sucked up some of her dust? Then I think of Dad unlocking the front door, coming to a dead stop in front of the stairs at the sight of vacuum tracks. Maybe next time.

The washing machine has finished filling, so it's safe to get in the shower. At my abode, I'm never sure if one of Magoo's meals is going to bubble up the drain, so I shower here once a week. My daily sponge baths are more than adequate to keep the undercarriage tickety-boo. Dad's words. Anyway, it's not good to use too much soap; it dries things out.

Between the shower tiles, microbial life flourishes. Dad doesn't have the same cleaning standards as the hospital staff. Once, on my way back from the cafeteria, I tripped over my own feet. Before I could untangle myself, Pat—the daytime cleaner—scooped up my baked beans and ran a mop over the spot. Pat smiled a lot but never spoke. I liked Pat. We knew all the faces after a couple of months, the cleaners, the people who brought the food trays and, of course, the nurses.

This brings on an unwelcome image of Dad draped over the nurse. I was in the hallway when I spotted them. It was late. I counted my heartbeats. Thirty. Granted, it was going pretty fast, but it was long enough for them to pull apart from the embrace. They didn't. And who knows how long they'd been there before I caught sight of them in the sliver of window?

Near the main entrance, Information Arthur looked up from his paper and winked as I strode past, yanking my hat down over my eyebrows to make it known I was not open for chatting. I was almost out the big sliding doors when Dad caught up.

"Speck, stop. That wasn't…" He paused and nodded at Arthur. "What it looked like."

"What did it look like?"

Maybe my sarcastic tone is why he said what he said next. Maybe if I hadn't gone all teenager on him, he'd have held it back. He got closer, lowering his voice.

"We're not all like you."

"Like me?"

"I miss her."

"So do I!" I remember how his hands dangled and his face scrunched. Until then, he'd never pitted his grief against mine. But she's my mother. He had a life before her, I didn't.

"Of course, but it's not the same for you. I need to be touched." In our lives, the Before, he was the first to defend my borders, arguing on behalf of my personal space with the school, ready to invent allergies if necessary. If I chose not to take part in gymnastic formations, that was probably for the best; our clan wasn't known for athletic ability. If I didn't want to bring boys around the house and kiss them when no one was watching us, all the better. But now, it means I am deficient in some way.

"She's right there. Touch her," I said, pointing down the hall in case he wanted to do it right then.

"But she can't touch me."

"No, she can't." It's precisely what I'd been telling him. She's not there anymore, and she's not coming back no matter how many months we spend reading the paper to her, stroking her hand.

"I don't have a lot of choices."

"Yes, you do."

"What? Treat her like one of your discarded animals?"

He should have just slapped me. The idea I'd put her on the To Die list was beyond awful. All I'd suggested was that he not talk to her like that, like she'd answer back or laugh at the joke. It was a pantomime I couldn't watch anymore. I walked out, him calling after me. The next day I found my abode.

While the dryer whirls, I venture up to my old room and have a lie-down. Sleep was of *paramount importance* in the Grey household. Attempts to stifle yawns didn't go unnoticed. Protests caused him to point out that a lack of sleep makes one irritable. "Roger," Mum would say in a meaningful tone, "leave it."

When I got a good grade, he took credit, saying it was because I'd always had the proper amount of slumber. Don't get him started on the lack of sleep these days. *The things modern society could accomplish if people just went to bed at a decent time.* Behind him, Mum would wink.

Dad continues to plead for me to live at home. I've told him enough about my place for him to form an opinion. I've tried to make it sound appealing—a studio, a bachelor suite, a Hobbit hole.

"Even Wombles like to go overground, Dot."

He doesn't understand my need to be away, but he stopped short of preventing me from moving out. His conditions were that I have an electric kettle with an auto shut-off and a decent bed. The store delivered the bed. So, I have the industry's best pillow-top mattress with a set of high-thread-count Egyptian cotton sheets, and a pair of luxury pillows (one for side-sleeping, one for back) between my cardboard night tables. At home, my single bed remains in my room, *just in case* I want to stay the night. And yes, my bathrobe remains on a hook in the downstairs bathroom.

WHEN I GET TO THE VETERANS' WING, THEY TELL ME GRAND IS IN his room. There's no response to my knock, so I crack the door and call out a hello to his room. Inside, the curtains are drawn.

"Grand?"

His head rises from the pillow, and he pulls back the blanket, patting the bed beside him.

"It's Dot," I say.

In case it helps him place me, I knock out a greeting in Morse on the door.

"Come on, then," he says. "You can warm your feet on my bottom."

Backing out of the room, I head for the nurses' station and find a familiar face.

"Is he getting fresh again?" Eileen asks. "Come on." She marches ahead of me. "Don't take it personally, sweetheart. It happens." After a bold knock, she shoves the door open and hustles over to the curtains, "Mr. Murphy, your granddaughter is here to see you. You called her this morning." More precisely, he left a message on Dad's answering machine, which still features Mum's outgoing message and probably always will.

The room plunges into daytime and he yanks the sheet over his eyes like a vampire. Eileen leaves us at the same busy pace she arrived. I pull up the chair by the window and wait for him to pop his head back out.

"Dad said you wanted to talk about the shelter?"

His nose appears above the sheet and he lowers the shelf of his eyebrows to peer at me. There's some groaning as he achieves a sitting position. I watch his face go through a series of adjustments. Inside his head, I envision a time machine, clicking and whirring to find the correct decade, slotting me into this present.

"You'll need to freshen the stock for winter," he says, glancing at the window. In the distance, the trees are fading into yellow.

"Wash all the blankets and get some canned peaches. Oh, and some nice bars of chocolate, fruit and nut." He smiles at the thought, revealing tea-stained teeth.

I should have known it would be about the *bomb* shelter, the bane of Mum's childhood. When my parents sold Grand's house, it was a curiosity for the potential buyers, a submerged bus shored up with soil and weeds. I wonder if the new owners dug it up when they did the big renovation.

"You should write this down," he says, miming a pen in his hand.

The Cuban missile crisis happened during Mum's teens. Grand dragged her inside and locked the door.

"Make sure the bins are clean," he says, propping himself up a little higher in bed.

Oh, the dreaded bins, the garbage cans they used as their toilet. In the shelter there was no privacy from each other, Mum said, visually or otherwise. Eventually, she convinced him it was safe outside, the crisis had passed. But he preferred it, spending most of his time in the shelter, neglecting the house. It was kind of a relief for Mum. Even then, though kind, he had bouts of confusion. The shelter kept him occupied.

It's simpler to scribble down his fallout list than make the argument for reality. *Jugs of water, radiation pills, first aid kits.* The family resemblance isn't hard to see in the frizz of his hair and the shape of his nose. But it's the way he moves that really gets me; the simple arch of his eyebrow brings her back. It catches me in the throat when I see it.

"There," he says, sounding satisfied, "now, let's have some tea, Dawn." I don't correct him. "Then you can tell me all about your day at school. What *are* you wearing? You look like a farm boy." He squints at my denim overalls. They're perfect for the shelter, roomy with pockets for everything. It's not something she would've worn, though. At my age she'd started with the floaty skirts that became her uniform. I envy him his imagined visits with her, critiquing her choice of pants, looking forward to a cup of tea without realizing he's already had his last conversation with her. I envy it greatly. I hate it and I love it and I want to scream the truth at him, but it wouldn't do any good. His mind would erase it, and the nurses would jot the incident down in a folder somewhere. Instead, I go off in search of tea because it's something I know how to do.

FIVE

ΩΟΩ

WHEN I ARRIVE MONDAY, EARL'S TRUCK IS IN THE PARKING lot. It's a relief, because sitting on the step, instead of a cat, or a dog, or a cage, is the new guy, Joe.

Earl's seat is reclined. Even the sound of my soon-to-depart muffler hasn't woken him. It unnerves me, seeing him sleeping, but a knock on his door rouses him. One eye opens and he reaches to turn off the radio.

"Well, well. Always nice to wake up to a fresh face."

Flattery is his automatic setting. I am anything but fresh.

"How long have you been here?"

He strokes his moustache. "Can't really say." Reaching behind, he grabs an empty cup and his lunch bag. "Couldn't get back to sleep so I thought I might as well head over. The motor makes me drowsy. I'm getting more and more like an infant. Too bad I couldn't get someone to drive me around while I snore."

"Morning," mumbles Joe, standing and stretching his back.

Earl flinches and steps ahead of me. Apparently, they've not been acquainted. I make the introductions and Earl shifts his cup and bag to offer his hand to Joe while I unlock the door.

"Didn't see your car," says Earl, scanning the parking lot.

"Oh, I got a ride this morning." Joe's shivering a little. I wonder how long he's been sitting on the concrete step.

"Well, we're glad to have you."

Earl heads for the office while I flick on the lights in the kitchen. A few of the dogs begin to sing.

"There's a fridge for lunches," I say. "Our weekly schedule. Coffee machine and kettle are here. Rubber boots are in the store-room there..." Joe follows me as I illuminate the shelter, asking the occasional question.

Back in the kitchen, Earl is filling the coffee machine. He's not one to enjoy silence for long. "So, Joseph, what do you do?"

"Actually, it's just Joe." He glances at me as if I'm to back him up on this. "Right now, I'm waiting tables at a seafood place downtown. Just taking some time off from school until...I figure things out."

"I keep telling this one she needs to get back in school."

They look at me, expectant. So, I retreat to the cat room around the corner to, allegedly, survey the cages and see if anyone needs immediate attention. My grades fell off in the last year of high school as I was mostly at the hospital. Anyway, I'm doing what I want to do.

When I return to the kitchen Earl's eyes are twinkling.

"What?"

He gestures behind me with his chin. Joe is in the storeroom putting on a grey lab coat. On his feet are Judy's prized rubber boots. Despite her lack of height, she has remarkably large feet.

"What?" says Joe, straight-faced.

Judy brought in her gardening boots because she felt the place needed cheering up. Who knew they made such things in adult sizes? The illusion of a pair of slender ankles and feminine feet is startling. Whoever designed them loves pedicures. Each toe has a different colour with an embedded design. When they aren't filthy, you can see the sparkles too. On the right calf is a tattoo of a dog raising its leg. That was what made her decide to shell out the money.

"They fit perfectly." Joe says, squinting at the toes. They spell out *Piss Off* in sparkles so you can read them when facing the wearer of the boots.

"Alas," I say, "they belong to the boss."

I dig in behind the layers of dusty boots until I find the right size. Mine are black with white polka dots, a high school graduation present from the shelter. *Dots, get it?* they said, as if all of my cards and gifts of the previous years were not adorned appropriately. But, just in case someone did not get it, I wrote my name inside a dot on each boot.

"Shall we?" I say gesturing in the direction of dogs.

Unlike Rachel, Joe says he's happy to clean the kennels while I walk. And he foregoes chatter, only using necessary words, so I'm not quizzed about my (nonexistent) social activity.

It takes a while to get Ozzy, the latest Shepherd-Lab mix, to finish outside. He's more interested in barking at a plastic bag blowing in the yard. So when I get back inside, the last dog, Bodie, has been waiting a while. Despite the warning sign, Joe is in with him. Bodie's hackles are down and there's no hint of a growl. Evidently, Joe is not on the list of men he doesn't like.

"What did he do?" says Joe, offering his hand to be sniffed.

"Bit a little kid. And didn't let go." Stitches were needed. An adult wasn't watching, so it's the child's story only.

Joe says nothing, just slips the leash over Bodie's neck.

"Oh wait, he's supposed to wear this." I reach for the muzzle hung on the door. "It can be tricky." Seeing it, Bodie turns his head, readying for the struggle.

"But no one's around," says Joe.

I sigh and hang it back up. It'll save time.

We go out together. I'm waiting for a stampede of small children to come through the yard and make a beeline for Bodie. The shelter's location makes this extremely unlikely, as does the time of day, but that's just the sort of thing that gets me in trouble, assumptions.

Joe holds the leash in two hands, keeping Bodie to the left. I'm impressed; it's just how the trainer taught us to walk the dogs. Judy arranged a session for the staff and volunteers last year.

"Do you have a dog?" I say.

Joe gives the leash some slack so Bodie can search out the winning fence post for his urine. Meanwhile, he tells me about the mutts his family has had over the years, always two or more and never on a leash, just sprawled out in the yard or across the kitchen floor so everyone had to step around them. It sounds like heaven. Wall-to-wall dog.

"The day I turned six," he says, "our neighbour's dog had a litter. I got to pick out a puppy. We called him Dipper. All brown except for one white paw." Bodie flops into a vigorous roll. Even this spiky grass must feel luxurious after the kennel. Joe smiles at him. "Every year Dipper wore a party hat for our big birthday photo. He always looked better in it than me."

A car pulls into the parking lot out front. I glimpse sunset orange. Must be Judy.

It happens so fast. A few pigeons land on the grass. Bodie springs to his feet, pouncing for the birds as if Joe weighs nothing. One pigeon is caught in a flurry of movement. Joe still has the leash, but he can't get the dog off the bird. "Off, leave it, drop it," he says. I grab Bodie's back legs, lifting him like a wheelbarrow, and pull away. Swinging his head at me, he finally lets go. Feathers cling to his chin, but he's lost the spark in his eye. The pigeon, thankfully, flies to the nearby roof.

All three of us are still panting when the back door thumps open and Judy is there, mouth pressed into a hard line. We must have been shouting. I release his hind end and straighten my hat. Bodie licks his lips, hackles still raised.

"Did you forget?" she says, referring to his lack of muzzle.

It's amazing how much people who know one another can communicate in a blink, or without one in this case. It's our ongoing debate: her insistence we stick to the safety rules versus my need to bend them, if only to make life more bearable for the doomed ones. I call it mercy; she calls it naive.

"Did he get you?" She's looking at the froth on my sleeve. In the scuffle I didn't notice his mouth on my arm. Pulling up my sleeve I show her the dented skin, red but unbroken.

"Just a pinch." I want to tell her the wheelbarrow technique came in handy, but I sense this isn't the moment.

"Morning, Joe." Judy waves me off and explains things to him with words like *liable* peppered throughout.

AT SUPPER, I PULL UP TO MY ABODE EARLIER THAN USUAL. JUDY SAID I looked tired and insisted I go home. I know she was still annoyed about Bodie. Anyway, she's right, my head feels like it has a layer of cotton wool around it and I can't stop rubbing at my eyes.

"Dorothy."

It's Magoo, out of his lair up the stairs, wobbling at the top of the landing. A cane is in one hand, the railing in the other, which should steady him, but both arms quiver like we're in the midst of a small earthquake.

"Hello, Mr. McGee. How are you?"

He shakes his head and points to his ear, so I shout this time.

"Oh well. Things are not what they once were. I've come to speak to you about something. Would you be so kind as to come up?"

My bladder says no; my mouth says yes.

"It won't be long until we have snow." One hand ventures away from the railing to showcase the crumbling asphalt driveway and overgrown garden beds, flowers long dried out. I nod as he tells me, patting his heart, about the warning from his doctor. It's T-shirt weather today, and last year it didn't snow until January. I try to concentrate on his words, but his accent is distracting. I've never been able to place it. Is he British or just a local who's big on enunciation?

I reassure him snow removal was my job at home, dialling up the volume of my voice. Mum had a bad back and Dad thought I needed to contribute to the household. Both snorted at the whole aerobics trend. Instead, they found ways for me to be *usefully physical*. If I make myself indispensable, maybe Magoo won't evict me if he finds out about Toby and Ori and everyone else.

"Excellent. My son is a bit of a drive from here."

Magoo has a son? My mind reels. I have to recast his entire life. There was a mother Magoo and a mini Magoo too.

He points out where the shovels are stashed, under the little patio at the back, and thanks me. I turn to leave, but I'm not yet dismissed.

"Did I see a car here the other night?"

"Just someone from work. Rachel." I'm not sure why I tell him her name.

His chin bobs up and down as if he's discovered a morsel between his back teeth. I use the moment to count the strands of hair left in the middle of his scalp. He needs a porkpie hat. That's what's missing.

"I did mention no parties?" No, he had not, but I'm in full support of that rule. He leans a little harder on his cane. His eyelids are swollen. Meanwhile, his nose whistles a little tune. "No parties, and no dogs," he says, examining my shoulder.

"No, sir," I hear myself say.

He continues to focus on my shoulder as if my eyes are located there. I crane my neck and discover a clump of fur—cat fur, mind you, not dog—I recognize the orange fluff.

"I work at an animal shelter." I pluck it from my shoulder and give it to the wind.

"That's right," he says, "you mentioned that. But you won't be bringing them back here? I don't mean to be a fuddy-duddy, but the doctor thinks I have sensitivities. There's not much that separates you and I."

What separates us is a custom-cut piece of Styrofoam at the top of the stairs. His son's handiwork? He assured me he wouldn't be *wandering through*. What was I to say? It was the only place in my price range, plus I could move in right away.

"You don't need to worry about that." It seems to satisfy him.

"Well, I must get back. My program is about to start."

I open the door for him and get a peek at his armchair in front of the chunky TV. It's just how I pictured it: threadbare corduroy, a TV tray with a faded country scene. Other than food, I don't think he's made any domestic purchases in thirty years.

"Thank you, Dorothy," he says, taking hold of the inner knob and closing the door between us.

I'M SLURPING NOODLES ON MY BED WHEN RACHEL ARRIVES, UNBIDDEN.

"Quick." I almost shut the door on her heels. "Toby's out."

"You ought to get a phone," she says, instead of hello. "Then people wouldn't have to pop in on you. Ted's in the car."

I push aside the tea cloth that is my curtain. Every year a fresh patriotic tea towel comes wrapped around Nan's tin of Christmas cake. So, I nabbed the Union Jack when I moved out. Behind Rusty is another car. I can just make out a head of spiky hair slumped in the driver's seat.

"Want to go to a movie?" She plops down on my bed, shoes on.

"It's not in the budget." It's almost laughable, the thought of blowing my earnings on something that may or may not amuse me for two hours.

Her eyes shift from me to Toby, wedging his beak under the door.

"Who's in the bathroom?" She squints at me, suspicious.

"It's just Abbott and Costello."

"The gerbils?" She seems disappointed. "Hey, you mind if Ted comes in?" She goes back to the door, pulling aside the tea towel like she has to make sure he's still there.

"No. I mean, yes. Sorry, it's just…" I point at the ceiling, indicating Magoo, whose TV is now silent, because he's probably gotten a glass from the kitchen and tipped it to the floor to use as a low-tech listening device.

"You're always doing that." She's looking at my fingers drumming the air.

"Habit." I tuck my hand in my pocket.

"We could get a coffee. Ted's friend works at a place near here so he gets, like, half price." She knows how to tempt a cheapskate. Noodles never fill me up.

"Just give me a few minutes and I'll get the comedy duo out of the tub." Too bad, they'll miss the drain tonight.

THE BACK SEAT FEELS FAMILIAR, LIKE I'M OUT FOR A DRIVE WITH my parents, except I spot a flattened box of condoms under the driver's seat and we're treated to Teddy's mixed tape of The Cure.

Ted wears a pair of round glasses, just big enough to cover his eyes, so the effect is similar to buttons. I think of John Lennon. *Imagine.* As I suspected, it's difficult to look at him without picturing the whole toe-sex thing Rachel described. It's like meeting a porn star, the one who has the most awkward lines, in a hushed elevator.

Rachel turns to look at me. "Did you see the thing in the paper?" As if I have a room in the budget for a newspaper. I nab it from people's garbage to line the bottom of cages when it's a week old. "You must have heard about the puppy in Pleasant Park? A guy was beating it with a stick." It's as if I am being whipped with a stick myself.

Ted mumbles something with a lot of *fucks* thrown in. Rachel translates. "Ted has ideas about what to do to him." As do I.

"The guy ran off. But then someone else near there called the police. They saw a man running out of the woods and get into a car, thinking he was a thief or something. Anyway, the cops grabbed him. The dog was taken to the emergency clinic. Broken leg, punctured lung..." We sit in silence for a minute. I've lost my appetite for my cookie, so I roll it into the paper napkin and stow it in my pocket for later.

"I'm going to be there when he's in court," Rachel says.

"Me too," says Ted. "Stare him down." Rachel pats his shoulder.

"We should all go," says Rachel, "get the whole shelter down there."

She's still new at this. We've done that before, waving signs outside, sending poisonous looks at the accused. It makes it that much harder when they let the person go or just give them a fine. But I'm learning it's easier not to say no to Rachel.

"Maybe," I say.

Before getting out, I alert them to the empty box of condoms behind the seat. For this, I am thanked profusely.

SIX

٥○٥

R USTY'S MUFFLER IS GETTING HARD TO IGNORE. MAGOO'S CUR-
tains quiver after I fire up. It's early, darkish. I roll down the
street like a farting rocket.

Mum helped me buy Rusty, sifting through the classifieds
in the paper. It meant they wouldn't have to drive me to the
shelter anymore. The fact I could afford it with my savings tells
you something. Rusty's original paint job, still in blotchy evidence, is also rust-coloured, as if the manufacturer knew to set
low expectations for future owners. Or maybe they painted all
the cars destined for the Eastern seaboard this colour, knowing
about our road salt.

The radio turns on without a key in the ignition. For the first
month of Rusty's residence in our driveway, I sat listening to talk
radio, my hands on the steering wheel like I was on a lengthy road
trip. Because of that, I also had the opportunity to learn about car
batteries and jumper cables.

Joe is waiting on the front step when I pull into the parking lot.

"How do you get here?" I ask. He's been here two weeks, and
he always arrives before me.

"Bus." He stands. "Sounds like you're in need of a mechanic."

"That and the money to pay for one." A muffler is probably at
least a hundred dollars. Isn't everything?

"Wow," he says, walking over to admire my wheels. "A nice Reliant automobile." He smiles at my bumper sticker: *This car is not abandoned.* "I learned to drive in one."

"Was it this colour?"

"I think it was burgundy." He bends to peer at the dangling metal. "The cops might pull you over."

"For being rusty?"

He laughs softly. I think it's the first time I've seen him smile. "For being noisy."

We move through the morning cleaning like a rust-free car running on premium gasoline. At lunch, Judy finds me in the boardroom. "Your dad popped in. Last night, after you left."

I suppose it was inevitable after all the unreturned phone calls.

She doesn't elaborate on his impromptu visit. I imagine him hugging Judy, gazing down at her saucy rubber boots.

"You should go." In her hand is a card for a therapist, a blank line for an appointment time not yet pencilled in.

"I have. Do you know how much one session costs?"

She's a balloon leaking air. "About the price of neutering a St. Bernard."

"Yes. And Dad can't afford that."

"He wants you to talk to someone."

"I did. That's all I did." Forty-five minutes of exploring my psyche left me completely dehydrated. "No solutions were provided by the professional." It was all questions and the quiet scratch of her pen.

"How about me?" She pulls out a chair as if we can start immediately.

"Judy. I'm fine. It's not about me." What I need is a mechanic.

She's inspecting me the way she does a stray cat. "Your eyes look sore."

"They're itchy."

"I've got some ointment in my desk."

"You're not supposed to do that."

"What?"

"Share eye ointments."

"It's brand new. Sheesh, Dot. This is me, professional animal health technologist. I know about contamination." She pushes her chair back and jogs to the ringing phone in her office.

In the corner, I spot a donation I must nab for Toby. It resembles a hanging abacus. He can do calculations while I'm at work. Bug hunting and a little bathroom splashing are not enough to keep him out of trouble. I'll just pop it in the car so I don't forget it.

Outside, I find a pair of legs protruding beneath Rusty. "I think I can jury-rig something here," says the legs' owner.

"To re-muffle me?"

"Yup." Joe inches his way out. "I'll need a couple of cans."

"You're a waiter, no?"

"Yes." But, he explains, he and his brothers compete to see how long they can keep something on the road. A case of beer is at stake.

"Should I be discouraged by the fact you're now using a bus to get around?"

"Probably."

I like that he can hold a straight face. Facial control is underrated.

"The vet's running late." I hold the door open for him as his hands are crusty from Rusty. "It's E-Day," I remind him.

"Judy said."

Speak of the devil, she's at the front counter, a rabbit in her arms.

"Dr. Trainer said she'd have her tech with her," she says. The rabbit appears to have fallen into a deep sleep.

"Oh." I head into the office to find the To Die list. Judy follows.

I scan the names. It's short, but not short enough, with one dog and two cats. We're always full to bursting with cats.

"Dot, you can take the occasional Wednesday off." Judy tucks the rabbit into a cage beside her desk. I suspect this one is going home to join her others.

It's not true, she couldn't cover my shift. We're understaffed. How many times has she said that under her breath while drawing up the schedule?

"It's just me and Earl on Wednesdays," I say.

"And Joe."

"He's a volunteer." They stick to cuddling, walking. Some do the cleaning, like Joe, but not many sign up for that.

"That can change." Her mouth is anchored low at the corners like she's suppressing a smile. Hiring Joe might mean cutting back Rachel's hours, because there is The Budget and The Board to control it all. It would make sense to have three of us here full-time. "I'll talk to him, see what his other work schedule is like." Her eyes focus on someone behind me. "What you got there?"

"Dot's exhaust," says Joe. He's been through the recycling and dug up some cans.

"Who eats Alphaghetti here?" Judy says.

"Earl." Maybe I shouldn't out him, I caught him burying a can in the bin one day.

"Anyway," says Joe, "between Alphaghetti and baked beans, we might have something. Is there a toolkit?"

"Shed out back," we say in unison. Judy tosses him a key from her drawer.

"He must like you," she says quietly, as soon as the door shuts. "Fixing your car."

"He's from the country. Country people are helpful."

"Stereotype," she says, pointing a finger at me.

"Truth," I say.

"I'm going to need some wire," says Joe from the doorway.

Jesus, did he hear that?

"There might be some in the shed." Judy clears her throat. "We patched up the kennels with it a while back. Have a dig around."

When he's left we share a wide-eyed look.

The front door chimes and Dr. Trainer calls out hello and moments later she's in the office. Despite working at a small animal clinic in the city, she looks like she belongs on a farm, trudging through muddy paddocks in her floppy shirts and rubber boots.

"Oh good," she says, seeing me, "Megan had to stay behind with a discharge. Want to give me a hand until she gets here?

Straight to it, with Dr. Sneaker.

"Sure." I stash my bag behind Judy's desk.

"Who's first?" she says as we walk to the back of the shelter.

"A spaniel." Always do the hardest ones first.

"*Biter. Dog-aggressive, cat-aggressive, nervous of men, guards food and possessions,*" she reads. With his floppy ears, freckled nose, and spot over one eye, Bodie is painfully cute. I think his looks have worked against him. People see him and move in for a hug. Dogs, especially anxious ones, don't like to be hugged.

"He's been adopted and returned twice," I say.

"You want to use the pole?" she says, crouching by his door.

"No, but I'll put on the gloves."

Even though he's botched his chances, I feel like, given time, I could help him. But the decision is not mine. It's not Judy's either. The Board has spoken.

I put a handful of treats in my pocket and carry the bite-gloves in with me. Settling on the floor a couple of feet away, I kneel and yawn broadly to show Bodie I'm calm. Dr. T. busies herself with the needle. "What's his weight, Dot?"

"About forty-five pounds."

Careful not to look at him, I jiggle the treats in my pocket. His nose lifts and he has the scent. Instead of standing, he shuffles forward on his elbows. Dropping one treat on the floor close to my leg, I put on the left glove while he's eating.

"Sure you don't want the pole?" She's at the door, ready.

"Yup, give us a minute."

With my right hand, I rub the scent of the treats onto the gloves and drop a few more nearer me. He stands and comes a little closer. I put on the other glove and scatter some treats on my lap. The next part will be tricky. Luckily, his first owners trained him, so he knows the basics. It's all in his file. "Bodie, down." I use the treat to direct him. "Over." It takes him a few seconds to decide. Smart dog. Eventually, he rolls to his left with his back pressed to me and allows me to run my hand over his side without flinching. I feed him while Dr. Trainer steps in.

"I'll do the hind end," she says. My job is to hold him still and avoid getting us bitten.

"Good boy." My heart slows; every time I do this it seems to gain in mass, weighing down my chest. My breath is too hot in my throat.

"Stay." Now I have to put my elbow on his neck to keep him from rising. The welder's gloves will stop teeth from penetrating my skin, but it will still hurt. I use my right leg to restrain his lower body. It's something I figured out on my own. It doesn't work for all sizes, but it's adequate for Bodie. I keep murmuring his name.

The prick of the needle makes him jerk. The seconds tick by as his muscles tighten. I hold firm. He snaps at me, missing. "It's okay, Bodie. Good boy. You won't be upset anymore." The tension slides away, his head dropping to the floor. I loosen my hold as I see it in his eye, the leaving. I remove a glove and feel for his pulse. "Poor Bodie."

No barking from the other kennels. Everything hushes, as if the others are holding this moment too. What is the scent of fear and dying? When we speak again, it's in softer voices.

I sit back on my knees and gaze at him, the curls and the freckles. I rub a hand along his side. A breath of air escapes his mouth in a rush.

"Someone cut his nails," she says.

"Me." She looks at me with her eyebrows at full mast. "They were cracking."

"But you knew he was—"

"Yes." A door opens and someone calls to Dr. Trainer.

"Back here, Megan." She turns to me. "He let you touch his feet?" Even non-anxious dogs dislike having their paws touched.

"It took a few tries. I didn't get them all. See?" He'd get a treat if I could touch a toe, then I'd hold his paw while he ate and so on.

She looks thoughtful.

"The owner should have done this," she says. "It would have been kinder." I don't think she means nail trims. "Owners drop them with us, sometimes, because they can't look. Guilt." She glances at me. "But a decent goodbye is the last gift you can give them. They should feel safe in these last moments."

Megan waits, a large black garbage bag in her hand. Dr. Trainer introduces us. She's a recent graduate of the Animal Health Technology program, replacing the previous tech, who left to start her own boarding facility.

"We can do this part, Dot."

My feet have gone to sleep. His back is still warm on my leg. Gently, I slide him off and give him a final pat, even though he's gone now. One treat is on the floor by his nose.

"I'll meet you in the cat room," I say, stepping past.

"What a beautiful dog," Megan says, the bag rustling as she opens it.

In the storage room, I grab the quilted winter coats, one of them shredded down the chest. But they'll still help a bit. Claws rip though flesh in a messy way. I have some impressive scars.

Dr. T. and Megan are crouching in front of a cage. A low growl comes from the farthest corner. This one will be nothing like Bodie.

"Here," I say, holding out a coat to each of them.

"Feral?" says Dr. Trainer, putting down the list and taking the coat from me.

"Yup, both of them." The cage to the right contains the other cat, whose ears are just nubs; a combination of frostbite and cat fights. Both have feline leukaemia.

Megan is slow to take the coat from me.

"Trust me, put it on," says her boss.

"Now," I say to Megan, "if you can open the cage door, I'll towel him. But get the gloves on first."

I know they must have practiced this in the technology program, but probably no more than a few times, whereas I have daily opportunities to swaddle cats that hate people. The sound issuing from the kennel is demonic. The soundtrack to a horror film.

"Okay, just gradually," I say. The key is not to get rattled when they swipe at you. Thankful for my glasses, I lean in and get the towel around him with one motion. The growl climbs from deep and menacing to a screech. I snug him under my left arm, vowing not to let go, and get him to the table in the corner. He's bundled like a burrito with one leg out for the needle. From the motion of the towel, you'd think there was more than one cat in there.

"I've got him. Hold the leg?" I say to Megan. Through the glove, he gives me a series of vicious bites.

Megan needs to hold his leg just so, steady enough for the needle, while pressing down with her thumb to reveal a vein. We're knotted together, me using all of my upper body to contain the squirming, shrieking mass with Megan's hair tickling my nose, while she gets close enough to do her part. Dr. T. waits to see the vein. She gets it on the first poke, thank Christ. There are other ways to do this, but this one is quicker and kinder.

"One down," says Dr. Trainer. "You're bleeding." Megan has a thin stream of red running down her neck. She didn't zip the coat up to the top, but I don't point that out. "Impressive, no? Just a fraction of our weight but they can do some damage." She pulls out a swab from her bag and offers it to Megan. "You've had your tetanus?"

"Yes." She winces as the alcohol hits the wound.

"Good. Here, dab some of this on too."

Inevitably, the second cat will be harder, having witnessed the ruckus of the first. He's completely silent, except for the thud of his fat tail on the wall, spelling *NO* in Morse. I start to repeat my towel trick, but he charges the door at the last second. Megan is startled and he slips through.

"Sorry," Megan says.

"Might have to use the box?" says Dr. Trainer.

"No. Not yet." I hate the box. It makes me think of the Holocaust. "Just guide him this way."

"I'm sorry."

Together, we corral him. It's done on the floor. Dr. T. can't get a vein. She has to try the other leg while he hisses and hates me. A claw yanks my hat from my head. I leave it tangled in his paw and reach around Megan to hold his leg for the vet.

At the end, we're all sweating in our big coats. Megan's mouth trembles.

"Here." Dr. T. hands me my hat. "You know, I don't think I've ever seen the top of your head."

"Did you think I was bald?" I try to pull the loop back through the other side of my hat. It will never be the same.

"Well, I did wonder if you were hiding something." Dr. Trainer lifts the cat while Megan holds the bag open.

"It's where I keep the codes for the nuclear weapons."

"Yes, that's what I thought," she says.

The tiniest plop grabs my attention. A tear landing on the garbage bag, followed by a sniff from Megan. Shit. Was it the deaths? The banter? It's not flippancy, I want to tell her, it's...coping.

"Dot, would you mind?" Dr. Trainer uses her eyes to point to the door.

"Sure. I'll be up front."

I close the door behind me and lean against it. The mumble of voices come through the crack. Megan apologizing. Then Dr. Trainer saying, "It's normal to cry. Expected."

Am I normal? Should I be able to just carry on with my workday?

Before facing people, I stop at the kitchen sink to splash some water on my face.

"Bad one?" Judy says as I enter the office. "Her tech just left. She seemed upset."

"Remember that feral we did together?"

Judy and I have done many together. The vet only comes for the dogs. We're equipped to handle smaller animals ourselves. Sometimes, we'll be having a glorious day, the sun shining, animals getting adopted by kind and responsible people, everything ticking along like we might be making the world a little better...Then, the phone rings or someone shows up with a box. I hate phones and boxes.

After a deep breath, she tells me to go find Joe. Apparently, he wants me to fire up the beast and see if the muffler will muffle.

IF I HEAR MY NAME MENTIONED MOMENTS BEFORE STEPPING INTO a room, I'm not above lingering for a few sentences. It's Rachel's voice and there's a certain tone to it that makes me stop. She's trying to get Joe's story on why he's spending his weekdays volunteering here instead of working at a paying job. He doesn't budge, offering the same words he did me. About wanting to help. But he looks a little rattled when I walk in, even though he's sitting in a kennel with three puppies.

"Hey," I say to Rachel. "Aren't you in class today?"

"The prof cancelled." I have to wonder about college. Not once in all my years at school did a teacher cancel a class and we all got to just go home. There was always someone ready to step in and drill us on math. It's not the first time she's shown up with time on her hands.

"Joe re-mufflered my car," I say to her, straightening my glasses.

"Well, we'll see," Joe says, disentangling from the pups and pulling himself up with the help of the cage door.

"He used a couple of cans and some wire."

"MacGyver," Rachel says, winking at me. "What happened to your hat?"

"Cat."

"A cat happened to your hat?"

"Exactly that." She doesn't smile. I'm rubbing off on her.

Outside, I say, "Sorry about Rachel."

Joe coughs. "Ah, she's nice." Crouching, he points out the cans, de-labelled and ready to do their best in their new role. "Just take it easy over bumps. I wired it up pretty tight, but it's not like a weld job."

Rusty coughs to life, singing a squawky but quieter tune than this morning. I run it for a minute, bracing for the cans to blast off under pressure, but they stay put.

"My neighbourhood thanks you."

"They're welcome." Hands jammed in pockets, gaze fixed on Rusty's rust.

Because he refuses to let me pay him, and against all my instincts, I offer to drive him home. He refuses. I insist. He accepts. *Shit.* What will we say without the distraction of work?

Dr. Trainer barrels out the front door, bag in hand. She has wet down her hair, but the first strands are already standing up. Spotting me, she comes over.

"Your wheels?"

"All mine."

"Impressive," she says. "Dot, thanks and sorry about today. It's been a wild week. Training a new person and emergencies..."

"Sure."

"On the weekend, when you're not here, you should come by the clinic." She digs in her bag and finds a wrinkled business card. "Just call and make sure I'm around." On cue, her phone rings, like it's remembered its voice. "Dammit," she says, rifling through another pocket of her bag. "I hate these things."

We watch her climb into her van, giving instructions about an antibiotic.

"I think," says Joe, who never received an introduction, "she wants to offer you a job."

"Really?"

"Just a hunch."

Sometimes, I'm told, I miss the subtleties of human communication. I suppose he could be right. Why else would she want me to pop into the clinic? But I couldn't leave the shelter. It's my world. Maybe she's been recruited by Dad, another person to plant the idea of going back to school.

Joe shrugs and heads for the door.

On the front step Rachel lights a smoke. Letting the match fall to the ground, she traps it with her toe and puffs smoke at her boot.

"They're filling out an adoption form for the orange tabby," she says of the people hunched over the front desk. "Hey, look." She sticks a boot out for me to see, turning it this way and that. "These are vegetarian."

"I'm not hungry," I say.

"Jesus, Dot." Reluctant smile.

"Mine are too." I stick out one polka-dot boot.

"I'm just saying, I didn't know you could get, like, vegan shoes. Did you? I got them from my aunt for my birthday. They're from England." Bad British accent.

"Very nice." My vegetarianism has not yet gone to my feet. After all, it's not as if I go on shoe-buying sprees. I have crickets to purchase.

"I'm going to court tomorrow," she says. "In the morning." The guy who beat up the puppy. The images come flooding back. Even though I didn't find out how old or what breed, I see Bodie yelping and cowering from the next blow. "Want to come?"

"Can't," I say. "I open tomorrow. Sorry."

"Right." She takes a long drag, nodding. "Guess it's just me, then. Ted's got a test."

"Are you going to hold up a sign or something?"

"By myself? No. I might take my sketch pad, try out live drawing. Apparently, it's a legit job for artists. Maybe it'll keep me from losing my shit."

She wouldn't be the first to get punted from the courtroom for yelling at the accused.

"He won't get what he deserves. You know that, right?"

She nods and blows a wonky smoke ring my way. We watch as it evaporates between us.

"Still," she says, "I'll be there."

JOE HAS TO WAIT WHILE I BRUSH AWAY THE FEATHERS AND REMOVE one small turd from the passenger seat. He protests, saying he sat in a wad of gum on the bus last week. When I start up Rusty he nods with satisfaction.

"Someone flipped me the bird this morning, like I *chose* to sabotage my muffler."

"People do that," he says, buckling up, "make their cars louder."

"Really?" I've never understood the need to be noticed, especially for doing something so unmistakably obnoxious. He tells me they're marketed as fart boxes.

So, just as Dad says, people will buy anything.

"Where to?"

"I'm in the North End. That okay?" He fishes in his pocket for some change to pay the bridge toll. I hear myself insist, even though it's an extra half hour for me each way. I tell him to pick a station from Rusty's full range of AM radio.

"How's your dad?" he asks. The question throws me off while I'm attempting to merge lanes. We shoot forward and a car's brakes scream behind us. How does Joe even know my dad? Not the commercials. "Sorry," he says. "He called when I was on the front desk."

"It's okay." It's an awkward crawl to the next set of lights, the person behind me, shaking his head and mouthing *fuck.*

"Sorry," Joe says again. "It's just, he sounded worried. About you."

"Right." Does Dad just broadcast our personal lives to everyone? "Have you ever had something happen to you and all the people around you want you to talk about it and, I don't know... emote more?"

"Yeah." He nods. "Talking about it doesn't change the past."

"Yes, exactly." Finally someone gets it.

A car horn blasts.

"You can go," says Joe. I've hesitated at a green light in traffic. Behind me, the driver rolls down his window so he can make his hand gestures more obvious. I want to slouch in my seat and let him pass, but we're hemmed in.

Joe's knee does a jig, but not in time to Hootie & the Blowfish howling to *let her cry.* Joe's knee is sending out messages. Possibly, he'd rather be in charge of the brake and accelerator.

"What is it?" he asks finally.

"I just want this guy to pass me."

"Pull into that parking lot. I'm in no rush."

That means a lane change. I put on the indicator and hope for a gap. The drivers to my right are looking resolutely forward. Eye contact might guilt them into letting me delay their plodding progress. This infuriates the man in the mirror, his left hand appealing to the gods of traffic.

"Is that *SOS*?" says Joe.

"Huh?"

Right, I'm tapping.

"Scouts," he says, rolling down his window. He leans out and catches the attention of a woman applying lipstick. She waves us in and makes the car behind her beep. What fun. I give her a thank-you wave. I don't think she sees it, as she's now glaring at the person behind her.

We pull into the parking lot. It's shared by an interesting mix of businesses: a scuba-diving shop, a beer store, a gas station, and, of course, Tim Hortons. We sit in silence for a full minute, me drumming the steering wheel, Joe with his face turned away as if the scenery is of great interest. He clears his throat a couple of times before offering to get me a coffee.

"No thanks, a muffler was enough for today."

Getting out, he leaves me to watch the unhappy parade of cars. If the caffeine queue is long enough, rush hour will peter out by the time we get back in line. The bridge tends to clog things, but after six o'clock, much like the drain in my abode's bathtub, it has a good burp and things loosen up. But Joe is too quick. Climbing in, he catches me smelling my hands.

"Sorry, that weird smell from the latex gloves," I say, placing my hands back at ten and two. Under the bite-gloves, I wear a pair of surgical gloves, in case the vet needs help getting a vein.

"Is it every Wednesday we...?" *We?* Is two weeks long enough for a collective we?

"Usually, yeah. All those puppies from last Christmas are getting too big now." Don't get me started on that.

The plastic coffee lid is giving him grief; he's trying to open the tab without cracking the rest of it. "Does it bug you?" he says, glancing at me.

I nod. "Have you ever seen an animal die?"

"Too many times." He takes a tentative sip and burns his lip.

My beeper hums and I grab it from my bag.

"Rachel," I say, tucking it away again, instead of *What the hell do you mean by "too many times?"* "All right if I get moving again?" He nods, though his lap is vulnerable to first-degree burns now he's surrendered and removed the whole lid.

After a few blocks he says, "My dad's a hunter." I picture a smaller Joe tromping through wet leaves in a bright orange vest. "I liked being in the woods. But I was no good at it." I glance over at him, but he's staring hard out the windshield, frowning, like there's a limp deer on the hood.

The rest of the ride is uneventful. The quarters land in the basket at the bridge's toll booth instead of under the car as they're wont to do. Joe finds a radio station playing Pearl Jam and his lips move to *I'm Still Alive.*

His home is a tiny, lime-green house with a view of a liquor store and a pharmacy. The driveway is car-less.

"You're all set for pain management, I see." I point across the street.

"It's a rental," he says, as if it would occur to me he would own a house.

The front door opens and a lanky guy comes out with an ancient ten-speed slung over his shoulder. The house doesn't look big enough to accommodate a person of his stature, let alone a bike. The screen door closes on his back wheel and there's a short struggle as he disentangles. "My roommate, Mike," says Joe. Opening his door, he calls, "Off to work?" Mike teeters on his pedals, then looks up, "Yup, I'm late. See ya, Moe."

"Always late." Joe smiles.

"No helmet," I say instead of *Moe? He just called you Moe.*

"Always helmet-less too," he says, unfolding himself from the seat. Once out, he pats Rusty's roof, clearing us for takeoff, I suppose.

Is it Joe or Moe? Mojo. Maybe his roommate has a speech impediment. Maybe my ears are clogged.

Alone at last, I turn up the volume. Elton John, yet again. He's taken his song for Marilyn and just switched the name. How would Diana feel, having Elton's Marilyn Monroe song retooled for her? Doesn't a princess deserve a song of her own? Nevertheless, I sing along.

SOMEONE ELSE HAS PARKED IN THE DRIVEWAY OF MY ABODE. THIS means Rusty will have to stay on the street. Making sure all the doors are locked—because thieves will not only steal your change for the bridge, but even a driver's much-needed back cushion—I head in. There's a notable lack of flickering blue light from upstairs. Whoever's here, they've interrupted Magoo's regular programming.

Inside, I'm greeted by Toby clanging on the bars. I hope whoever is visiting Magoo doesn't point out the noise. At least Toby doesn't say much; he favours whacking at the side of his cage when he sees me, as it usually produces a snack.

The second I undo the latch he hops out and zones in on a bug.

The upside of having an apartment dominated by a Posturepedic mattress is you can sit and make supper. I slather some hummus on a slice of bread and eat it in five bites. Ori, perched on my shoulder, gets a nibble.

A knock on my door makes me pause mid-swallow. What if I just don't open it?

"Dorothy?" It's not Magoo's voice.

"Just a minute." Ori must be tucked in and Toby shooed into the bathroom.

The man says nothing, but I can tell he's leaning in, trying to see around the edge of my Union Jack. Toby loves the tub but likes to head there at his own pace. I receive a peck for rushing him.

I open the door a crack. He introduces himself as Stan Junior, Magoo's son, looking beyond me as he talks, towards the cage condo in the corner.

"You'll be doing the shovelling?" he says, bringing his gaze back to me.

"Yes, it's not a problem." Ever so slightly, I start to close the door, but he's not done.

"Also," he says, "your car. The noise woke him—"

"Oh, my muffler. I had it fixed."

"Right." He squints at Rusty, parked at the curb. "Oh, and he wanted to make sure you don't have any pets."

"He told me no dogs." My voice climbs an octave without my permission.

"No dogs?"

"That's what he said." I grip the doorknob a little harder.

"The doc says his lungs aren't sounding good." He rubs at the stubble on his chin. "Might be something in his environment irritating him."

I know the feeling. My left eye twitches. He waits for me to say something. Offer to evict myself? Or find homes for my brood?

Upstairs, Magoo's TV turns on. Stan Junior glances at the ceiling.

"He's got a nasty cough and a rash." He scratches his arm, looking at Abbott and Costello, both standing with paws braced against the glass to follow the action.

Mum liked to say silence speaks volumes. Magoo II seems immune to it, though.

"I used to play down here. Rode my tricycle on rainy days." He points. "Banged into that post more times than I can count."

"I'll try to avoid it."

He laughs through his nose, muttering something about me not having enough space for that, then reaches into his shirt pocket for a piece of paper.

"My number, probably good you have it. I'll be around more anyway, to check on Dad. Doc's orders."

Closing the door, I listen to heavy, slow steps climb to Magoo, where a full report will be given. At least Toby was quiet in the bathroom. He could ask me to leave. Or tell me. Maybe there's another tenant prospect. Someone like myself, equally unreflective and in need of cheap rent. But would they shovel? I think not.

Magoo's TV plays a commercial, drowning out the crickets along with any decent eavesdropping. A knock on the bathroom door brings me back. The door opens inward and Toby refuses to back up, peering around the edge at me.

"Come on out."

I leave it for him to wrestle open with his beak. Crows seem to welcome opportunities to solve problems, whereas I'd be happy with some monotony.

SEVEN

ᕙᕗ

A T TWO AND THREE, I WAKE UP WITH A COUGH. AT FOUR, I
decide to flip on the light and fumble around for a book under
my bed. I find the one Mum gave me on self-defence just after I got
Rusty. The book's cover has an angry-looking man being walloped
by a petite woman with a tidy ponytail. It promises techniques for
disarming people of knives and guns. I study the pages on weapon
removal. A quick side movement, smack the arm away and down.
I try the moves while propped up with my luxury pillows. It must
jiggle something loose in my chest; I end up in a full-on coughing
fit, carefully muffled into my pillow to avoid waking the house. This
doesn't bode well for getting back to sleep. I need to take something.

Movement upstairs, while I wait for the kettle to boil. The
TV turns on at its usual blare, then down to a whisper. It must be
Junior. I turn up my White Noise Freeway and flip to the chapter
on defending from dog attacks. *Avoid getting bitten.* Good idea.
Control the head seems to be the prevailing advice throughout the
book. I might be able to teach them a thing or two about this topic.

The toddy is a tad stronger than what Dad used to make. He
tucked miniature bottles of whiskey in with my tea kettle, along
with the recipe. But I don't have a shot glass for measuring.

I crawl under the blankets to enjoy it, fully expecting it to anes-
thetize me. The taste is still not my cup of tea, but I like the warmth

spreading down my throat. Collapsing onto my pillows, I try my sleep technique, counting my breaths until I reach something that is not my world but has all the echoes of it. I'm running and Mum is with me in the form of a colourful blur, an impressionistic Dawn. Her feet make an odd pattern. Is it a message? Then I'm chasing her. The code fades. Colours blur as if I don't have my glasses on. Roaring traffic is everywhere. I'm straining for the faint message. I wake up with it just out of reach, my alarm blaring.

"Have you looked in the mirror?" Judy sits at her desk with a rabbit in her arms.

"I don't like to reflect."

"Well, you ought to. Your eyes look infected now."

"It's just a cold." Am I slurring?

I brought another toddy to work in my travel mug, just to warm my throat, more honey than whiskey this time.

"You'd better not be contagious," she says. "I have a lot of work to do in the garden this weekend." The garden is for her rabbits. Judy is the only person I know to grow pots of dandelions. Bunnies love them. Lately, she's been working on making it safe for the rabbits to dig burrows in the garden, lining it with chicken wire that extends underground.

Earl pops his head in and reports the cleaning is done. "Young Joe is just finishing up the cat room."

"Thanks," Judy and I say in unison.

"His name's not Joe, you know," I tell Judy as soon as Earl leaves.

"Hm?"

"His roommate called him Moe."

She gives me a look. "Probably a nickname, *Dot*." She enunciates my name, as proof.

"Well, if he's working here you ought to know, that's all." My voice sounds like it's down a tunnel.

"I'm on the radio in"—she checks her computer—"five."

"What's this week's topic?"

"Black cats and Halloween."

I rub the back of my neck. The ritual satanic sacrifice sea-son is upon us. Every holiday has its dark side for animals. At least Halloween doesn't try to disguise itself with satin bows like Christmas and Easter. It's grinning vegetables and gore made edible with candy.

"You doing anything this year?" asks Judy, running two fingers along the forehead of the rabbit.

"I hadn't thought about it."

"You ought to come to my place. Help hand out candy. We can watch a scary movie."

I shudder.

"What? You don't like scary movies?"

"No. Kids in costumes." A ninja turtle kicked me in the stomach in Grade Five.

One eyebrow arches; I envy her ability to do this. "Fair enough. You could keep the rabbits away from the door. One always gets nosy."

She's talking to me, but her eyes are on her computer, so I leave her to her prep and find Earl starting a load of laundry. "Decision time," he says, pouring in the bleach. He hands me a quarter from his pocket. "Your call."

"Heads." It arcs in the air, glinting in the flickering fluorescent light, and lands on tails. I sag.

"Two out of three?" he says.

"Nah, you've been stuck on the front desk lately. I could use a sit-down anyway."

From the office comes the sound of Judy using her radio voice. I pull out the cat book and listen to the messages, jotting down details. Each one is urgent, as if it should be our only priority.

When we adopt out cats, we stress they not be let outside—cars, predators, feline leukaemia, non-vegetarians...they're better off indoors. People just nod, hoping to shorten our lecture.

Underneath the book is the paperwork for Oliver. It looks like someone wants to adopt him. All the references have checked out. A single woman working from home. She lost her old Lab last year. Lucky Ollie.

My coffee tastes strange. The whiskey has done something to my tongue. How can people drink this stuff for pleasure? Judy catches me feeling for the glands in my neck.

"Really? You're on front today? Dot, no. Go and look in a mirror."

"The coin has spoken."

"You and Earl can handle the back. There's a cat that needs a flea bath. Joe can do this." She holds up a hand to keep me quiet. "He filled in the other day. I already talked to him about it. Right?" She's looking over my shoulder. There he is, hands jammed in pockets.

"Morning, Moe," I say, sliding off the stool. He looks startled but doesn't correct me.

Judy points at the toes of her boots: *Piss off.* It's meant for me, not Joe. Succinct.

IN THE CAT ROOM, I LOCATE THE FELINE IN QUESTION, STILL IN A carry case. Judy has doodled a flea on a sticky note, alongside a sad face. Not bad. I wonder if she sat in high school history class perfecting parasite sketches while the teacher droned on about the War of 1812. Getting down on my knees, I peer into the crate and let the cat assess me. Whiskers poke through the bars and there's the low rumble of a purr. A fluffy cheek presses against the door.

"So, you're one of those?" I say to her. "All 88 for now." Sadly, the bite-gloves cannot be used for this job because it's rare the claws don't come out, with even the sweetest of them. "I hope you can forgive me."

I have a long-sleeved shirt and my lab coat on. Nevertheless, I once witnessed a cat completely remove Earl's T-shirt during a bath. It snagged the fabric at the bottom with its claws and climbed while he tried to keep it in the water. Eventually, the shirt went right over his head and ended up tangled in the bath. I had time to survey his fuzzy shoulders while I did the lathering. Earl wouldn't look at me for the rest of the day. It couldn't have been comfortable, wearing a lab coat as a shirt.

Earl meets me at the sink with the requisite bottles and towels. He's already warmed up the water in the sprayer. Clearly, he plans to lather and not lose his shirt.

"Her name is Buttercup," I say, opening the door. "The new boyfriend has a dog that chases her."

"You never know," says Earl. While I doubt people's stories, Earl's always the optimist. Somehow, he continues to like his own species.

Buttercup purrs and rubs her head against my chin until the water touches her bum, but I'm ready. With a firm hand on the scruff of her neck, I lower her into the sink.

Earl hums "Islands in the Stream" as she yowls. It sounds a lot like she's saying *Out. Owooot.* But she's not struggling. Someone will fall in love with her.

"Here they come," I say to Earl, who reaches up and snatches a flea from her forehead without pausing his crooning. Her white fur makes it easy to watch them flee from the sudsy water.

The steam soothes my eyes and throat. That and the humming must make me drowsy. My glasses fog up, or maybe my sight blurs, because the next thing I know, Earl is pulling me out of the sink. Buttercup claws at my chest. I've never heard Earl's voice go this high—it sounds like he's shouting through a wool blanket. Lowering me to the floor, he grabs a towel for Buttercup who scrambles to the top of the fridge leaving a soapy trail. Cups and utensils clatter to the floor in her wake. I want to help, but I'm in a dream where my limbs won't obey.

Judy's boots are beside me, then her furrowed forehead. Buttercup yowls. Rubber shoes squeak on the floor. Judy turns my chin toward her. "What happened, Dot?"

"Gravity," I say, my tongue thick.

"Think she fainted." Earl is steadying a stool so Joe can reach the cat.

"How do you feel now?" She's got my wrist, taking a pulse.

"Funny," I say, instead of *I could throw up any second now.*

"I want you to go in the office and lie down."

It sounds like quite a journey. Between Judy and Joe, I'm lifted to my feet.

"She's pale," says Joe like I'm not there.

"I wish you guys would stay home when you're sick," says Judy.

"Just tired," I interject. They'll be suggesting a doctor next.

In the office is one of those pieces of vinyl furniture meant for a waiting room where you don't expect people to make themselves at home. It's long enough for a reclined torso but has no use for a set of legs. Judy tells me to curl up on my left side and shoves her wastepaper bin near me, "in case you have to puke." That word, the *p* and the *k*. I suppress a gag.

"Joe, keep an eye on the front and see if Earl needs a hand?" I guess he nods, as I don't hear a reply. A blanket is placed over me. It must be from one of the dog's kennels. I drift, just about to fall into that inky pool of sleep, when Judy booms, "I think you should stay awake." Her face hangs above.

"Don't have a concussion," I think I say aloud, but I'm not sure because she keeps talking over me.

"Maybe your dad's right about a few things. This weekend, no popping in. You hear me?"

"No pop."

"Feeling better?"

Inside, my organs flutter. "Stomach's in the wrong spot."

"Then stay." Her hand signal is the same she uses for the dogs. "I'm going to make sure they're using a flea comb on Buttercup. Don't puke."

That word. Mum used to say *barf*, which made me think of dogs, oddly comforting. I call it *ralph* and inwardly chuckle whenever I meet someone with that name. No matter what it's called, I always resist.

"Dot, you gave me a scare," says Earl. I open my eyes. He's groping in a gym bag, soaked from the waist up. His cheek has a thick red line leading into his moustache. "I could smell a little something on your breath this morning." His voice lowers. "Didn't know you liked the sauce." He locates a crumpled shirt and gives it a snap, as if that will make it instantly presentable.

"I don't," I say. "Just when I'm sick...ish."

"Here." He holds out a package of mints. "A breath freshener."

My stomach does a little leap at the smell of spearmint, and there's no longer any holding back.

Earl pats my hat as I spit the last of it into Judy's waste bin. "Better now?" I nod. He hands me a tissue. "Not much there," he says, tipping the bin. "You're a lightweight." His eyes crinkle. "Dot the sot."

"Great." A new nickname.

"Sorry, Sot. Want me to drive you home?"

"I can take her," says Judy from the doorway. "You and Joe hold down the fort."

There's a tone to Judy's voice that tells me I'm better off with Earl.

"But my car..."

"We'll figure that out later."

I'll be stranded at my abode. My place is beyond reasonable bus routes.

"I think I'm better now." I straighten my glasses and my spine.

"I don't think so," Judy says.

THE TRASH BIN ACCOMPANIES ME IN JUDY'S CAR. I'M ANNOYED AT this bodily betrayal.

"Which way?" she says as we pull out.

"Left then left again. Right at the bottom of the hill."

It's murky outside. We head through the industrial park—two words that don't belong together—populated with dusty oblong buildings and the occasional fumbled attempt at landscaping. Leaves are rapidly abandoning the few trees in the park. They scuttle along the curb, accompanied by fast-food wrappers and squashed coffee cups.

"I heard Earl." She glances at me. "You were drinking last night? Is that what this is? You and Rachel?"

"No." I explain about the toddy, but the corners of her mouth are still turned down.

"But you and Rachel have been hanging out?" We drive into a wall of rain and Judy struggles to find the right setting for her wipers.

"Not really. What's wrong with Rachel?"

"I knew girls like her in school, that's all." She must feel me staring, using my silence to prod her on. "It's just that you don't really hang out with anyone your own age, and I'm not sure...she's the best influence." I leave a gap of silence so she can hear how maternal she sounds.

"She's an artist. Like Mum. They have a different way of seeing things."

"Rachel is an art *student*," she says, "who still lives at home and shows up late for half her shifts and calls in sick every second weekend. Now which way?"

"Up," I say, pointing to the hill that will take us to the highway. We gain speed and I clutch my trash bin.

"Magazine Hill," says Judy. "I used to think it was named for, you know, glossy magazines." Maybe she thinks we need to keep talking so I won't ralph in her car. "But nope, it's explosives."

"Stay in the right lane up here," I say, hoping I won't explode on Magazine Hill.

The rain stops. There's a line on the pavement as if we've entered a new land. After avoiding the subject for a full week, Judy brings up Toby and asks if I've tried the rehab place again.

"Right lane still," I say in response.

Judy takes a deep breath and lets her shoulders drop. She turns on the radio. They're in the middle of a missing person report when she switches to music. Unlike Joe, she doesn't lip sync but belts out all the parts, including the harmonies. I'm treated to her version of "Losing My Religion."

"You're quite a distance from the shelter," says Judy, turning onto my road. The family abode was closer. Over the past few months, I've started to enjoy the longer drive; it gives me time to transition from one world to the other.

The driveway is empty when we glide to a stop in front of Magoo's. Perhaps Junior has gone. I thank Judy for the drive and place the bucket gently on the floor.

"You rent the whole place?" She eyes the house.

"Just downstairs."

"Ah. I can come—"

"I've got it from here." I sway a bit as I hold onto the door to stand. She narrows her eyes, frowning.

"We'll run the car back to you after we close."

"Thank you." I try for sincere eye contact, but Ralph lurks, so I close the door and gingerly make my way down the empty driveway. Judy idles while I fumble to open my door.

Toby is aflutter to see me. Locking the door, I make it to the toilet with my hand over my mouth. There's plenty of time to contemplate the hygiene of my bathroom floor. More than one tiny turd is on the floor beside the toilet. It inspires the complete emptying of my innards. My stomach is a collapsed balloon.

Bed. Soft pillow. *I'm ready*, taps Toby. So, I take my chances and let him free-range while I close my eyes. Sinking into cotton luxury, I prop one eyelid open. Toby bounces past. There's nothing like trying to stay awake to make you fall asleep, a technique much touted by the Sleep King

A variety of unwelcome noises raise my lids. Knocking: one, two, three. Pause. Knock again. *SSS?*

"Coming." I place a foot on the floor and find it's unusually cushioned. A roll of toilet paper has been sculpted and fluffed. Only the bathroom light is on. The world outside has dimmed.

"Dot?" says the shape behind the tea towel. Friendly.

"Coming." A little louder and better enunciated this time.

Toby perches on Ori's cage, trying to reach in. Whiskers poke out the side. He blinks, *Thou art unfit for any place but hell.* Toby's back is to me, so I attempt to nab him but I'm sluggish and he slips away, laughing. Everyone is annoyed. Five pairs of eyes follow me. The delinquent crow gets to have all the fun. The silent crickets are a judgement in itself.

During my forty winks, the garbage and my bag were raided. At least the paintings haven't been touched, still swathed in paper, tucked behind my woolly walls. He'd have gotten around to them eventually.

"Dot, it's...Joe."

I crack the door. The porch light casts shadows under his eyes.

"Sorry. I fell asleep."

He holds up my car keys.

"How are you getting home?" I say, instead of thank you.

"Judy's coming." He glances toward the road. "I think."

"Thanks." This would be the moment someone else might say, *Come on in, can I offer you a drink...*but I lean out the door and peer toward the road.

"She was right behind me when we left." He rocks back and forth on his feet. "Feeling better?" he asks his toes.

"I'm hoping I didn't flush my stomach down the toilet."

"Yes. That would be bad for the plumbing."

Both of us glance towards the street as a car approaches.

"She was right behind me," he repeats as it continues past.

My beeper hums. Leave him out here or invite him in or offer to drive him home?

"Come in, if you want."

Opening the door, I flip on the horrific overhead light.

"You should see my pla—" he steps inside "—ace." He gapes, then rearranges his face.

"Toby's work. I fell asleep and he had a wingding."

"The crow?" He stoops, reaching for his laces.

"No, leave them on. Yes, the crow." Toby fluffs and gurgles.

There's nowhere to sit but the bed. I'd love to just lie down, but I sense people don't do that with visitors. So we stand inside the door, surveying the wreckage.

"Want some help cleaning?"

"No, I'll get it later." With the help of a towel I corral Toby toward his cage. His blue bandage is still intact despite everything.

"Do you like rats?"

"Rats?" Joe eyes the floor.

"A hairless rat, retired from academic life." He looks genuinely worried. "Ori, my rat."

Bzz, says my pager.

"Sure, but do you want to answer that?"

"I can't. I don't have a phone." I step over the trail of garbage and find Ori glaring through the bars. *And who, may I ask, is this?* I reach in and lift his warm, leathery body in Joe's direction.

Joe steps away from the door but seems undecided, hands anchored in pockets. Sitting on the bed, I boost Ori onto my shoulder and locate the pager. Rachel, yet again.

Joe picks up the mangled garbage bag and starts to shove things in.

"Really, you don't have to." But he carries on.

"Crows can count, you know." He's picking up a slice of moldy bread. "A family lived near us when I was a kid. I used to gather up acorns for them." He pauses and hands me my wallet. "Anyway, I wanted to be fair, so I'd make piles so each crow could get some. But they'd always go for the biggest one first. Every time. Even if it had just one extra."

My door opens without even a slight knock.

"Joe," says Rachel. "Jesus, Dot. What happened?"

I hold my beeper up. "Give me a chance to respond?"

"Sorry. Judy left me a message asking if I'd fill in for you tomorrow." She's looking at Joe holding a butchered tampon in one hand. "What happened?"

"Stomach flu," I say. "I guess." Because I don't like Earl's theory that I just couldn't hold my drink. Joe carries on gathering the flotsam and jetsam on my floor. "But I'm empty now."

Joe picks up my self-defence book and places it on the bed. Rachel reads the title upside down. "Working tomorrow?" she says to Joe.

"Mm-hm." He knots the top of the bag and carries Toby's toilet-paper sculpture to the bathroom. Rachel takes a seat beside me and we listen to Joe washing his hands.

"I've been trying to call you. You were right about that guy with the puppy," she says. "They let him go. Not even a fucking fine. The witnesses couldn't be sure it was him."

I don't always like being right.

"But," she says, "I followed him afterwards, so I know where he lives."

"Where who lives?" says Joe, not hiding his eavesdropping.

Before Rachel can fill him in, I interrupt: "Wait—you tracked him *to his house*? Weren't you scared he'd see you?"

"I kept my distance," she says, and pulls out a spiral-bound pad from her bag. She's drawn him looking back, sharp shoulders hunched in an oversized sweatshirt. She's left the catchlight out of his eyes, so they're just dark holes.

"It's good," I say.

"Thanks." A flicker of a smile as she tucks away the pad. "But, get this, his place is on this road I didn't even know was there. And it's got a massive fence in the backyard." She looks from me to Joe. "I'm going back out when it's dark. I want to know he doesn't have any more dogs."

"Not alone?" Joe and I say at the same time.

"No, Ted's coming."

"Her boyfriend," I say to Joe. "What are you going to do?"

"I don't know. I mean, they didn't charge him, so it's not like he can't have animals. Right?" She nibbles a hangnail. Her thumb is a deep yellow from smoking. "So, we need evidence."

My neck's too hot with Ori draped behind my hair. Has Magoo II cranked the heat? Is he trying to smoke me out?

"But what if it wasn't him?" asks Joe. Like Earl, he still has hope for humans. "Maybe he was just in the wrong place—"

"It was him. I felt it," says Rachel a little too loudly for my abode.

"Okay," says Joe, hands up in surrender.

"We'll just surveil." Her voice is quieter. It sounds like cop talk. I suspect Ted the film buff's influence.

I move to the head of the bed, sink back into the pillows, and listen. Rachel talks about what she doesn't want to find in his backyard.

Out of things to tidy, Joe's untethered hands rake through his hair. He always looks too warm in his flannel shirts, even outside. His face is quite symmetrical. Evenness, I've read, is an appealing trait, something to do with the health of our species. I just want someone to stroke my head while I fall asleep.

Headlights swing across my tea towel and go out.

"Don't tell Judy," says Rachel of her plan. "She's kind of pissed at me for being late last week."

"Speaking of." Joe stands, making no promise of discretion. He pulls the towel aside and peers out. "I won't keep her waiting." He opens the door and Judy's there with a plastic bag.

Uninvited visitor number three steps in. Judy's face holds a similar expression to Joe's when he first saw my abode, except she doesn't rearrange her features. "Why's everyone in the bedroom?"

"It's a...studio," I say.

"Right, a studio." She puts a toe behind the heel of her boot to lever it off.

"Leave them on," says Rachel, like we're roomies.

Judy straightens up. "Well, I just wanted to drop this off. Soup. From my favourite place. Amazing food. I made a stop—sorry, Joe—still warm. Eat it." She gets this way when she's stepping into her management role, speaking in snappy commands like she's remote-controlling people.

"Thank you." Ori sneezes.

"You're welcome. Your hair just made a sound." She puts the bag on my mini fridge. The crickets start up. Three heads turn to locate the source.

"Get some sleep." Judy gives me an appraising look, taking in my jittering hand. "Right, everyone out. This one needs her rest. Dot, I've got cough syrup in my bottom desk drawer, the good stuff. No more toddies."

I try to say yes, but a cough rumbles deep in my chest. The room goes silent. Judy grabs the garbage can and plunks it beside me.

"It's okay, I'm empty."

"If I see you tomorrow morning, you're fired," she says with an index finger aimed at me. I nod.

Joe has the door open, October air funnels in, damp leaves and a hint of wood smoke. Judy switches off the overhead light and they're gone.

It seems I now have clearance for unconsciousness. I try for a weightless place where Mum paints, Ori perched on her shoulder. She's covering a long string of code with the scene of a mother dog and pups in a field of bright flowers.

There's a knock. One, two. Someone says my name, but not the right one. A shape beyond the tea towel. "I'm very asleep," I say quietly enough that I don't wake myself, and close my eyes to search for the painting. Trust the door is locked, ignore the knocking, the gruff "Dorothy."

"Fuck off," I whisper, and it seems he does.

EIGHT

ᴓ

THE SUN MUST HAVE MOVED. UNTIL THIS MORNING, I'VE NEVER seen it inside the abode. It's illuminating my tea towel, casting reds and blues on the wall. This calls for the temporary removal of the Union Jack.

A yellow sticky is on my window. I have to open the door to get at it, letting in a blast of frosty air. Large letters on top: *Don't park in the driveway.* Smaller letters add: *Please. No more than one visitor at a time.* The last few words crawl sideways up the note, as if they too aren't welcome in the small yellow square. I'm glad I told him to fuck off.

Magoo never mentioned the driveway was off limits. After all, Magoo I is *carless.* Out in the cold sun, Rusty is blocked in by a truck with a load of lumber dangling off the back, an orange ribbon tied around the longest piece. Is he going to nail my door shut?

Something squishes underfoot. Standing on one leg, I find a splodge of bird poo decorating my heel. I don't have a vacuum or a mop. There's a broom, courtesy of Magoo—bristles worn to nubs—and no dust pan. At home, I liked pretending the vacuum was a clumsy droid, not quite as advanced as R2D2. We'd encounter the occasional alien species, such as earwigs. All of it, satisfyingly, sucked up. Maybe R2D2 could come for a visit. Of course, the noise alone may call for my immediate eviction.

Thumping steps from upstairs prompt me to re-curtain. The tea towel stays in place but it'll need fresh tape. Judy won't miss a roll from her stationary hoard, and I know where the key is.

When I go to make the bed I spot Rachel's sketch pad on the floor. I study the drawing, the man's crooked mouth and lightless eyes. She said he was smug. I try to picture her skulking around his property, attempting to scale the fence, or knocking on his front door. Maybe he doesn't answer the door. Maybe he's in the shower, or wearing earphones while counting grams of heroin in the basement, or hosting a boxing night for ex-cons, or standing on the other side of the door with a semiautomatic weapon and a nasty smile. My defence book has plenty of advice for a physical attack, but there's only so much you can do if someone starts shooting at you from the other side of a firmly shut door or window.

And did Ted go with her, as promised? They argue regularly. Rachel could mess with his name, call him Teddy Bear and make him feel diminished. Or Baby, another pet name people throw around. *Hue Bare* called me that during my First Time.

Heavy feet descend the outside stairs. I ready myself for a knock. A shape continues past my door. Maybe he'll unblock the driveway. After a few minutes, there's no rumbling truck. Magoo II carries the lumber from the truck to the side of the driveway, laying it down in a messy stack. Judging by his expression, he's not an enthusiastic carpenter, nor one to view this as a welcome dose of daily exercise. He's noisy about it too, each piece allowed to clatter on top of the next. Straightening, he holds his lower back and swears silently at the sky. Men should not use that word. Maybe it's meant for me. Does he know I'm watching? I open the door and give him the royal wave.

He calls out a hello and asks if I got his note.

"Dad's not doing so well. Had a bit of a fall yesterday."

"I'm sorry. Is he in the hospital?"

"Nah. He's in bed." He points to a window at the front of the house. Thus, the note about visitors. I imagine Magoo in bed, listening to me retching. "Now I've gotta build a goddamn ramp." He coughs and spits awfully close to Rusty's front tire. "Anyways, I'm gonna need the driveway for the construction project." He sighs to let me know how much he dreads his task. "I've gotta use my vacation time to do it. And my vacation money." The last bit is muttered as he heads back to the truck to get another piece of wood.

"I can move my car."

"Nah, I got it all untied. You're gonna have to wait till I'm done." He's got a piece of plywood to put on a new pile. "You supposed to be at work?"

"I'm sick." He gives me a look that says he knows what kind of sick people my age get. Something ugly wells up but I squash it down. "That's why people were here last night, dropping off my car—"

"Don't tell me. Tell Dad. He said he heard a bunch of people." He shrugs like he's the most easygoing guy in the world.

AT 11:30 I'M SITTING ON THE EDGE OF THE BED HOLDING MY CAR keys. Faint sounds of the trumpet make it through the floor. Toby rouses at the sound, chattering along to the show's theme. I imagine Magoo propped in a cloud of pillows, glad of the companionship of the working-class folk down at the Rovers Return Inn. At last Magoo II moves his truck.

It feels good to get in the driver's seat. Sunlight on my skin. My feet tingle as they dry out. I pass a drugstore, but remembering Judy's cough medicine, decide to save my cash for crickets.

Joe is at the front desk. He doesn't see me right away. He's explaining about spaying and neutering to a woman who has her index finger planted on a picture of one of the puppies.

"Afternoon," I say and move past them to the office.

Earl is at Judy's desk, hunched over a bowl of, yes, Alphagetti. He seems a bit put out to be discovered.

"Dot," he says, plucking the letter F from his moustache, "good to see you back on your feet."

"Top of the afternoon to you."

"Still not sounding so good," he says, reaching for something behind a stack of files. "She dug this out for you." He bangs the bottle on the desk. "With any luck, it won't have you...talking on the big white phone." The bottle has a line of brown goo dripping down one side. I remove my glasses to read the fine print.

"Best to plug your nose when you take it," says Earl between spoonfuls of letters, "then the taste doesn't hit you until it's well down the hatch."

"I'll try that. And where's Judy?"

"Talking to Rachel in the back." He lifts his eyebrows.

"Did she hire...?" I cock a thumb in the direction of the front desk.

"Young Joe? I stay out of those things, as you know."

That's right, Earl's leave-it-to-Judy policy. He's retired from decisions. I leave him to the remains of his bowl, with a few paragraphs left to slurp.

Getting to the bathroom involves passing the front desk again. Joe is with the same woman; he's moved on to nutrition for large-breed dogs.

In the bathroom, I turn on the lights to measure out the brown goo and I forget, just for a moment, not to reflect. So, I see it all in one blinding glance. It's not just the plucked hat and the sore eyes. My face has new hollows and the pasty skin doesn't help. This is why I don't do this. There's enough going on inside without worrying about the outside.

The second spoonful of goo is the worst, as I have to unplug my nose to pour. Is it possible for your stomach to shudder? Fresh fumes are like a cool wind within. Taking an experimental deep breath, I find the cough reflex subdued.

Earl's in the kitchen, pouring a mug for each of us. He hands me the cup and we clink a toast to medicinal sludge. "You going to work with the volunteers this afternoon?"

He shrugs. Of all of us, Earl is the least likely to snap at people. He has a knack for slowing things down and getting them to listen without raising his voice.

"Unless Judy has other plans for young Joe."

"I think I'm on front desk for the rest of the day," comes Joe's voice from behind. The puppy woman must have gone back into the dog room. That leaves me without a job for the moment, so I head off in search of tape.

Judy catches me hunched over the supply drawer, and it makes me jump and drop the tape.

"Just put a fresh one up there this morning, Dot. Give me those glasses. They're always smudged." She plucks them from my face, leaving me stranded. "You're not even on the desk." She's blurry, but I catch her tone. "Joe is. I thought I told you not to come in today."

"You said *this morning*."

She shakes her head slowly.

"Most people would understand that to mean to take the day off, Dot. But since you're here, are you up for doing a supply run?"

"Sure. Is Rachel here?"

"Cleaning the cat room. Take my car. It's got a bigger trunk."

"Why is she cleaning the cat room in the afternoon?" We always did that before lunch.

"We need to make room for the new cages." Seeing my blank look, she goes on. "The hoarder?"

My heart slips a few inches and rests atop my deflated stomach. "Where?"

"A couple of hours from here; they didn't release all the details. But the rescuers said they were puking from the stench of...Sorry, you okay?"

"I'm empty." I pat my stomach.

"Over a hundred in there. Cat shelters took most of them, but there's still a dozen without a place to go." Looking at her watch, she stops. "A reporter's supposed to call in a few minutes. Then I have to get on the phone to find some fosters." She claims to hate talking to the media, but she must be on their list; every time there's some awful story, they give her a call.

"Were there any dogs?"

"No, Dot...the dogs were dead." Her voice catches. "Here's the list. You know the clinic in the South End?"

How can a person think they're helping animals when they're sick and dying around them?

I wait until I hear her pick up the phone, then make a detour. All the cat cages are in the centre of the room, so they have just a few feet's distance to look at, or purr at, or threaten one another. A fuzzy arm reaches out, trying to connect with the cage opposite, in which a ginger cat has pushed itself to the back corner. The room crackles with feline energy. Buttercup is immune. Now flea-free, she presses against the bars, purring as if I had nothing to do with her bath ordeal.

Rachel is on the top bit of the stepladder that says in large red letters not to stand on it. In her hand is a rag that should have been wrung out better. Drips slide past her rubber glove to her sleeve. She grunts as she reaches for a corner.

"You here to help?" she says, sensing me.

"I'm heading out to pick up supplies."

"Fuck," she says, not quite reaching the spot.

"Here, just get down and we'll move the ladder." Climbing off, she glances at the door. A stream of volunteers moves past.

"So, I was there last night."

"Just you?"

"No, Ted too. Jackass," she mutters. "Never mind."

They watched from the safety of the car for a good hour," she explains. Ted offered to fill the time with some groping. "Totally not taking it seriously." That's when she decided to get out of the car. "I peeked through the fence. There was a tire swing and a chain attached to a tree. Oh, and a wire cage, nothing in it from what I could tell."

"A dog kennel?"

"No, like what we use for rabbits and guinea pigs. Anyway, around ten, a car pulls in the driveway and it was him, Dot." She swallows. "When he opened the front door, there was barking."

"Shit," I say.

"Fuck," she agrees. "We have to go back." Her eyes lock onto something behind me. "Almost done."

Judy stands in the doorway. "Dot—"

I feel ten years younger all of a sudden, caught where I shouldn't be.

"—good thing you're still here. Make sure there's a flat of canned food, too." And she's off, chasing a volunteer.

"She hates me," says Rachel. I tell her she's imagining it. "Oh, yes she does. I can tell by the way she talks to you. She, like, sags when she sees me. Every time. But you, you're her right-hand woman."

"I've been here a long time."

"I know. I'm just stressed. Next week's my first crit." She rinses the rag and climbs back on the ladder. "That's when everyone gets to judge your work—and trust me, they don't hold back."

"The nest thing?"

"No, I still have a few weeks on that. But I did this whole series on cats." She shakes her head. "They're going to crucify me."

"What's wrong with cats?"

She shoots me a look over her shoulder.

"In art school? No sunsets and no pets." She stabs at a stubborn bit of dirt. "I don't know what I was thinking."

"They probably don't want pastel kitten posters." I say. "But when it's not as advertised, they come to us." I've only seen the one sketch from her, but I know she can capture a mood.

She turns and squints.

"Show them this." I point to an old tomcat in the corner, watching us with one eye.

"Thanks. They're still going to tear me to pieces."

"I'd better go." But she's lost in thought, staring at the wall she's supposed to be cleaning.

"Rachel?" It seems I've woken her from a dream. "How about I go with you next time? We can take my car." It sounds like it will blend right into the neighbourhood, and I need to see things for myself.

She winks at me and smiles.

It's a half hour to the cat clinic with Friday afternoon traffic. The pace suits me fine. In the car alone, no one criticizes my fidgeting. In school, tapping my desk irritated the teachers so I hid my hand in a pocket. Then they thought I was hiding something. The principal took it up with my parents. Mum relayed all of this to me with a snort.

"Pills, he said. You've always had one hand going. They should focus on the ones who can't read a book."

Despite her defence, I tried other things: biting my nails down to nothing, then the cuticles. I ground my teeth, scratched, rocked and pulled at the loose threads of my sleeve. The first time I ever experienced stillness was when I touched Archie, the sheepdog Mum pulled from the wrecked car. Feeling that trapped message within but no language to let it out unlocked something in me.

Right now, though, I don't control it. It helps my lungs somehow, tapping out the names of my animals on the steering wheel. Bridge traffic slows. Below, a container ship glides into the channel accompanied by a tugboat. What a different day we each have—people in their cars, the tugboat captain, the crew aboard a hulking ship from another part of the world—all consumed with private shitstorms of worry. All of us trying not to bump into things.

Then I hear Judy's voice on the radio. A sound bite in the story of the hoarder, offering insight, the vagaries of legislation, the appalling number of cats. Anger is evident in her voice. They cut her off when she starts to talk about euthanasia. Next is a psychiatrist who says it's *a disorder*. It might start out well, he says, with the collector attempting to rescue the animal, believing they're the only one who can care for them. It grows into *a compulsion*. They move on to the rising cost of food just as I descend the ramp from the bridge and loop onto the road that will take me south.

It's an all-cat clinic, which is evident by the sign, a pair of triangular ears on the letter C and the silhouette of a Siamese with its tail underlining the words. One of the resident cats, known as Margaret, sits on the reception desk with her hind leg in the air, performing a thorough inspection of her anus. My entrance does not disturb her task, despite the loud clang of the bell on the door. This is something I admire greatly about cats—not the necessity of cleaning with their tongues but their utter indifference. Meanwhile, Elizabeth reclines in a small doughnut bed behind the desk. She raises her head and meows. One might get the impression the place is run by felines.

Eventually, an exam room door opens and a tech comes out, apologizing. Her name tag says *Alex*, but she doesn't confirm or deny this. She's all business. Her ponytail is yanked free on one side. "Trying to get a vein on a Sphynx," she tells me in a lowered voice. I nod and follow her to the stockpile of donations in the back. A wall of stainless-steel cages holds the day's patients in various stages of recovery. A Ragdoll looks at me woozily and emits a sound like a creaking door. "Four dental extractions," says Alex, reorganizing her ponytail. She tells me about the drama of the morning, without checking to see if I want to hear.

"Of course, it's not as bad as the shelter after Christmas," she says. It turns out Alex worked there before going back to school, before my time. Together, we haul sacks of litter and food out to Judy's trunk. She asks if I knew Birdie, then describes an entirely different woman than I knew, full of ideas to improve the place and make it more efficient. When I tell her about Birdie's sudden departure she shrugs and says, "Burnout." After, she's keen to get back to the vein hunt, so I thank her and get on the road.

IN THE SHORT TIME I'VE BEEN GONE, THE PARKING LOT HAS FILLED up. News travels fast. People rush in, ready to tuck a cat under each arm and do their part. Naturally, it doesn't work that way. There's a procedure, we'll spend the rest of the day explaining. None of us excel at that. Judy's car will have to hang on to the supplies a little longer. I park at the end of the street and make my way to the back door. Earl is in the yard hanging tight to a leash with a Shelter Classic on the other end, a term coined by us for the ubiquitous Shepherd-Lab mix. The young dog is trying to get a tug-of-war going.

"Leave it," says Earl in his dulcet tones, removing the leash from the dog's mouth.

"Earl," I say, instead of hello.

"Dot." He glances up. "Leave it."

I take a seat on the concrete step and watch him remove the leash once more and pop a treat into the dog's mouth. He's coaxing him into a down position. The dog is less interested in the leash now, watching Earl's hand go to his pocket. He must be about nine months; the family got him from a newspaper ad. He was the best Christmas present ever. Shelter Classic.

"How are things inside?"

"Down," says Earl, producing a treat. "Judy's twitching."

He glances at me and the dog nips his finger. "Ow," he says, pulling back. This must seem like good fun; the dog bounces onto his hind legs and pushes off Earl's chest with his paws. Earl just turns, presenting the dog with his back. You need a good centre of gravity to work with these ones. It's not their fault. Everyone encouraged it when they were pups, inviting them up and making happy noises.

"Anyone interested in this guy?"

"Not yet. What he needs is a young person," Earl says. "A jogger." A familiar assessment.

"Will you take him home?" Some weekends Earl fosters the Classics, to get them ready for adoption. I've never seen Earl's place, but I picture plaid blankets flung over old furniture and a stockpile of canned pasta. He's still considering his answer when the door swings open, nudging my back.

"'Scuse us, Dot," Joe says. It appears he's converted some cat adopters into dog walkers. I hold the door and let them pass. They receive the grand tour of the yard: favoured pee posts, poop bags, trash bin. "Wrote down a phone message for you," he says, before leading them back in. "It's up front."

Inside, the dogs that aren't being walked are in full protest. All the washers and dryers are going full tilt. A heap of stained blankets overflows the nearby basket.

"You're back," says Judy. "Where's my car?"

"Bottom of the sack," I say, our term for the cul-de-sac. "The lot's full."

"Right," she says, sighing. I'm recruited to print off some signs for the front, filling people in on adoption procedure for the new cats

—no different from the usual one—and forbidden to use Comic Sans or a paw-print border.

The trick is to get past the front desk to the office without making eye contact with anyone in line. Paper is good for this. I grab a list from the kitchen and do my best perplexed expression as I sidle past Rachel, who is talking to a woman in a flowery hat. Even so, Rachel tries to grab me with her left hand, but I shake her off. More people are beyond the flowery-hatted woman, also attempting to get my attention.

"Dot," Rachel says, and I realize she's actually pushing a piece of paper at me. "Your dad. Again."

He's going to come by my place this evening. He's going to take me to supper. He's figured out a way to make me call him back, which I will do, I tell myself firmly, just as soon as I've done the sign.

Only an hour left of being open. I stand at the printer while it clears its throat and silently compose an excuse for Dad. If I tell him I'm working, he'll talk to Judy. If I tell him I'm socializing, he'll know I'm lying. Sick, it is. It's not far from the truth, which is the best sort of lie.

Cracking the office door, I see Rachel has cleared the line for the moment. She must be in the bathroom; the fan is running. I grab the tape and set to papering the doors and windows. I'm humming the appropriate tune—*do this, don't do that, can't you read the sign*—when Rachel appears, her eyeliner thicker.

"You know what one person said to me? I'm a hypocrite for not letting them help. Like *I* make all the rules around here."

"I've had that one."

"God, here comes another one."

"Maybe they'll read the sign first."

"Dot," she says, hand on hip, "people don't read signs. Oh, Joe wants to come with us to the abuser's place."

Two people, both in hunters'-orange toques, are standing at the window reading my signs, their lips moving. I'm willing them to read it and leave.

"Sure," I say, crossing my fingers. They come in anyway and ask to have everything on the page confirmed. Rachel abandons me to the task and I'm now, by default, On the Front Desk.

There's not a moment to make a phone call, and before I have a chance to lock the door and turn off the lights, Dad is here.

"You're here," I tell him.

"You didn't get my message?"

"I did." *But I didn't expect you to show up at the shelter and stand in line to speak to me.*

"We'll go to that place you like? You can leave your car here and I'll drop you off after."

It's harder to lie to people when they're right in front of you. He knows this. He looks at my hand, on the counter between us, index finger vigilantly still.

"I'm not quite ready."

"I'll wait in the car."

I watch him go, slumped and wrinkly but resolute.

My coat is in the office. Judy is at her desk, stroking another rabbit.

"Can I trouble you for some more anti-cough medicine?"

She reaches into her drawer without looking and pulls it out for me. This makes the rabbit open its eyes and wiggle its nose. On her screen is a lengthy email. Apparently, it's worthy of a frown.

"You heading out?"

"Dad wants to take me to supper."

"Good. Eat lots."

My stomach twists a bit at the prospect. People always encourage me to eat more. Others dream of such problems. But I don't see how it's any different from people being told they should lose weight. Either way, you just look wrong and need to be fixed. I'm all edges; it's how I've always been.

In the car, Dad looks at me and says, "Steakhouse?"

Wouldn't that make his day? For me, all the fixings from the salad bar: iceberg lettuce, sad tomatoes, withered carrots. For Dad, filet mignon (because he loves saying it), a mountain of oily chips with vinegar, and a sprig of wilted parsley.

"No thanks." Something free of dead animals.

"McD's." He waits, a half smile on his face. "You used to love their ice cream."

"I was uninformed."

"Just pulling your leg."

We join the traffic snake and inch our way toward our usual, the only vegetarian place on this side of the bridge.

"How's the store?" I ask.

"Kelly's at the helm." His longest employee. I called her Aunt Kell when I was little.

"That's good." Without her, the store would have been closed last year.

A truck pulls out in front of us, a half ton with a dog in the back. Dad glances at me. He knows I don't like it. His hand floats over and pats my shoulder.

"Sorry, Speck. Not everyone feels the way you do."

He started calling me Speck after we watched a space documentary when I was ten. It's meant to remind me we're all pretty insignificant in the grand scheme of things, something we both find comforting.

"Why even have a dog?" It's not like it's a summer evening. True, some dogs hate to be enclosed and love to gulp fresh air, but this one is huddled, unsmiling.

"I heard from Pete last week," he says in an obvious attempt to change the subject. "Remember him?"

"Of course, your Pete pal."

Without Pete, Dad may have stayed in England instead of crossing an ocean to start his empire of sleep. Dad's English teacher foisted a pen-pal assignment on him and pow, I exist. *Kismet,* Mum said. For years, Pete and Roger wrote to each other. One summer Dad flew over to Canada and stayed with Pete's family. They rented a cottage on the Northumberland Strait and he was hooked. All that space. Here, he'd be able to get ahead. In England, he'd never have bought his own business right out of school.

"He called?"

"No, an email. Look." He points to the paper on the dashboard. A giant, grainy garden gnome underneath the email. Pete poses beside it. Underneath he's written, *Hanging with my gnomies. Gnome pun intended.* Dad pulls into a parking space. "Fourteen this time. How am I supposed to top that?" Their tradition is to purchase postcards of roadside attractions and write a message using as many puns as space allows. The email format makes it possible to expand the word count.

I shrug. "A garden of possibility for a...fertile mind, don't you... gnome?"

"You're a whiz with this stuff. You and your mum." His eyes shine.

My stomach tenses. "I'm really not hungry."

"Come on, Dot. Look, we're here. I'm not taking you back until you swallow fifteen thousand calories."

"Dad." He's never grasped the calorie thing. "That would be a week of food."

But he's out of the car and coming around to open my door, not to be chivalrous, but because the inside handle is useless. "Bloody hell, it's getting worse," he says, wrenching it open.

"Anyway," he continues, "I called ahead and they reserved a table."

"You can do that?"

"Guess so."

Inside, it's just the staff. One of the four tables has a sticky note: *Rezervd.* Dad sees it and elbows me. "Do not," he says, *pull out a pen and correct the note.*

We settle in and Dad pockets the note.

"You know we have to order at the counter, right?" I say, draping my coat over the chair.

"Just get me what we had before." He pulls out his phone and squints. "I'm just going to check in with Kelly."

I select some things from the display case for him and a bowl of lentil stew for me. I think he likes the ones that look like pastries, it takes him back to his stodgy English youth.

When I rejoin him, he's bellowing into the phone at Kelly like it's a walkie-talkie. Luckily, it's a short conversation.

"You know," I say, "she *can* hear you."

"Yes, but I can't hear her."

"You aren't holding it right."

"The thing's too small," he says, placing it on the table in front of me. I flip it open and closed a few times.

"But you had to have it." A friend picked one up for him in the States when they first launched last year.

"The world is getting closer and closer to *Star Trek.*"

"And this makes you...?"

"Captain Kirk." He smiles. "Is your pager still working?"

"Mm-hm."

"All right." He pockets his phone and leaves the follow-up question dormant. Luckily, the food arrives. It's not until he's polished off his first spanakopita that he starts in, with practised offhandedness, on the agenda for our meeting.

"You ought to visit her in the new place."

I slurp my stew.

"It's nicer than before. Softer."

"I can't."

He runs a hand through his hair and comes away with several strands between his fingers. He stares at them, irritated, before brushing them off on his pants.

"What, is Rusty not running well? You can't get away from work?"

"You know why."

"She'd like it," he says, pushing a stray hair off the table onto the floor.

"How do you know? Did she tell you?" He flinches. "I'm sorry."

"It's all right." He wipes his mouth with a paper napkin, smearing feta down his chin. "I'm going to pay."

We're on different planes of understanding. I've explained repeatedly in notes, over the phone, and through clenched teeth. He will not cross to my side and I can't go back to his.

When he returns he brings two cups of tea. I'm mopping the remains of my stew with pita bread.

"See? You were hungry."

"Acknowledged." I push my tea bag down with a spoon, watching it stain the water.

"You feeling okay?"

Now we'll review my sleep habits, the state of my pillows, whether I am getting the requisite amount of daylight to keep my circadian rhythm in good working order.

"It's just a cold, but I'm on the mend."

Miraculously, he doesn't prod. Outside, a pair of joggers stumbles past, toes barely lifting high enough to avoid tripping. Dad gives me a look, conveying his disdain for the North American self-improvement industry—from Jane Fonda to Richard Simmons—as if we're all *training for the Olympics now.*

"Mind the speed bumps," he says, watching them skirt a line of idling cars awaiting fast food.

My pager bleats. Dad pulls back from the table like I've pinched him.

"Just a friend from the shelter, probably." I glance at the number. Yup, it's Rachel.

"You know that was for *us*," he says, eyeing the pager.

"I'm aware." He got it for me in my last few months of high school so I'd know if anything happened at the hospital. People thought I was a drug dealer. "Well, Judy has the number. And Rachel."

"What could possibly be that urgent? In my day, friends made plans, they didn't have to page each other like it was a ruddy medical emergency. You're not a vet." That's a cheap shot.

It's not my fault he told everyone I'd be off to vet college after high school. Just because you work with animals, people assume you'll become a vet, like it's the only option. What if you don't have the math or the chemistry or the money to get through all those years of school?

"It's fine." He nibbles at a cuticle. "You just make me worry and I'd appreciate less. Less worry."

"I'm sorry. I'll call more. The shelter gets busy and then I'm tired."

"I can get you a phone. Take this one."

"Dad." We both know I can't afford the minutes. They say one day we'll all have a phone in our pockets. Not me. Even if they make it cheap. I'd rather write. Now, emailing people from a phone—that, I'd like. "The pager works." He's made his finger bleed. I pass him a paper napkin. "I'll use the codes. Okay?"

"Okay, Speck." But he's not looking at me, he's standing up with his empty mug, a wad of napkin balled around his finger. "Okay."

NINE

⚬◯⚬

THE SATURDAY RECEPTIONIST AT DR. TRAINER'S CLINIC IS NOT A rat person. Not entirely surprising. Other than Mum, Rachel is the only other rat person I've met. And, even among rat people, there aren't a huge number who gravitate toward the hairless variety. The receptionist, whose name I don't catch in the kerfuffle that follows, mistakes Ori for a hunk of flesh attached to my neck. It's the first time I've seen someone faint from fright. Of course, I might have done the same thing if I saw someone's bulbous, blinking goitre on the move. Luckily, a carpeted cat tree breaks her fall and she rebounds in no time.

It turns out she's A Fainter. That's why, explains Dr. Trainer, she's on the Saturday shift: there are fewer surgical procedures on the weekends, or fewer scheduled ones. In an emergency, the fainting receptionist is not a reliable assistant. Plenty of things can happen on a Saturday. Apparently, the last incident was a chocolate Lab with a face full of porcupine quills. All of this, Dr. Trainer imparts in a hush, despite the fact she's closed the door to the exam room.

I don't ask her why the Fainting Receptionist hasn't been fired, because she turns her attention to Ori.

"I'm not really an exotics vet," says Dr. Trainer, gazing into Ori's eyes. "That's my partner, Ian. But I can tell you right now, Dot, he's going to need antibiotics." She stops and listens to his breathing. "How old is he again?"

"Two-ish." She looks hard at me, weighing her words. "I know," I say, "ancient."

"Primordial. For a rat."

"He lives in his head a lot," I say, lifting him so she can get the stethoscope under his chest. "Doesn't expend a lot of energy."

"Right." Her mouth twitches.

I think of telling her about his appreciation for art, but she's busy listening to his heart.

"Is your place damp?" she says, gazing off, the way vets do when plugged into their stethoscopes.

"Not exactly." My floors aren't wet, per se. I cough and her head snaps up, eyes narrowing.

"I'm not really a human vet either, but you're not looking so good."

"Just getting over the flu. Sorry." In my haste to get here at the appointed time, I neglected to wash my face.

She runs her hands along his abdomen, feeling his whole hind end and then, to Ori's obvious mortification, she lifts his rubbery tail and examines his anus. *I'm sorry*, I blink at him, *this is undignified but necessary.*

"Rats are prone to respiratory illness. I'd recommend a dehumidifier and make sure he stays warm, too." She scribbles something in a folder while I try to remember if there's a dehumidifier in the cobwebbed corners of the family attic. "I'll get you the antibiotics. The exam is on the house."

"Thank—"

"But"—she holds up a gloved finger—"I want to talk to you about something."

I nod and wait while Ori scales my arm, finding the nape of my neck where he settles to await the topic of discussion.

"He really does have a wise face," she says, shaking her head. "Anyway, our Saturday situation, as you've witnessed, is a little lacking." She indicates the thin wall that separates us from the front reception. "I feel like I'm poaching from Judy. I know you're full- time there, but I wondered if you'd want to come in on Saturdays."

"To work."

"Yes, to work here. For a paycheck."

"I'm not a tech."

"I know. But you have a way."

"So, I'd be up front with customers?"

"Well, no, we're not replacing our receptionist. God knows, she could use some more iron in her diet, but she's Ian's aunt, so..."

"Just Saturday?"

"Mm-hm. For now. You'd assist me, care for the animals in recovery, prep for Mondays, clean. It's a half day, unless we get an emergency—"

In my pocket, my beeper sounds at the very utterance of the word *emergency*. Dr. T.'s eyebrows rise. It's Dad.

"Can I think about it?" If I say no, will she charge me for Ori's exam? Is this an offer I can refuse?

"Of course."

"Do you think I could use your phone?"

"Judy has you on call?"

"No, it's my dad."

Line three is all mine. I even have the privacy of the exam room for the call.

"Oh, the perks of this job," she says, closing the door.

Dad sounds tired. Grand is asking for me. That means one of the nurses has phoned because he's insisted. Grand can be persistent. But it's not an urgent situation. I've learned that by now. It's not like I'm there within minutes, so by the time I arrive, he's often moved on.

"Where are you?"

"At the vet with Ori."

This makes him pause. No doubt it's due to memories of Mum speaking out of the side of her mouth in a squeaky voice.

"Could you go see him?"

Dad knows I see Grand most weekends. But every once in a while, I forget. Satisfied with my lukewarm yes, Dad signs off. A customer has entered the store.

"Love you, Speck."

We leave the clinic with a small bottle of medicine and a page of instructions. She gives me a wink as I take it from her and reminds me to think about her offer.

AT THE SHELTER, I LEAVE ORI BUNDLED IN THE KENNEL, SPENT FROM his trial of being examined. It's busy. Rachel is at the front wearing a lopsided lab coat and a tight smile. We make the briefest of eye contact as I slip past to the office. Inside Judy's desk drawer, I find a lot of rabbit kitsch—everyone's go-to Judy gift: a tea cozy, several buttons, and a set of (rather creepy) candles—before the eye ointment.

Locking the bathroom door, I squeeze some into my right eye. It closes reflexively and I stand with my head tilted back, tears dripping down my cheek before inflicting the left with the same treatment. I have to wrench it open with my fingers as if it belongs to someone else. I follow the whole procedure with a dose of anti-cough goo, holding my nose until it's well past my tongue. The misery of being a living thing, feeling things. I want to stay in here with the light off, indefinitely. But someone knocks, a panicked voice asks if I'm done. Outside is a desperate mother holding the hand of a toddler. It's already too late by the pong wafting from his pants. Muttering apologies, I retreat to the back. My eyes aren't ready to drive just yet.

Oliver isn't in his kennel. Instead, there's a mountain of a dog, who, despite being seated, is eye-level with me, his tongue lolling from his mouth as he pants, drool cascading from his chin. We gaze at one another, and when I don't say anything, he plants a paw on the gate between us in a high-five. There's nothing on the kennel to indicate who he might be.

"Did you eat the dog that was here?" I ask him.

"Dot, meet Button. Button, Dot."

"It's Saturday," I tell Judy, who really has a knack for appearing silently. "You shouldn't be here."

"I know, I'm heading out. We're a little short this morning." She clips a card to Button's door. "Good thing, though. I had to peel the owner off this one. Divorce. He couldn't take him with him. I've never seen a grown man cry so hard."

The card reads *Button, 18 months.*

"Is this right?" I point at the weight. Perhaps the zero is in the wrong spot.

"Yup, one hundred eighty pounds, give or take. So, only staff can walk him. Damn near pulled me off my feet when the guy left."

"Where's Ollie?"

"Adopted. You didn't know?" Fastest adoption yet. Ollie needed someone that could handle his separation anxiety, and Judy was worried about him staying with us for too long. "You *just* missed them. She was due to pick him up Monday but called and asked if she could come today instead."

"But I didn't get to say goodbye."

She pats my shoulder. "Say hello to Button instead. He's lonely." She starts to walk away then turns back. "How's the crow?"

I tell her about his latest feats, including the opening of my fridge.

"You ought to get him out in the fresh air. Let him stretch his... wing."

"Sounds risky."

"How else are you going to know if he's healing?" She leaves us without giving me any suggestions about how to go about it. Am I to borrow a leash from the shelter and take him around my neighbourhood?

Button's card says he's a Great Dane mixed with a Newfoundlander.

"That makes you a Great Newfoundlander, I suppose." He pauses panting, so, probably a yes. "Mind if I come in?" He high-fives me again, so I open the door and squeeze in. The first thing he does is plant his nose on my left shoulder, and ever so gently, using his front teeth, takes the metal button on my overalls and starts to pull.

When I tell him no, he backs off right away with an apologetic wag.

"Buttons. So that's your thing." The card also says he's had two gastro surgeries (button removal, no doubt) and he likes to be vacuumed. I run my hands along his sides, smoothing his coat. Part horse, part bear, he leans into me and I have to use the wall to brace for his weight. We both slide to the floor. He rolls to his back and reveals his belly. There's a rectangle of shorter fur where they must have shaved him for surgery.

I stay with him, feeling his heart slow. Eventually, the drooling peters out and he falls asleep. Then, and only then, do I slip out.

WHEN I GET HOME, MAGOO'S RAMP IS UNDERWAY, THE SCREAM OF an electric saw masking Rusty's rumble. The driveway is littered with sawdust and tools. The framework is in place. Magoo II bends, waistband dipping too low, as he cuts a piece of wood. When he catches sight of me the saw jumps in his hands. He says that word again—the one he shouldn't use unless he's a woman, and a bold one at that. I brace Ori against my neck, his heart hammering his own curses, while I pick my way into my abode.

My tea towel hangs open. I suppose Junior has been peering in the square of glass, taking in the sight of my un-vacuumed abode, plotting my eviction. In the bathroom, I grab my *I heart Wombles* beach towel, tuck it over the top, and squeeze the door shut. There. Full coverage. Visual privacy. It helps muffle the electric saw's shriek.

Something is off about Waldo. His head is larger than it should be. When I get closer, I see the issue. He's shedding. *Look away, I'm hideous.* He turns his head in that decisive way of lizards, dismissing me.

Toby fiddles with his door handle, so I oblige and unlatch it. He swaggers over to my bag and roots inside. There's nothing in there to harm him, so I crawl onto my bed and watch him pull out three dollars and forty-six cents, Judy's eye meds (I swipe the tube from him before he pecks it open), keys, Dad's old sunglasses, a hair elastic, an origami rabbit (for good luck), and Dr. Trainer's business card. I grab that before he can turn it into a sculpture. She'd said I'd help prep for procedures and watch surgeries if I was interested. That would have been exciting before the accident. Now I'm just tired.

Junior's hammering ceases and there's muffled talk. A tapping at my door. It's tentative, polite, familiar, shave-and-a-haircut-two-bits. Lifting my beach towel, I find Joe facing my door but carefully averting his eyes, as if to avoid my potentially nude appearance. Behind him, staring right at me, is Magoo II.

"Hang on," I say through the glass, "I have to get Toby in his bedroom."

When I open the door, Junior has another piece of wood lined up for cutting, his hairy posterior to us.

"Sorry," says Joe, stepping inside and glancing at the construction site. "He's not very friendly."

I shut the door before sawdust can flutter in. "He's traded a beach in Florida for building a ramp."

"Right."

"And he thinks I'm up to something in here."

"This was in Button's kennel, I thought you might need it." I hadn't even noticed the pager was missing. "Good thing he didn't chew it up."

"No, buttons are his thing. Thanks."

He takes a seat at the foot of my unmade bed while I cram things back in my bag. I give him the origami bunny so he'll have something to occupy his hands.

"I'm thinking of heading out to that place Rachel told us about. With the dogs." He smooths the rabbit's ears, not looking at me.

"You know how to find it?"

"Rachel drew me a map." He pats his shirt pocket. "Want to be my navigator?" He's unfolding and refolding the origami like it's a Rubik's Cube while I silently tally my excuses, but in the end, I want to go and see things for myself.

"Just let me get Bungo out of the bath."

When I return, Joe has scooted around the corner of the bed to face Toby. He pulls a treat from his pocket, all the while lavishing him with praise. Toby moonwalks over and accepts the offering.

"Mind if I?" he says, touching the latch.

Toby steps out, and instead of making a round of the abode in search of mischief, he sideways-shuffles up Joe's arm. He's never done this with me. Has he been observing Ori?

"Um," says Joe, trying to turn and look at him. Toby, more gently than usual, taps six times on his head.

"I think he'd like you to stand up."

Joe walks a tight circle as if he's balancing a book on his head. From his higher vantage, Toby tries to snag the Womble towel with his beak. When they pass the light switch, Joe pauses and Toby plunges us into darkness, light, darkness, light.

"Prankster," says Joe, moving back towards Toby's bedroom.

"That's the crow code." I'm thinking of how they saucily look down from electrical wires like they're working out how to steal your car keys and go for a joy ride.

"He seems like he's getting better." He's saved a treat to tempt him back in. "Not that I'd know, really." I move in to lock the door behind him. "When will you release him?"

Already, the thought of him leaving is too much, despite his wily ways. If I had a larger place, I'd build him a proper enclosure so he could be outside. That would be a good, safe life for him. The trouble is, I don't know when that might happen. An extra half day of work at a vet clinic probably won't make me wealthy.

"It'll be a while," I say, putting on my coat.

BEHIND RUSTY IS A LITTLE GREEN TRUCK. JOE CLIMBS INTO THE driver's seat and leans over to unlock the passenger side. I guess I'm used to Dad's car, because I just stand there until he leans over a second time to shove the door open.

"Coming?"

When he starts the engine, a blast of guitar blows my hair back, or it would if I didn't have it secured under my hat. He ejects the cassette, apologizing. I pluck it out to see what Joe listens to at such a volume. Pearl Jam. He tunes the radio to a conversational volume and we're off, at ten kilometres below the speed limit.

"So," I say, "your roommate doesn't call you Joe."

He's a keep-the-eyes-glued-to-the-road kind of driver, so I observe his profile, and there's an extra blink.

"Oh, that." He risks a look my way. "Joe's my middle name."

"So, your first name's Moe?"

He swallows, which is oddly noticeable despite the beard.

"Morris. Same as my dad. I go by my middle name most of the time. Some of my friends call me Moe. Actually...Mojo, but never mind."

"Oh." He's given away the unwanted nickname. Mine is Dotty, but I don't share that.

We're approaching a set of lights. They turn amber and he brakes, coming to a full stop long before the red. A car swerves around us and accelerates through the intersection in the nick of time.

"Want a coffee?" He's spotted a drive-through ahead and rifles through his console, unearthing a hole-punched card. "Two more and I get a free muffin."

"Things are looking up for you."

He gets me a cup of tea, a string wilting over the edge, a scum of bubbles on the top. It's horrible, but I sip it to legitimize the lack of conversation.

Getting back on the road takes some time as Joe waits for a sizeable gap in the traffic before venturing out.

"You never drive to work," I say. *And yet, you own a truck.*

"No, I...I only drive in the daytime." He pulls his lips into his teeth like he's eating his words.

"Okay." It's meant as a prompt, but no, his eyes remain on the road, vigilant. Is it his eyesight? We take the old road, passing houses with people raking leaves, holding their lower backs, yelling at kids to help *for cryin' out loud.* In one spectacular tree, I spot a murder of crows, dark shapes among the bright orange.

I ask him what made him want to volunteer at the shelter.

"I love animals." I wait for more because that's a mere opener for most volunteers to get into their bigger story. "But, it's more about...getting over some stuff." Eyes ahead.

"It's a left up here." I point.

"Really?" He squints at a leaning road sign, the name unreadable.

"Looks like it." Rachel has photocopied an actual map and illustrated the landmarks alongside the highlighted road. "So, it's helping? With getting over stuff?"

"Yeah," he says, "I think so. Last year was kind of rough." *Tell me about it.* But he doesn't. I tap my finger soundlessly against my thigh instead of inquiring about the nature of the *stuff.* Then I spot the turn.

He slows even more. The asphalt is pocked with holes. We're close. I point, spotting an old fishing boat. It looks as if the land has sucked every drop of moisture from it, leaving only the bones. "Okay, turn right."

A metal post missing a street sign leans next to another signpost reading *Dead End.* That's why she drew the map. There's no way you'd find this without help. Joe slows us to a crawl. Sickly trees have sprouted on either side of the road's entrance. If you weren't looking, you wouldn't even notice it.

"There's the fence," Joe says.

"Maybe hang back a little, in case." My gut is on the move again. Joe pulls over.

"Weird," he says, eyeing the crumbled sidewalk. "It's like they started to build a neighbourhood."

"The dump isn't far." I roll down my window and listen for dogs.

"Right. Probably what stopped them building more." He pulls the lid from his coffee and reaches for his muffin. "Want half?"

I wave him off. How can he eat at a time like this?

"What's that one?" He's looking at my right hand, tapping the armrest.

"That? Oh, it's twenty-one."

"Okay?"

"Phillips code? Telegraph operators invented it. Kind of like Morse shorthand."

"Neat," he says, without a shred of mockery. "What's twenty-one?"

"Stop for a meal."

He chokes on his muffin, but luckily, it's actually a laugh. I'm not required to do anything, which is good because I've only performed the Heimlich on a stuffed golden retriever.

"We kept a list of them tacked on the fridge and added some of our own."

"You and your dad?"

"No, Mum. Grand—her dad—taught her." Much as she hated the bunker, she loved code. You run out of things to do in the dark. Grand would only keep a lantern on for so long. "And she was the only kid in her class who could pick a lock."

"She sounds great," he says. "I'm sorry." His voice catches and he clears his throat.

I know I haven't told him anything about my family. Is it Judy or Earl filling him in on my life? I try to imagine how it comes up, what they say when I'm out of the room.

"This one's six." I tap my empty cup. "*I'm ready.* Seven is *Are you ready?*" I tap it, twice.

He blinks at me as if he has to wake up.

"Yeah. Sure." He crumples his napkin, stashing it inside his cup, and lets out a long breath. "We'll get a little closer." He coaxes the truck to start. It groans. It gives me time to imagine hitchhiking back to my place, getting in Rusty, and coming back with jumper cables. "Don't worry," he says, looking my way, "the battery's good."

A beat-up car is in front of the house, vast stretches of rust pocking its dulled olive paint. The tires are inflated, so it must come and go. Joe swings around at the dead end and pulls behind the car. He sits, pulling at his beard, engine idling. Obviously, he's not had any training on a stakeout. My window is closest to the house. I yank my hat down a little lower on the right side. I have that prickly sense of being watched.

"I'm going to knock," says Joe.

"What?"

"It's okay." He leaves the engine running and heads for the front door with a bouncing step. Should I climb behind the wheel? All by itself, my hand taps *caution.* Joe's knock is a standard *bang-bang.*

He turns his back to the door, one hand anchored in a pocket, and studies the clouds. He's not great at looking casual. He tries again. *Bang-bang.* There's a crescent window in the door. He peers in, then tries the doorbell. He turns and shrugs at me as if *oh well, whatshisface isn't here.*

Climbing back in, he puts us in drive and cruises away.

"No one answered." Clearly.

"What was your big plan?"

"Say hello."

"And then?"

"I don't know, something would have come up." There's a sheen of sweat on his forehead. It's a breezy day. I don't think he's a wing-it kind of guy. "I just thought, what if it's a big misunderstanding? You know? Maybe we ought to rule that out."

"But no one answered." I say. So, we know nothing new.

He turns onto the rutted road and weaves around the worst of the potholes.

"It's a mess in there." He describes the front room, stacked with crap like those photos Judy has of the hoarder. He tries to find the right word for the smell, without success. From his face, I can tell his muffin is in danger of reappearing.

"It could be coming from the dump," I say. "Could you hear anything?"

"No," he says. "You?"

I shake my head. "If dogs were out back, they'd probably bark."

We glide to a gentle stop at a four-way intersection. If I were holding a full beverage without a cover on it, I wouldn't have spilled a drop.

"You know, I think the speed limit is sixty here." *Not forty.* Maybe he just got his license.

"I'm in no rush," he says.

THE RAMP IS IN PLACE WHEN JOE PULLS UP AND MAGOO II'S TRUCK is gone.

"They might have been inside the house," he says, putting the truck in park. "Rachel said she heard barking, right? Why not just report it to the animal cruelty people?"

I know why, having had phone calls at the shelter from people suspecting their neighbours of abuse or neglect. To go inside, they need the police. The police need a warrant. To get a warrant, they need something more.

"What about next door?" he says. "They'd know."

Unless people live in a house with a large crack in the front window, the house number hanging sideways from a rusted nail, I'd guess the neighbours are long gone. Another one had a little lamppost out front, snapped off halfway down and left dangling. Sure, people procrastinate about things, but the whole street?

"So, we'll go back," he says. "Maybe at night."

My heart is made of lead. When I started at the shelter, I imagined cats in need of a good grooming, dogs awaiting an ear massage. No one tells a twelve-year-old people intentionally hurt animals, even Mum. I push the truck's door open.

"Wait," he says. "My number." He pulls a piece of paper from his pocket and hands it to me. "Just, you know, if you need anything, I'm here. Okay?"

I nod, taking it from him. As I watch him drive off, the paper folded in my palm, I wonder if he's asking me out or trying to be my big brother.

TEN

≈

A SUNLESS SUNDAY MORNING ON THE OTHER SIDE OF MY WOMBLE towel. I clean the bathroom floor with what I have on hand, a damp cloth and my bony knees. Toby balances on the toilet seat, jiggling the handle just enough to start a flush. Judy keeps rattling on about him needing to *stretch his wing*. What's wrong with a cozy life with easy access to food and furry friends? But I'll take him on a small outing, if only to prove her wrong.

The sky is white and painful. I put Dad's sunglasses on, but they slide off if I tilt my face, so I'm forced to walk with my nose high, toting an excited crow in his travel cage. Magoo II's truck has returned in the night. My heart trills until we're shut in the car. I'll bet he's watching from a window, reminiscing about the time when the basement was his domain. It's a relief to drive away.

I head away from the city to my private roadside retreat, discovered on a trip back from yard sale-ing with Mum the weekend after I got my license. We'd had lunch, and because I was the driver, she had a beer or two. Her bladder wasn't going to make it home, so I pulled over at the first spot I could. When she got back to the car, she was bright-eyed, insisting I follow her. Beyond the squat evergreens festooned with litter, just a short way down a dirt path, was a gurgling creek sloping through the trees. We sat next to a miniature waterfall for a bit, imagining a different life where water ran behind our house, instead of traffic. When I'm here I pretend she's beside me. It's not the beach, but no one bothers me.

Toby tries to poke my hand through the bars as I cart him to the creek, his way of hurrying me along. I have a book and an old towel. We can settle in for a bit and Toby can enjoy the sky from his cage. As soon as I set him down, he lets me know he has a different plan, working hard to undo the latch from the inside. This one doesn't have a lock, so I have to hold it closed with my fingers. After a few stabs from him, I give in. How far can he go with one wing?

As soon as I open the door, he hops out and swaggers over to the stream like he's just purchased the land. He eyes me before dipping his beak to the water. I squat in the spiky grass and watch him. My pocket is jammed with treats, and I toss one his way as a reminder I'm here.

He manages a sort of bath, flicking water my way. His bandage, dotted with mud, begins to sag. I read the same paragraph four times. It's just marks on paper, like squashed bugs. I can't focus with him free-ranging. Every few minutes I move a little further downstream to stay near him.

Just as I'm thinking to snare him with the towel, he tilts his head at the nearby trees. A crow caws three times. Seconds later, the others glide into view. Answering, Toby lifts his good wing, hopping toward them. I toss a peanut, but he doesn't even look. One swoops down and makes off with it, landing nearby to work the shell open. If they're interested in him, they don't show it. I toss a handful in the other crow's direction and his mates join him on the ground, snatching them and retreating, eyes on me. Toby ignores his peanut and hops their way, gaining a little height before landing awkwardly. Trying not to panic, I stand, ready to chase them off, in case this turns into a Hitchcock film.

But after a few minutes without peanuts they take to the trees, chattering to one another, bobbing their heads and grooming themselves. Toby circles the trunk below: *Wait up, guys.*

There's conversation above, discussion of this odd, grounded bird with a blue sash. They've chosen the tallest tree, bare of its leaves among the tangle of pines. Toby makes a new, piercing noise. Except for clanging his beak on the bars, he's quiet at home. He clicks and cries as they lift off.

"Toby," I say, rattling my pocket, trying to get close enough to head him off. But he starts after them, farther into the scrubby trees, easily navigating under low branches where I can't go. I have to find a different route while keeping my eyes trained on him. I try creaking and clicking like a crow. No one is fooled, and I'll need my last few peanuts to get us to the car. If I can get him to the car. He could keep going deeper into the brush.

The crows belt out a burst of caws. We both pause as they fly over, a beat of wings moving back the way we came. Toby's high-pitched cry hurts, hopping and reaching with one wing. His gift of flight taken away, he's anchored to the ground with me and a handful of peanuts.

A full hour later I get close enough to wrap him in the towel. I'm numb as I close the cage door and head for home.

On the drive back, he cries. I open the windows to let the sadness blow off with the wind. His voice rattles through me. So much for this sip of freedom. He'll resent me even more now.

When I open the car door, Toby goes quiet. A curtain shivers in a window upstairs. Inside, I transfer him to his big cage and dig out Judy's soup leftovers, tucking some into his bowl as a peace offering. He angles his head to get a look but doesn't budge from the perch.

I just want to lie down, but my overalls are stiff with dirt. Ori blinks from under his blanklet, a bid to accompany me on my laundry trip.

To keep the autumn wind from his skin, I wrap his cage. Magoo II is there, mug in hand, atop his new ramp.

"Do I wanna know what you got under there?" He smiles at his own joke, trying to sound like De Niro.

"Ori," I say, hoping he'll leave it at that. "Nice ramp."

"It's coming along. Got to stain it today if doesn't rain." He frowns at the clouds. "What's Oreo?"

"Orinoco, my rat."

His face slackens. I peg him as a non-rat person, so I try to set him at ease. "A domesticated rat, not the wild kind. Hairless." It doesn't seem to raise his spirits. "He won't cause an allergic reaction for people with that kind of sensitivity." Of course, Bungo and the comedy duo have full furry coats, but never mind. Their surface area is minimal.

"Oh." He has a gulp of caffeine. "Where you taking him?"

"To my dad's."

Before he can form another question in his sawdust-addled mind, I bundle us into the car.

EVIDENTLY, DAD STILL FOLLOWS THE GETTING-DRESSED-IS-OPTIONAL-on-Sundays credo. He stands at the top of his dusty stairs with a cup of tea, an echo of Magoo II but sadder. His forehead is still asleep, but he manages a smile.

"Hello, Speck."

"Afternoon, Dad. Okay if I do laundry?"

"Aye, I have a month of knickers to do." He winks, badly. "Pulling your leg. I'll put the kettle back on."

"Coffee for me. Please."

"Traitor." It's not that he doesn't drink coffee, just not at home, where tea rules the cups.

Installing Ori on my shoulder, I sort the darks from the lights. His whiskers tickle the side of my neck. *Home sweet home, where a bald rat can roam.*

"Final gurgle," calls Dad down the stairs, knowing I don't like coffee to sit on the burner for long.

I find him in the kitchen doing what he refers to as "cooking." Two slices of bread—not sprouted grain or whole wheat, but the kind you can roll between your fingers and it returns to its doughy state—slathered with Marmite, adorned with a pale slab of tomato, and topped with thick slices of cheddar. This concoction is broiled in the toaster oven and topped with another condiment. It could be mustard, steak sauce, or ketchup. Maybe all three.

I decline his offer but make myself a piece of the nutritionless toast with a thin layer of Marmite. In elementary, it was a good way to keep people away from my lunch. I've recently discovered it's packed with vitamin B. So, it pretty much compensates for the bread.

"You know," I tell him as we create crumbs together, "this bread can be used as a poultice."

"Nice."

"It helps pull the gunk out of an abscess." I pass Ori a nibble of toast.

This doesn't deter Dad. In fact, he locks onto my eyes as if to show me how unbothered he is by my morsels of truth.

"Speaking of pus," he says, wiping his mouth. "How about those eyes?"

"I've got some stuff for them."

"For yours or Ori's?"

"Both."

"He looks all right."

I hold my arm out so Ori can descend onto the table.

"I wish you wouldn't do that," says Dad.

"What? We're both finished. It's only logical he be allowed to assist with the cleanup." Ori settles onto Dad's plate, his front paws delicately picking up the larger of the scraps. Frankly, he's a much neater eater than either of us. "Any chance of there being a dehumidifier in the attic?" I say, remembering Dr. Trainer's advice.

"There's a better chance of it being in the garage."

TOGETHER, WE VENTURE INTO WHAT WAS DESIGNED TO HOUSE A motor vehicle but, in our case, has become an oversized box of memories. I brace for it. Dad has to use his shoulder to coax the door open. We stand in a hallway of cardboard. I have the flashlight because the overhead light burned out last year and replacing it would require digging out the ladder at the far end of the room.

"Now," says Dad, eyes shut to summon spatial memory, "we had to use it when the washer flooded the floor that time."

"Right," I say, trying not to think of Mum laughing hysterically as the washer belched foam. My first attempt at doing the family laundry. That means if it's in here, it's five to six years in. "It's a tad fire-hazardy in here, wouldn't you say?"

"You need it for your flat?" says Dad, avoiding talk of decluttering.

"Vet's orders," I say, casting my beam of light along the shelves at the back. "There. Is that it?"

"Bloody hell," Dad affirms. "I'll shove these ones aside, you see if you can get in there sideways." Glancing back at me. "Not that you're any wider front-on." A jab at my undereating again. "Think you'll be able to lift it?"

"You ought to see me in action with the bags of food at the shelter." I flex and pat my bicep to indicate the well-concealed strength.

He waits until I have it in my grasp and am executing the lift and twist to say, "Come with me this afternoon, just for a short visit? For me."

"They won't want me there when I'm sick."

"Did you get to see Grand yesterday?"

In answer, I cough. The elderly don't appreciate a visit from a germ-wielding person either.

Dad sighs and takes the machine from me, shuffling backwards to the door.

"I'm worried about you, living in that flat at your age."

"It's fine."

"Judy said it's dank."

Ah, it's as I thought. Is there a weekly, or daily, conference discussing my behaviour? Although, to his credit, he has not tried to visit me at my abode.

"It was not at its best when she was there. Speaking of which, may I also borrow R2D2?"

FRUSTRATED WITH MY *DAFTNESS*, DAD LEAVES ME TO FINISH MY laundry. I narrowly avoid a farewell hug by ducking into the bathroom when I hear him collecting his car keys.

"Stay for supper?" he calls through the door.

"Sorry. I have something. With a friend."

"A friend?" The shift in his tone is operatic. His hopes for me as a girl with a gaggle of friends—mates, as he insists on calling them—reignited with one white lie.

"Just someone from work." I clear my throat to indicate the need for privacy, beyond the visual. No one wants to hear a small or large splash when hovering near a bathroom door.

"Right then." The front door closes.

UPSTAIRS, I GATHER CLOTHES FROM MY CLOSET. ORI TUNNELS UNDER the sheets, settling down at the foot of the bed as a barely noticeable lump. I swear I hear him sigh.

From downstairs, deep in the folds of my bag, comes the song of my beeper. It has been many hours since I heard from Rachel. More than twenty-four, now that I think of it. For once, I'm able to call her back.

On Sundays, she cleans kennels and walks the dogs. It's a far more relaxed environment without the people. I can hear her chewing a piece of gum as she asks about the drive with Joe. She seems disappointed we didn't see more, just a pile of junk through the window.

"A car was there." I feel the need to defend us. "It was daytime."

"Anyway," she says, "I did a little research, and guess what hanging tires are used for?"

"Fun for small children?"

"Training dogs to fight."

My stomach clenches. I learned a bit about dogfighting, like it or not, at a weekend seminar on handling the neglected and abused. The instructor, a large, sad-eyed man in rainbow suspenders, said these dogs are conditioned with taunting, starving, and sometimes beatings. We'd have to be cautious, deliberate in our actions so as not to trigger them. In other parts of the world, dogfights still happen out in the open. Here, there are rumours, but during my time we've never had anything at the shelter. I hoped that meant these things just didn't happen around here. More likely, those dogs are taken to the provincial shelter across town, or maybe they don't catch them here. At the end of it the instructor recommended not trying to rehabilitate the dogs ourselves but working with a professional behaviourist.

"Dot? Did you hear me?"

"Why tires?"

"I guess it makes their jaws stronger. They use thick chains, too, so they have to build muscle to move around..." She trails off, just as unwilling to think of it as me. I think of the smaller cage in the yard and wonder what he had in there.

Neither of us says anything for a moment. I listen to the excited bark of a dog on her end of the phone and try to erase the images in my head.

"So, I've got Mum's car tonight and I'm borrowing Ted's video camera."

Ted can't go because he has a shift, so she's talked Joe into it. But, knowing that the guy could be training fight dogs, she's nervous, as she bloody well should be, and would feel better if there were three of us. The thought of that kind of thing happening here with no one stopping it makes me livid.

"I can't hear you," Rachel says. "There's interference on the line."

I realize it's me, tapping *SOS* on the mouthpiece, so I switch hands and ask her what time we're heading out.

WHEN I PULL UP AT THE APPOINTED TIME, SHE ISN'T THERE, BUT Joe is. He climbs in and we sit in silence, watching for Rachel.

"What's that one?" Joe says, looking at my hand tapping the wheel.

"Oh, nothing. *Waiting.*" Mum used to take forever to leave the house. After five minutes I'd start transmitting, tapping the horn. The neighbours didn't like it, but it worked.

"Here she comes." She pulls alongside us. All of her windows are down, an odd choice for late October.

"There's a spot after that road you went to before," she says, taking deep breaths out the window. "We might be able to get to his backyard that way."

We agree to follow in my car. That way, I can drop Joe off afterwards and she can be home before the car's curfew.

"Forgot to ask you," says Joe, after we're on the road. "Did you go see the vet?"

"I did." I'd forgotten his prediction. "And you were right."

He nods, satisfied. I tell him the details without mentioning I didn't give her an answer.

Theme music comes on the radio. It's the bossy woman who gives people advice from her booth in New York. Sometimes I listen, finding it oddly comforting—not her hard-hearted counsel, but the level of turmoil in the lives of others. But most people probably don't enjoy it, so I switch to a music station for Joe.

"Do you think you'll be a vet?" His knee bumps up and down to the music.

"I don't know. What about you?"

"Engineer. That was the plan, anyway. Things kind of fell apart in second year." His knee loses rhythm.

"What sort of engineer?"

"Mechanical."

"Ah," I say as if I know all about the different kinds of engineers. Mental image of Joe in a train conductor's cap. We hum along to Garth Brooks, which must make him think of Toby—a bird with *friends in low places*—because he asks how the wing is doing. I recount my unplanned journey through the trees.

"Birds start to lose it if they don't get enough mental stimulation. You know?"

"I know."

Ahead of us, Rachel's brake lights come on; she hangs an arm out the window and points. We go past the leaning street sign onto a dirt lane. It looks like the land was cleared here, maybe for the next phase of building that never happened. Spindly trees have sprouted, threatening to overtake the bit of road left.

Rachel parks and gets out, bolting for the back door to pull out a plastic bag. When we join her, I see there's a brown paper bag inside seeping liquid. I don't need to get close to know what it is.

"Let me guess, you plan to light it up on the doorstep," says Joe.

It must contain a week of crap.

"Where'd you get it all?" I ask.

Does Rachel smuggle shit home from work like I do with the toilet paper? But no, her neighbour has a mastiff. It's only occurring to her now the smell might stay in her mother's car permanently.

"It'll be fine." Joe has a knowing look.

This seems to relax her enough to get back to the plan. Pulling a flashlight from her pocket, she points at a narrow opening in some prickly shrubs.

"All right," says Joe, "but it's best if we don't use a flashlight."

"Right," she says, turning it off. "Hang on, I need to get the camera out." She pulls out a little Sony and fiddles with the buttons until a small screen lights her face. She points it at us. "It's pretty grainy, but it should work." It's better than what we see on our security video at the shelter.

Joe leads, gently pushing the branches out of the way with gloved hands. I take the middle and follow in his steps, trying to be as silent as him. Rachel is not as careful, cursing as thorns catch her loose hair.

Before we even approach the fence, I hear signs of life. Joe halts and I bump into his back. Puppies. I stare, waiting for my pupils to adjust. From here, we can make out the upper floor of the house and the top steps to the yard. The pups are playing, yipping and growling in their high, buzzy voices. Joe turns and whispers he's going in for a closer look. Rachel prods me in the back, none too gently, until I relay the message. She tries to get around me but I hang onto her jacket, anchoring her in place.

We watch his progress, knees in a deep bend, stepping with toes, then heels. His dad must have taught him some hunting skills. At the fence, he leans in, going still. The back door opens and we see someone in a hooded sweatshirt emerge with two bowls. Is it him? Rachel vibrates at my side. I give her jacket a firm tug to let her know I still have her. The screen door slams. Joe turns and makes his way back to us in the same halting gait.

"A mother and six puppies," he says when he gets close enough.

"In a kennel?" Rachel says.

"No, they're loose."

The screen door slams and it's the same hooded guy with a dog on a leash. He struggles to keep from being pulled down the short staircase, grunting as the dog strains forward.

A thin voice calls from in the house. "Waylon."

"Just gimme a sec," he calls back. "For fuck's sake," he mutters as he muscles the big dog over to the tree. He goes out of sight, but there's the soft clink of a chain.

My grip on Rachel hurts my hand. I let go but she doesn't seem to notice. We're rigid, eyes wide, like prey in the darkness. Without saying anything, Joe creeps back to the fence, picking a different vantage point.

Again, the door swings wide and Waylon comes out with a garbage bag. He struggles to heave it onto his back and makes for the side of the house. A latch clicks, then he's back in the yard. He hawks and spits. There's a sharp yelp from a puppy. Both of us flinch.

Before I realize it, I'm moving, like Joe, towards the fence. Luckily, the puppies are making enough noise to cover any snaps and crunches.

Just as I reach the fence, headlights swing through the cracks. A car door slams. I have a partial view of him. He goes to a gate at the side.

"Over here, bro."

Another hooded creature appears, roundish, slumping and smoking. He's permitted into the fenced area and I see the puppies for a moment as they clamour for his ankles, pale with dabs of dark on them like someone splashed paint around the room. He grabs one of them and lifts it by the scruff, dangling it above the others.

"Think you got it in ya, bud?"

"You seen his dad," says Waylon, kicking at the ones trying to climb his legs.

A small fire starts in me. The creature drops the dog. Just lets him go, and he lands with a yelp. I cover my mouth.

"Fuck's sake, that's my investment, numb-nuts."

"That him?" says the Dropper, looking at the tree. Tied to the tree, the brawny dog strains at his collar.

"Damn straight," says Waylon, in what must be his most sentimental tone.

"Heard he took the other one down in, like, five."

Chilling laughter ensues, and I imagine euthanizing them both, Dr. Trainer getting a fat vein and me with a jumbo needle ignoring their pleading eyes. Joe is at my shoulder, leaning in. "Just wait," he says in my ear, as if I'm about to vault the fence and take them both out like the Terminator.

"Looks like a good set up, why're we movin' 'em?" asks the Dropper.

"People been coming around." He juts his chin at the street. "And my fuckin' harpy aunt."

"She doesn't even leave the house, what's she gonna do?"

"Her goddamn mouth works just fine, and she can use the fuckin' phone."

"Shit, you're just trying to make a living. Why they got to make it so hard?"

The pup has found his mother. I hadn't noticed her before, huddled close to the fence. She greets him with a full licking. Meanwhile, the others have moved away and are making a game of tugging on a tattered blanket.

"You taking 'em all?" says Waylon, flicking his cigarette butt into the bowl of water for the dogs.

"Fuck no, not in my ride. Dice is coming. I'm here for the other thing."

"Seriously? You're making the drop?"

The Dropper responds by pounding his chest like a flabby gorilla. Waylon heads for the back door then turns and points a finger.

"Don't get 'em riled up."

With Waylon gone, the Dropper moves for the mother and her pup. She goes stiff as he gets near. But he crouches and just looks at her, watching the pup rooting for a nipple in the curl of her belly.

"Fuckin' dogs," he mutters in an oddly tender tone.

Waylon returns with a lunch box and hands it over.

"Spiderman?"

"It's all I had," says Waylon. "What's wrong with Spidey?"

"Nothing, if you're eight."

"Just take it. When's Dice coming?"

"After his shift." He rolls back the sleeve of his sweatshirt to look at a gaudy watch. "In, like, fifteen? Anyway, I gotta fly."

"Don't do what you did last time," says Waylon.

"Not my fault. You shoulda seen her." He licks his fat lips and heads for his car. His *ride*.

Inside the house, the phone rings and Waylon sprints for the back door.

We could call the police. But I think it might be too late, and what if they don't care about the dogs, only what Spiderman is hiding?

"We've got to get the pups out before they move them," I whisper to Joe, my index finger tapping *SOS* in the air. He nods like he's thinking the same thing.

"Rachel's shit?" he says.

"Yes."

I move back to where I left her, with her view of the back door. She's visibly trembling, trying to work the buttons on the camera.

"It won't turn on," she says. "Did you hear them?" I nod. Now, proven right, she's shrunk.

"Never mind the camera, we're going to get them out of here." I take it from her and lay it on a flat rock.

I tell her how we'll do it. Joe is already heading back to the car for the bag of crap. One of us will use it as a distraction. She's wide-eyed at the thought of entering the yard and making off with the pups.

"What if he comes out?"

"How fast can you run?"

The door slams and Waylon reappears. He flops on the top step and lights a cigarette. In between drags, he massages his forehead and mutters to himself. He's a runt, but a malicious one. Then the phone rings and he scrambles for the door again.

By the time Joe returns and plops the bag on the ground, Rachel looks like she's going to throw up. She wants to call the police.

"Someone is coming for them," I say, "and I didn't see any pay phones near here, did you?" Now would be a good time to have Dad's phone on me.

"I'll go around front and light this thing on fire," says Joe. "As soon as you hear him, go in. Then head back to the cars."

"How?" Rachel is openly crying now.

"Just grab as many pups as you can hold and go," I say.

"What about the mother?" says Joe.

"She'll follow her pups." I hope.

"And the one that's tied up?" Rachel says.

Took down the other one in five minutes.

I shake my head. "First, the pups."

Joe's beard hides his expression, but I can see his twitchiness.

"You have matches?" I say. He nods, pulling a lighter from his pocket. "Okay."

"Okay," he says, not moving. "Um, if something happens. Just you two, get out of here."

"For crying out loud," I say. "No. Just light it, hit the doorbell, and run." I'm calm and angry. I'm Grand in World War Two. With a few major differences. "Just make sure it's a good-sized fire before you knock."

Joe leaves with the bag. When he's halfway, I signal to Rachel to follow me. We need to be ready to get inside that gate. I flatten myself against the side fence. Through the cracks, puppy noses snuffle at us, whining.

There's a series of knocks. Moments later, Joe is running in a crouch and the three of us make for the gate and wait until we hear a shriek, followed by curses.

It's not easy to move at great speed and look inviting to puppies at the same time. I drop to the ground and use my Tweety-Bird voice, scooping up two and bundling them into Rachel's arms before her fear can drive them away. Joe stuffs two inside his coat and is trying for a third wriggling pup. One nips at his beard. That leaves me with the one who was dropped earlier, cowering behind his mother's haunches. She has heaved herself to a standing position. I sink to my knees a few inches from her and let her sniff me.

In the house, the aunt screeches at Waylon to tell her what's happening. He curses and slams things, which must mean he's back inside, probably looking for something to put out the fire. Behind me, the dog on the chain growls.

"Come on, let's go," I say to the mother. She's quaking on her thin legs. Her eyes are large, the bottom lids drooping as she looks at me. She allows me to reach out to the pup.

"Dot," says Joe. "We've got to move. Now."

He's at the gate, one pup sliding lower than the others. Rachel is gone. I crawl over to the pup and pick him up. In my arms, he goes floppy. Tucking my fingers under the mother's collar, I tug her along with me. We make it through the gate. I want to sprint, but the mother hobbles beside me. I can't leave her. Then I see Rachel, coming back to us with her arms empty.

"Where are they?"

"In your car."

"Here," I say, passing over the pup. "Go."

I crouch down to the mother and get my arms under her. Normally, I don't think I'd make it more than a few steps with the weight of a milk-filled pit bull in my arms, but adrenalin is a wonderful thing. I'm almost to the back of the fence when I hear him behind me.

"What the fuck?" he snarls, footsteps pounding the ground. I try to go faster. "Stop!"

That's not why I stop. My grip is loosening, and I realize I have to let go of the mother if I'm going to fight back. I put her down as gently as I can before turning.

"You," he says. "You little bitch." He's coming closer, letting me see his pinched face. He's my height, maybe shorter. He hasn't pulled out a weapon yet. So, I let him get close enough to deliver a kick to his groin. But he lurches to grab for the dog and my foot hits him in the nose instead. Bloody, screaming and cursing with one hand to his face, he still reaches for the dog, but she's not having it either, snapping at his fingers. A telling snap. He goes down and then Joe's there, pushing me towards the car, lifting the dog. Together, we catch up with Rachel in the tunnel of brush.

"Get back here, you little c—" Waylon wails.

Rusty's windows are filled with wet noses. I open the back door and grab one flopping pup while Joe plonks the mother into the back seat. He crawls in with her and I close the door on them.

Rachel is behind the wheel with her teeth bared, eye makeup all over her cheeks like Alice Cooper at the end of a gig.

"You okay to drive?" I say.

She nods, her teeth in a wacky smile. "We did it," she squeaks.

"Follow us, okay?"

Before I can get into my seat, one of the pups leans on the horn, emitting a nasal, shaky groan. It doesn't matter. We have them. I climb in and attempt to buckle the belt while the pup nibbles at my ear. Puppy perfume is intoxicating, but I have to get us out of here. Something tells me Waylon doesn't give up easily.

"Okay?" I say to Joe, who has his arms wrapped around the mother.

"Just don't brake too hard," he says.

"I don't plan on using brakes." I turn the key in the ignition and there's a slight hesitation, a moment in which I imagine a world of horrors before it rumbles to life. The headlights illuminate the dust left by Rachel's departure. We're facing the wrong way, so I have to swing us around, and as I do so there's a sway in the bushes. We can hear him over the motor, but more noticeable is the thing he's holding.

"Jesus, Dot," says Joe, twisting in his seat.

"I know."

"Get down."

In the rear-view I see him take aim. I ram my foot onto the gas and we're almost to the turn onto the road when we hear the blast. Nothing shatters or bursts into flame.

"He's down," reports Joe.

"What? *He* shot at *us*," I yell.

"Don't think he knows what he's doing."

He's never shot a gun before? Luckily, Rachel disregarded my instruction and is ahead of us, making the turn onto the potholed road, tires screaming.

"How are they?" The pup in the front seat slid along the bench during my U-turn and got sucked onto the armrest as we accelerated.

"The pups are fine," he says.

"And her?"

"I'm not sure, but you can slow down now," he says. But I'm trying to keep up with Rachel, swerving around the larger potholes in the road. "There's no way he's following us," Joe says. "What happened to his face?"

"I kicked him."

"In the face?"

"I was aiming for his balls." The pup is crawling around the floor, trying to sniff my feet, getting too close to the pedals. Reaching down, I try to lift him, but he wriggles.

"Watch out!" says Joe.

I correct just before we hit the ditch. My heart skips five beats and then gets back to work at high speed.

"The pup, he's—"

"Just pull over for a sec. Dot? Pull over."

I take his advice. We transfer the pup to the back seat.

"You're shaking," he says.

"And sweating." My inner Grand must have fizzled away with the gunshot.

"Yes, that too," he says, peeling the mother's bum from his lap. "I'll drive. You stay with her." I hesitate, having seen his daytime driving. "I can't have something happen to you too," he adds.

"What do you mean?"

He shakes his head. "Nothing."

"No, no. I'm okay." I get us back on the road.

Rachel is long gone when we reach the stop sign to the main drag. As I get back to regular speed, the tension eases until I hear Joe curse under his breath.

"What?"

"Ford Mustang."

"Okay?"

"That guy, from Waylon's."

He's right on our bumper, mouth flapping, with a phone jammed to his ear. Of course, even small-time drug dealers have moved on from pagers now. It's one of those cars with a nostril on the hood.

"Just keep driving," Joe says, as if I'd stop and hand over the dogs. "But not to the shelter."

"Where, then?

"Take a left up here."

My hands are locked on the steering wheel, but I'm not speeding. The guy blasts his horn, making one of the pups startle and fall to the floor. He stays right on our tail for several minutes, letting us know we can't shake him.

"We have to get rid of him," Joe says.

"I know." I think of James Bond weaving through tight European streets in a sporty car, cafe tables airborne. But this is Rusty, and we're going only slightly more than the speed limit. I keep waiting for him to pull alongside us and try to run us off the road. But he's not, he's waiting us out. Doesn't want to draw attention to himself, maybe? We're approaching a strip of businesses, all closed for the night. Then I spot a doughnut shop, brightly lit.

"There!" says Joe. Both of us spot the cop car at the same moment. It's ready to pull out of the drive-through.

I slow down so they can get on the road ahead. We cruise along, well below the speed limit, willing to go everywhere the police do, which is, as it turns out, towards the bridge.

"You have change?" I say to Joe, catching his eye in the rear-view.

"Sure do."

And that is how we shake him. The Dropper doesn't have the toll for the bridge. Of course, the shelter is in the other direction, but Joe's right, we don't want to lead them there.

"My place. Okay?" says Joe.

"You're allowed dogs?"

"No, but it'll be fine."

ELEVEN

⠀

"RACHEL," I SAY, KILLING THE ENGINE IN FRONT OF JOE'S HOUSE. Is she at the shelter waiting or sitting in her stinking car with the Mustang pulling in behind her? "We need to call her."

"Right," he says, disentangling from the pups. "I'll do that."

"Here." I toss him my pager. "The number's on there."

Joe disappears into the house while I watch for predatory cars. As soon as he's out, I climb over the seat to join the dogs. Until now, I haven't had a good look at the pups. One jumps down onto the floor and circles, finds a balled-up newspaper, and squats. I realize that I, too, need to pee.

"I forgive you," I say to her as she leaps to tackle one of her siblings. She's got a brown patch over one eye like a monocle and the shape of a jaunty cap covers one ear like Mr. Peanut.

"Peanut, you're the party animal, I see."

The smallest one has his front paws on the door. He's got the shape of an English saddle on his back. The other three are knotted beside me on the seat, soaking up the heat of their mother's bum. And the mother is pressed into my chest, unmoving. I long to get her into a warm tub to clean off the stench of that place, feed her a meal, give her a bowl of water free of cigarette butts.

Joe reappears and motions for me to roll down the window. "Rachel?"

"She's home," he says, reaching in for the smallest pup. "She heard the gunshot, saw us behind her." Way, way behind her. "And she didn't know what else to do."

"And now?"

"We've got this under control." We do? We do. "She'll meet us in the morning."

It takes us longer to get them all in the house than it did to coax them in from the yard. Whatever life the mother dog had in her seems to have seeped out. Maybe she was in the grip of adrenalin too.

Drugstore flyers cover Joe's bedroom floor. He's nabbed a cushion from the couch to serve as a bed for the mother dog, but she crawls into his closet instead, making a nest of laundry.

"Where's your roommate?"

"He had to work through Thanksgiving last weekend, so he went home." Right. The feast. A bit contentious in our house, Dad saying I could just have the roast veggies. The ones cooked in the liquid of a dead bird. What bothers me most is how much I like the smell, so I just stay away.

Joe's room contains one double bed, unmade, a real wooden side table with one of those clocks that flips the numbers like a rolodex, and a poster of the convertible from the ending of *Thelma & Louise*, forever flying from the red cliff. His choice or a previous tenant's?

He sits on the bed, then gives a boost to the pup with the saddle who slides in next to his hip. The other two join their mother in the closet. I take the floor cushion and two pups scramble across my lap. I'll just sit for a few minutes, until everyone is settled.

I'm guessing they're about five weeks, still feeding from their mother. Thin coats, pink bellies, triangle ears. I bury my face in Peanut's belly and breathe in the puppy smell. She catches the end of my braid and chews. The other gazes, drunkenly, into my eyes. It must be naptime, you can almost watch their energy dwindling. I'm no different, sliding down on the cushion, the dogs gathering into me for warmth. My eyes won't stay open, but something occurs to me.

"Did you lose someone in a car accident?" My words are slurred.

"What?"

"In the car, you said something like you can't lose me, too." I'm so sleepy that I'm now doubting I even heard it.

"Oh. No, not that," he says. I crack a lid open and he's pulling at his beard. "I was just stressed."

"I should get going." But I know it's not going to happen. My face is leaden. I tip sideways and find the softness of the couch cushion, filled with puppies. I receive a lick on the ear. Just forty winks, then I'll head for the abode. A dream is waiting for me, I'm in the car again but the mother dog is driving.

"Dot, I'm sorry about your mother," Joe says. Or does he? My mouth won't work to respond. I think I open my eyes. There's a blanket on top of me that wasn't there before.

Then someone says I'll need an umbrella unless I'm a duck. "Achy Breaky Heart" blares until there's a whack and Billy Ray ends on *tell my arms to go back to the farm*. I rasp my thanks to Joe for intercepting before the chorus.

"Time?" I say, taking in the dim room.

"Six thirty-two."

The pups have made use of the newspapered floor in the night. I slide out from under the exquisite warmth of what looks to be a homemade quilt and rub my crusted eyes. I find my hat a few feet away and put it back on. Joe is fully dressed on his bed, with a pillow over his face and English Saddle in his armpit.

"Just wait until we tell Rachel that we slept together," I say.

He tosses the pillow aside and blinks at me.

"Kidding."

"You slept, I did not."

"Sorry."

"It wasn't you." He swings his feet to the floor and finds his shoes. "I've just never stolen a litter of puppies before."

"I've never been shot at." I kneel in his closet to check on the mother. My two puppies defected after I fell asleep and found her. She's on her side with one of them over her neck like a scarf. Her stub of a tail twitches when I put my hand on her side.

"We ought to get moving if we're going to get there before Earl."

JOE BEGS FOR A DRIVE-THROUGH COFFEE. OTHERWISE, I WOULD NOT have stopped with the party happening in the back. He gets me a bran muffin without asking. "For doing all the driving," he says, plopping a little brown bag in my lap.

Do I look like I need bran?

"I have a shift tonight." He yawns expansively.

"Where is the restaurant?"

"On the waterfront, Sea Breeze, with the big plastic lobster on the sign?" I shrug. "Next to the ice cream place."

"Ah."

Now I place it. In the summer you have to walk around the ice cream shack's lineup of drooling customers, the vented scent of freshly made waffle cones mingling with seafood.

The rain goes from a gentle tap to a downpour, challenging my wipers. In the back seat, Peanut leans against the window, frantically licking at the drips.

"Let's just say we found them outside, okay?" I have to speak over the drumming of the rain. "The dogs."

"Okay," he says, but it sounds more like a question. He's watching my hand on the steering wheel, relaying my message silently.

"A couple of years back, Judy fired someone for bringing in a dog that was, supposedly, being neglected." I remember him well. He was desperately thin, some sort of basset hound mix, a breed more prone to being overweight than underweight, with their stocky legs and fondness for napping. It turned out he was a beloved family dog with a thyroid problem. His family had him scheduled for surgery when the shelter worker intervened. "It made the news. You didn't see it?" Joe shakes his head. "Anyway, Judy's not a fan of vigilantes."

"This is totally different." He turns in his seat so he can dangle a hand over English Saddle.

"I know. Still, it happens. People drop off litters overnight."

"But there's the security camera, right?"

Good point. I can just say it was at the end of the tape and the camera didn't catch it. It probably is anyway.

"You think she'd fire you." The way he says it makes it clear he thinks it unlikely, but he hasn't known her as long as me. She'd certainly fire Rachel. But he agrees not to say anything.

No sign of Earl or Mustangs when we pull up. I let out a long breath, unaware it was trapped all that time. As agreed, I climb out and unlock the door while Joe carries the first two pups in, closing the doors to the kitchen.

Midway through the shelter is the room where we stash supplies. There's an odd-shaped kennel, mostly used as a place to stack bags of food. I have to shift it out of there to make a spot for the mum and pups. While I do this, Joe brings in the dogs. Unlike the other rooms, there are no windows. But it's clean.

There's the usual morning serenade from the back: echoey, staccato yips and howls.

Joe carries the mother outside and sets her down gently on the soggy grass. In the daylight, ridges of scars are evident on her narrow back. Her legs quiver as she squats for a pee.

"I don't think she got out much," says Joe.

"I wonder how many litters she's had." Her nipples are swollen and raw. The hair has been worn off her belly entirely.

"You all right?" says Joe.

"Me? Absolutely fine." He glances at my hand. If it's not *SOS*, he doesn't know what I'm saying. I'm not a good liar and I can't stop thinking about my own animals. I've never left them on their own at night.

"That's good," he says, heaving her into his arms. I hold the door while he carries her inside. "You sure did some damage to that guy's face..."

I'm about to recommend my self-defence book when the front door chimes and Earl's voice calls out hello.

"Shit," says Joe. I concur. It's too early for us both to be here, already in full swing.

"You finish up with them and I'll head him off," I say, moving towards the kitchen where he'll likely be getting the coffee started before he's even removed his coat.

"Morning, Dot," he says, eyes atwinkle. "Thought I'd have to wait outside, but you're already here."

"It's a good thing, too," I say, trying to figure out how I normally talk. "We found someone on the step. More than one, actually."

"Oh dear," he says, pouring the water into the machine. Then "We?"

"Me and Joe. Joe and I." Which one is it?

His brow furrows while I fill him in. Is he looking at me differently? Twice he glances at my hand, which I try to keep still. Too still?

When he sees them clamouring at the kennel door he goes weak at the knees. Joe squeezes out to switch places so Earl can lower himself into the thick of puppies. Any other questions he might have turn to observations about the pups. His moustache is a wonderful plaything. They topple him and he lets out a series of giggles that don't match his age. Meanwhile, the mother curls on her blanket in the corner.

"This one has a butterfly on her back," he says. "Look at that."
I point out Peanut then excuse myself, so I can fill out the intake
forms for the dogs in relative peace.

The office is dim with the blinds closed. I leave them shut and
sit at Judy's desk chewing the end of a pen. What to put on their
kennel card? Less is more. We found them when we came in this
morning, a tad earlier than usual. Why were the two of us so early?
I'll just leave it for now. Let them assume.

When I'm done I go back to the pups and clip the card to the
kennel. They've polished off their bowl of food and formed a landscape of snoring lumps. We did the right thing.

JUDY COMES IN LATE, CRUMPLED AND LIPSTICK-LESS.

"I think I caught your thing," she says, narrowing her eyes. That
makes me realize, aside from being a tad dishevelled, I'm feeling
remarkably refreshed. "I'm only here for the morning, then I'm
going back to bed."

I motion for her to follow me to the back and meet the dogs.
She lays her forehead against the bars with a deep sigh.

"How?" she says. "How did they leave them?"

"I don't know, some people lack a heart—"

"No, Dot, were they tied or what?"

Think fast. "The mother was. The pups were...in a box."

She nods. "They usually abandon them a lot younger." She
lets herself in the kennel and squats by the mother. Tails thump
as the pups rouse. "Hello, darlin'," she says to the mother, "you've
been through the wringer." She runs a hand along her back, being
gentle with the scars. "Looks like a puppy mill, but they wouldn't
have abandoned them. That's a lot of profit." She shakes her head.
"Weird."

"I don't know," I say, with an oversized, innocent shrug.

"I'll call the vet, see if she can come have a looksee." Then she turns her attention to me. "You need to fix your braid, it looks like you slept on it."

With my hand I feel a nest of hair pulled free below my hat on the side. It would have been nice if Joe or Earl could have alerted me. Do they think I style it that way? "Right."

THE REST OF THE MORNING FOLLOWS A FAMILIAR PATTERN EXCEPT for the stirring in my gut, which is only partly caused by hunger. Maybe I had too much coffee; my fingers are twitching. I keep them busy with extra work, skipping my morning break.

Rachel finds me bent over the sink, scrubbing dried-on bits of cat food from a dish. Luckily, Joe was able to call her before she came in, heading her off before she could tell Earl about last night. Leaning back on the counter next to me, she speaks out of the side of her mouth.

"I called in the address, anonymously, so Animal Control can check it out. The other dog's still there."

"Rachel." Earl sounds jolly. "You've come to see my new babies?"

She's lured away, feigning astonishment. Not a bad actor, I must admit.

Moments later, Judy sneezes in, making a big production of it, groaning and flailing for the box of tissues. I hand her one.

"Dr. Trainer will be here at two." She pauses to honk into the tissue. "Can you dig up that box for me? I need something for the bunnies at home. I have a heck of a time cleaning out the small enclosure when they're underfoot."

"The box?"

"The one the pups were in? I couldn't find it." Is she looking at me strangely? Or is it just her swollen sinuses? "It must be a strong one to hold them."

"Right." Foiled by a cardboard box.

"I'm heading out as soon as I've made a couple of phone calls." She grabs the tissue box and heads back to the office.

I FIND JOE IN THE CAT ROOM UP FRONT. HE'S TRYING TO SCOOP OUT a steaming turd from the tray while preventing Buttercup's escape. We try to keep on top of the smell in the adoption rooms. It doesn't take much for visitors to get the idea that the animals dwell in squalor.

"We have a snag." I tell him about Judy's giant box request. Lacking Rachel's acting chops, he turns pink and pulls at his beard.

"Maybe next door?" he says. "In their dumpster." It's some sort of research company next door. Maybe they'll have such a thing.

"Right, just distract her if you see her looking for me?"

Nipping out back, I first check our garbage because you never know. But it's full of the usual sacks of fermenting poop and cat litter. I go around the side because otherwise Judy might spot me through her office window.

My heart stops when I see the nostril car, idling in the lot. Both of them stare at the front door, unaware of me, squashed against the fence. Waylon's nose is covered in a white bandage. I can't hear what they're saying, but it's clear they don't agree. Waylon makes the shape of a gun with his hand and shoots out the front of the shelter, blowing on his—also bandaged—index finger when he's done. I just stand there, trembling, until they rip out of the cul-de-sac, tires squealing.

I DON'T FIND A BOX FOR JUDY BECAUSE I COLLAPSE AT THE SIDE OF the building and have a long talk with myself, despite the wet ground seeping through my pants. My finger taps my leg, *right thing*. We did the right thing.

In my pocket, the pager purrs. It's Dad sending a hug. My bottom lip quivers and I bury my head in my arms to stifle it. I wish to turn back the clock a full year and have them both. I don't want to know people like Waylon. Despite the heat in my face, I shiver.

What would she say? *No good deed goes unpunished.* Probably. She'd pat the floor by the couch so she could braid and unbraid my hair.

Judy drives away without seeing me and eventually Joe comes out, calling my name, jumping when he finds me hunched by the building.

"Did you see them?"

"Who?"

"Waylon and the Dropper."

He crouches, examining me. "What happened?"

I tell him about the handgun and it comes out just like that, *the handgun*, so I back up and explain things in a less alarming way.

"Maybe we should have called the police."

"We didn't have time." He's firm about it. No need to go down that road. "The dogs are safe now."

What if they're watching the shelter? What if they follow me? Jesus. It's not like Magoo would even be up to calling 911.

"Come on," Joe says, offering to pull me up.

I thank him but boost myself awkwardly, avoiding his hand.

PROMISING TO RETURN BEFORE DR. TRAINER ARRIVES, I HEAD FOR Rusty. All the way home, I scan the rear-view mirror for nostril hoods and/or drivers in nose bandages. The rain has stopped, leaving a gunmetal sky and clumps of wet leaves. People have decorated for Halloween with plastic skeletons (one hopes) and sheets draped to look like ghosts. It's hideous, as intended, I suppose.

When I cut the engine, I hear it, a muffled cry like a distressed baby or a Siamese cat. The hair on my arms stands up. Mercifully, Magoo II is not there, or his truck is not.

The screeching continues as I fumble with my keys. Toby goes quiet when he sees me in the door, his last cry ringing in my ears.

"I'm sorry."

Toby turns his back and drums the bars with his beak. One day he's hopping his way to freedom (and certain death) in the woods, and the next he's trapped in here with perfectly edible food out of reach. I open his door and he heads straight for a hapless sowbug.

Upstairs, a faucet turns on and I hear the whoosh of it down the pipes. This sends Toby swaggering off to the bathroom. Despite missing a meal, everyone seems fine, if a little rattled.

I put Ori's medication in the little syringe from Dr. Trainer, then coax him from his blanklets to dribble the solution into his mouth, filling him in on recent events.

The moment I close my door, Toby bursts into his pitchy caw. I try to ignore it, walking away; maybe it's only meant to get to me. To be sure, I sit in the car for a minute, window rolled down. If anything, he's louder. Even if Magoo's hearing aids are dead, he's bound to hear this.

So, I traipse back inside and load him into his travel cage.

RACHEL HOLDS THE FRONT DOOR FOR ME.

"He's trying to get me evicted," I say, placing Toby's cage on the kitchen table. "Any sign of the vet?"

"No, but Dot..." She swallows, her face paler than usual. "Joe told me about them coming here."

"You're fine, I'm the only one he saw."

"But they must know it was us." She gestures out the door like they're still idling nearby. Would they recognize Rusty? "We have to call the police."

"You know what that means?"

"Of course."

"What if they charge us?" I'm whispering, hoping she'll follow my lead.

"We didn't, like, break anything, we just...entered."

"And took. We could lose our jobs."

"So what? It's fucking minimum wage, Dot."

I stare at her. It's not the money, not for me.

"We'll talk about it after," I say, closing the kitchen door between us.

DR. TRAINER IS LATE, SO I WAIT IN THE KITCHEN WITH TOBY, WHO seems to enjoy the bustle around him. Earl hasn't seen him since that first day. He digs into his lunch and finds some cheese.

"A noisy boy, are you?" He slides a chunk through the bars.

"I'm not sure what to do about him." Judy won't like me bringing him here every day.

"He's a wild bird, Dot." Earl doesn't look away from Toby. "He wants...up."

"But he can't fly."

Earl pauses as if weighing his words, but he's saved by the chime of the front door.

Dr. Trainer backs in, her bum pushing the door open, a case of canned food in her arms.

"The good stuff for the little ones," she says, catching sight of us. "My treat." She plunks it on the counter and turns to me. "This the same crow?"

As if I'm making a habit of bringing crows to work.

"Toby."

"Ah." She comes close and clucks at him. He cocks his head, regarding her. When no food appears he turns his attention back to Earl.

"I have to get to the clinic in an hour. Putting down a lovely old retriever. One of my very first patients."

"They don't live nearly long enough," says Earl, a refrain around here.

"No, they don't," she says. "Then again, some people keep them around long past when they should. Then you wonder who it's really for. He's been struggling for months. If it wasn't for pain meds, I doubt he'd have gone this long."

Earl clears his throat, catching her eye.

"Right," she says, glancing at me. "I don't mean your family, Dot—"

"Of course," I say, turning away to avoid that hangdog look I get from people. Silence behind me as I shrug into a fresh lab coat.

"Lead the way," she says, heaving her bag from the floor.

One look at the mother and she's echoing Judy. Puppy mill.

"We'll just do it in the kennel," says Dr. Trainer, tossing her coat onto the stacked bags of cat litter. "She's been through enough."

I go in too, to keep the pups from mobbing her while she does the exam. Their teeth are like needles, so I tempt them with a towel I've twisted into knots.

"You've got a heart murmur, girl," Dr. T. says to the mother. She picks up a paw and frowns. "What did they do to you?" She shakes her head then gently rolls her to the side to examine her nipples. "Not your first litter, either."

Afterwards, she takes each pup aside and I make notes as we identify each one by their markings.

"They're in good shape except for being a little underweight." She stands and shakes a leg. "I'm too old for this cross-legged stuff. Get them started with the food I brought? Keep a close eye on the mother, I don't like the sound of her heart. She'd be better off in a foster, once the pups are weaned and they're ready for that. Give them a few more days together."

"What about those marks on her neck and back?"

She lets out a long sigh.

"They restrain them for breeding. I'll get you some cream to rub in her pads. It's from standing in her own...waste." She shakes her head, putting her things back in her bag before Peanut can make off with her stethoscope. "You'd think they'd treat them better, if only to protect their investment."

We squeeze out the door.

"Give any more thought to Saturday?" she says, glancing around.

"I've been kind of distracted..."

She nods.

"How's Ori doing with the meds?"

"Good, I think."

"You ought to be seeing some improvement. Keep me posted." As we go through the kitchen she stops to look at Toby. Earl has left, so we're of interest once again. "Let's have a peek, see how that wing's healed."

She reaches in and cups him between her hands, bringing him out. He doesn't struggle, just keeps his eye fixed on her as she lifts the wing up and down.

"You took off the bandage."

"It was getting to be a mess." Mud and grit from his forest trek.

I watch how she stares into the middle distance as she feels along, like she can see his bone structure there. Then she's back.

"Well, I'm no avian vet, but it feels like a good mend." She places him back on the branch and closes the door before he can hop out. He taps on the bars. *Important business.*

"Sorry, Toby," says Dr. T. "No apricots today. You bring him in often?" She shrugs into her coat.

"Just today. He's started screeching."

"Probably good. Crows don't make great room—" Her phone rings, high and horrible. "—mates. They're probably getting anxious. Worst part of the job."

I watch her slump to her car before heading out back. Button is lying down, resting on his elbows to look out, which puts him at about standing height for a normal large dog. His kennel card has been modified with a red pen. Only staff are permitted to walk him. *Heavy staff*, someone has added in thick marker. Despite his gentleness, once outside, he's determined to leave this place, perhaps head for home or just go to the sea, following his Newfoundland heritage. I shuffle in, avoiding the puddle of drool, and slot myself between his head and the wall. He leans, bending his head backwards to an impossible angle to look at me.

"Sometimes we can't go home, buddy." I wrap my arm around his woolly shoulders and feel for the thrum of his heart.

"Hey, Dot." Joe is leading one of the shelter specials back to a kennel. Both are damp on top, muddy on the bottom. Outside Button's door he stops and sets to towelling off the dog but ends up having a tug-of-war instead. "Have it your way, then." He pulls a treat from his pocket and snatches the towel back the moment the dog goes for it. He's catching on.

"Doing okay?" he says, not looking at me.

"Maybe I should've told Judy." Lying makes me nauseous. I sense she already knows and is just baiting me.

"You know, I could call the police and just leave you out of it."

"What?" It doesn't compute, why would he take all the blame?

"That way, it's only me that lied," he says as if I don't understand.

"*Who* lied." The correction comes out automatically, I can't help it, I do that when I'm agitated, point out trivial mistakes. He stares, confused, the colour draining from his face.

"I mean," I say, "it's not *that* lied but *who* lied. Grammar. Never mind..." Dad's right, the only place corrections are welcome is in English class. "Sorry."

He waves off my apology and goes to put the dog back in his kennel.

I must have touched a nerve; his must be as jangled as mine. Yet he's willing to take all the blame. But it wouldn't make any sense. How would he have done it alone? And why would he have lied? I have created a fine mess in an attempt to keep things simple.

In the end, it's me who calls the police.

OUR BOARDROOM FEELS TIGHT WITH THE ADDITION OF TWO PEOPLE in bulky uniforms. Their arms can't lie flat against their sides with all the gadgets strapped to them. I imagine donning the outfit, like folding into a Swiss army knife. I wonder if their hats have secret compartments. Can they take them off and toss them like boomerangs? I'd like a hat like that.

I'm questioned last. They took Joe first, then Rachel. By the time they get to me, I'm aquiver. Does it show?

We settle on opposite sides of the table, framed by stacks of files. They take my name and address and a description of Waylon's property. Then we go over it, complete with dates, times, and smells.

"Why," says the woman, who could easily be Dr. Trainer's sister, "did you not call us when you saw evidence of the dogfighting?"

I explain the logistics of finding a pay phone and our plan to present them with evidence they could use. I sense their frustration. Under the table, my finger broadcasts anxiety. "That's why we went last night, just to look. But they were going to take them away..." I forget to breathe.

"You all right there?" says the cop looking up from her pad. Constable Something.

"I just, I have trouble with stillness."

This gets a nod and another note jotted.

As I talk, they study me. Yes, we employed a blazing bag of shit as a distraction. *Oh God, could we be charged with arson?* Yes, I struck him. *Assault?* They even write down the name of my self-defence book, a title I'm able to recite from memory, along with the name of the author. Yes, Waylon shot (ineptly) at us. I notice the cop with the squinty eyes suppress a smile at that one. I'll bet they have some stories from firearm training. I give them the license plate of the nostril car, just the vanity plate on the front, *GANGSTA*.

Once we've gone through it all, they ask to meet the dogs. I don't think the mother has moved since her exam this afternoon. The pups scramble to greet us, stepping on one another, squashing a fresh turd in the process. Joe moves to clean things up and Peanut, dodging grasping hands, prances off to the kitchen. The cops *apprehend the fugitive*, forgetting to keep straight faces. Officer Squinty tells us about the shoe-eating terrier he had as a kid.

It's long past supper when they leave, handing each of us a card.

"We'll be looking into the gun," says Squinty. "The dogs are handled by the provincial cruelty investigator."

They repeat we should call *them* first if anything happens and not take the law into our own hands.

Rachel is all smiles afterwards, offering us cigarettes, which we both decline, telling us we worry too much. She has time to kill now, wanting us to celebrate in some way—preferably with liquids—but we both say no.

"Don't you have a date or something?" I say, glancing at the clock.

"Nah." She tucks the cigarettes away. "We broke up."

Behind me, Toby clangs six on the bars, *I am ready*.

"I have to get him home."

"All right," she says, embracing me. I lightly pat her back. "Relax, will you? They're on it. Need a ride, Joe?"

"No, I'm good." His hands sinking deeper into his pockets, averting the hug. Clever. Rachel pats his shoulder instead.

"All right, rain check then," she says.

I follow her to the door, locking it behind her, and turn off the lights. We watch as she gets in her mother's car and cranks the driver's window all the way down. No sign of a nostril car.

"Aren't you supposed to be working tonight?" I'm remembering him yawning this morning.

"I swapped my shift with someone. I'll work a double on the weekend."

"Well, you're not taking the bus." I aim to sound decisive. Standing at a dark bus stop sounds like a bad idea to me.

"I can call Mike." The roommate with the bicycle?

They could be around the corner, waiting for my car to pull out. I don't say it, but I'm not ready to be alone.

"No need. Just give me a hand with Toby?"

In the car, I notice Joe sniffing the air.

"Yeah, one of them peed back there." It's not like I've had time to detail the interior. To compensate, I give my cardboard pine tree a little rub. It twirls below the rear-view mirror, releasing its faux forest scent.

"You all right, Dot?"

I don't answer immediately because he sounds like he actually wants to know. So, I give him an honest answer.

"I'm not sure. You?"

"Too tired to know." He yawns to illustrate his point. "But do you feel...safe?"

"From Waylon?" They said they'd be looking into it. "Not until they tell us they've found something."

He nods and we drive on listening to Toby's rattles and clicks, more bearable than his earlier cry.

"I think he's trying to say something." Joe turns in his seat. "Hello?"

Toby answers, "Hello," with his gravelly voice, like when I'd talk into the fan in the summer and it would break the sound into something more machine-like.

Joe laughs, delighted, "I didn't know he could talk."

"Neither did I. Maybe it was Earl and his chunks of cheese."

"Hello." Three more times he does it, then stops, perhaps due to the lack of edible reward. Maybe he thinks we're daft, repeating ourselves.

"You have my number," says Joe. I pat my pocket and there's a soft crumple. "Good, call me if anything happens."

"The police might disagree with that advice."

"If you need to talk or anything."

I don't remind him I'm phoneless. Sometimes it's the comforter who needs reassurance, not the comfortee. I have Ori's counsel. I idle as he walks to his front door, finding an uneven paving stone with one toe, but catching himself before going down. He gives me a wave before shutting his door. From there, I imagine him stumbling to his bedroom, still strewn with newspapers, and landing face down on his bed, snoring into his pillow under the flying Thunderbird with Thelma and Louise clasping hands as they fall.

I'M GROWING TO DREAD SMALL NOTES TACKED TO MY DOOR. THIS one is not from Magoo II. The cursive loops tidily between the lines. *Dorothy, please come and see me this evening if you are in prior to 9:00 P.M.* My throat tightens and my hunger retreats. It's half past seven.

After installing Toby in his regular cage, I walk up the new ramp. It switchbacks like a bank queue. Junior has stapled down a lively green AstroTurf as an anti-slip solution.

Magoo is propped at the kitchen counter when I knock. His window in the door isn't covered, not even a tea towel for privacy. God, the door is unlocked too. No wonder seniors get burgled. He waves me in.

"Dorothy, thank you for coming to see me." With a shaking hand, he removes a tea bag from his cup.

"How are you feeling Mr. Mag...Gee?" *Almost said Magoo that time.*

Turning, he glowers, reaching for the fridge handle. "I've always said"—he removes the carton of milk—"growing old is a privilege when one considers the alternative." Naturally, he spills as much milk as he splashes into the cup. "But, of late, I am reconsidering my motto." I want to take over, wipe up the milk, put the carton away, but it's clear I should not interrupt his monologue. "Being housebound is unpleasant at best. When one is obliged to listen to the discordant screeching of a bird at all hours of the night, *unpleasant* is no longer the correct term." The carton is returned to the fridge, leaving a milky puddle on the shelf that will reek in the days to come. "Do you, Ms. Grey, understand?"

"Yes, sir. I'm very sorry."

"Can you"—he takes an unsophisticated slurp—"promise me there will be no follow-up performances of last night?"

I pull my lips in, considering an answer that doesn't involve lying.

"I see," he says, squinting at me. "Then I'm terribly sorry to say this, as you have been otherwise cordial and prompt with payment, but I must serve you notice for the end of the month."

"That's this Friday." I say it slowly so he can realize his error. "This. Friday," I repeat, louder, pointing at the floor as if we're about to step on Friday.

"I believe you are correct."

I can't find a new place by then. This is why people have leases, I suppose.

"Dorothy, when you arrived I made it clear it was just to be you, not a menagerie of critters."

"No dogs, you said."

"Absolutely no dogs," he says, looking alarmed.

"I don't have a dog." I enunciate, lifting my voice a little higher this time, almost shouting.

"My son complained to me about the chirping of crickets while he was here? All this time, I thought they were outside."

"I keep them for my gecko, and the gerbils like—"

"Dear me. No matter. It's the bird that's the bother. Unless you can promise I won't hear one squawk, rattle, or screech from below, I'm afraid I must insist."

Right on cue, possibly realizing it's long past supper, Toby lets out a series of piercing caws. Magoo, rather dramatically, puts down his bone china on the counter with a clack, splattering his cardigan in the process.

"I'm so sorry." I'm desperate to wipe his counter and make him a new cup of tea.

He removes his hearing aids, placing them on the counter, an unwelcome sight on a surface meant for food preparation. Nevertheless, it's an effective way to communicate the conclusion of our meeting.

"I'm sorry," I say, almost shouting and then I bow, as if we're a pair of samurais. He dips his head in response and I let myself out, winding my way down the anti-slip ramp, my heart sinking.

By the time I hit the end of Magoo's queue, my face is wet and my nose is streaming. Unlocking my door, I pause to wipe my face on my Womble towel.

"Hello," says the culprit.

"Hello, Toby."

"Hello."

Due to my blur of mucous, it's not feasible to feed them just now. I toss a few peanuts to quiet him down. I sag onto my quality mattress, letting my mind do its worst. Waylon's face twisted in fury, Magoo with his dismissive nod, Toby hopping away into the forest, Mum trapped in bed...

"Hello."

"Hello, Toby."

I open his door and head to the bathroom to rinse the wallowing from my face.

Not long after I've seen to my menagerie, the pager warbles. Toby gets to it before me, pulling it from my bag. It clatters to the floor at my feet. It's Dad, using another code I have to look up. *Come over.* Come over? It's past his bedtime.

Minutes later, a single knock at the Womble window. Peering under the towel, I see Dad. He talks to me through the glass.

"Judy called. What's this about police?"

Oh no, already? I crack the door open so he'll pipe down.

"Is she mad?"

"Is SHE mad?"

Clearly, I've asked the wrong question. He lists a great number of reasons why the alternate meaning of *mad* applies to my behaviour.

"I agreed to you moving out as long as you kept me in the loop. You're only eighteen, for God's sake."

"When Grand was eighteen—"

"Never mind Grand. When he was eighteen, the world was mad." He pushes the door wider.

"It still is. Please, Dad. This is my sanctum." Am I whining?

"Just come home. For one night. Bring Ori."

Toby hops onto the bed, fully aware I'm unable to shoo him off.

"I can't."

"Where's your car?" he says, turning to scan the street.

I point in the direction of my car, a few blocks down the street. He's gone ahead and parked in the driveway, without asking, but I won't have a chance to address that particular breach of the rules because he's taking the grand tour of my abode with his eyes.

"Bloody hell" is his opener. "Dot, this is not a bachelor suite." He gapes at my blankets with their missing squares, repurposed into Ori's blanklets. I didn't cut them from the edges, as I have an ounce of creativity in me. They're a pair of square eyes halfway up, like windows. "That," he points, "was on my bed when I was a child." I don't often see him angry; his upbringing didn't allow for it. Vast gaps are in his sentences where, I presume, others would utter a long string of expletives. Without offering to remove his shoes, he goes into the bathroom and stares at the mirrorless wall, then back at me. "This...this is...not a home, Speck."

"I'm looking for a new place."

He shakes his head back and forth, back and forth, then, seemingly, brings a stop to the movement by tidying his hair.

"Is it...really so...bad to live with me?" He goes to the foot of my bed, precisely the spot I've attempted to scrub clean of one of Toby's turds, and sinks down before I can warn him.

Toby hops over to his feet and says "Hello."

Dad blinks at him. "Hello." They do a back and forth until Dad is removed from the list of possible sources of food.

"She'd be...gutted...if she saw this." He's not telling me this. It appears he's telling Toby, who is having a go at his shoelaces. "She despised that bomb shelter."

That's not entirely true. As a small child, before Grand decided they should move in, it was the hippest thing about their house. Sure, their yard lacked a swing set or even a paddling pool, but the shelter was almost a playhouse, with the right amount of imagination. A place in which Mum was permitted to make elaborate mud pies, and noise, with the occasional friend.

"Tell me, though, what inspired you to be a vigilante?" He looks away from Toby, who might, if someone doesn't monitor the situation, actually remove the entire shoe. "Why...did you not simply call the...police?"

Again, with that.

I jog his memory about the abuse case; I'd told him about it when I was doing laundry that day. He gives one slow blink for yes.

"We would've called them if there had been time. It all worked out in the end."

"Yes, well, you don't have a…a TV, or a radio, or a bloody telephone, so you don't know." He waits for me to offer evidence to the contrary. "They seized a weapon and drugs from the property." It was on the late news. He watched the TV coverage, says there were speculations about gang connections. "And here you are in a…basement with a…flimsy door."

My heart is a butterfly. "They did? But that's a good thing. Did they mention the other dog?"

More hair tidying.

"Yes, they showed the dog chained in a filthy yard."

"Did they—"

"One of those SPCA people had it. It was wearing a muzzle because it might be a fighting dog?" One hand messes the hair all over again. "You were, and still could be, in…danger." He rearranges his face into something softer, less exasperated. "Tonight, you'll come home with me."

Crickets.

"I'm fine."

"Really? You park your car, walk a few blocks and you think that will…be sufficient. These people are…different."

Upstairs, footsteps creak. Magoo is making his bathroom trek a little earlier than usual. Dad stares at the Styrofoam divider, his left eye twitching. Magoo can't accomplish it in a single stream, it's a series of splashes, and he doesn't allow the yellow to mellow. He's a flusher. We wait for the whole performance to conclude.

"The police gave me their business card."

"Well, that would be grand if you had a phone." He scans the abode to see if I've been honest about this detail. He's getting a little testy. "You can have a hot shower at home and a good breakfast in the morning."

My stomach gives a little leap. But, I'm not so easily persuaded.

"It's not just me." I indicate Bungo on his mezzanine level taking in the show, Toby pecking at the eyelet of Dad's left shoe, Abbott and Costello arguing about ballplayer names, and Waldo, who is camouflaged for the moment.

"For...God's sake, Speck, you leave them all day for work."

"Not the same."

"Right then. I'll stay here." He removes his shoes, leaving his jacket on, claims one of the pillows with a little shaping punch, then climbs under the (relatively clean on the underside) duvet and shuts his eyes. Not a word as I tuck Toby in for the night.

TWELVE

⊙⊙⊙

D AD LASTS UNTIL THREE IN THE MORNING, AT WHICH POINT HE swings his legs over the edge of the bed and sits facing my "flimsy" door. He doesn't ask if I'm awake before he begins.

"She sheltered you. From people," he says, as if he hasn't told me this before, that I haven't responded with *Not everyone needs a herd of friends.* It's conceivable that I'm asleep, hearing none of this, so I stay silent.

"God, I miss her. But." By the shaking of the bed, I detect the pause to mop his face on a sleeve. "She's what your nan called a *one-off.*" He laughs quietly. "Good reason to fall for a person, if you ask me." The dark sharpens the other senses, so I don't need to see the liquid of his eyes or the bent back. "She didn't have a mother. Just Grand. Imagine that." My grandmother died when Mum was a baby. "So she had this need in her. I suppose that's what all parents do; try not to mess up the way their parents did. We just botch it differently." The middle of the night is ripe for revelations. That's why we should be asleep. "I'm rambling."

"And slurring a bit," I say, not sounding any better with the pillow hampering my lips.

"Now she's...out of reach, you're not prepared. I know you think I'm the one who's delusional. But I'm a grown man. You're just—"

"A speck."

"No." He pivots. "But you're at the start. You should be in college. It doesn't take much, you know, a couple of bad decisions when you're young. I could tell you stories." No need, I've heard about his dropout friends, a dead-end job for one, prison for the other. It's part of the well-worn story of how he came to Canada. "Then you get this idea about yourself that it's all you can do and you forget your dreams. Don't forget your dreams, Dot."

"I'm not, I'm working with animals." Living the dream.

Long, shaky exhale followed by a cough.

"But it's such a sad place, Speck."

Maybe I shouldn't have only told him about the surrenders, the neglect, the fleas, the worms, the shivering, and the merciful deaths. Perhaps I should have peppered my stories with the occasional happy ending. Those things happen all the time too.

"I'm not sure how a person can cope with so much...misery."

The bed shakes and he sniffs. I reach a hand out from under the covers and pat his back.

"I'm helping. That's how I cope."

"But you won't let me help you."

"You ought to go home and get some sleep," I say.

"I haven't gotten a full night since she went to sleep. Not once."

"She's not asleep, Dad." I say it softly because it's painful for us.

"There's still hope, Speck. While her heart beats."

"I know." I'll give him that.

THE TROUBLE WITH NOT SLEEPING IS THERE'S NO DIVIDER BETWEEN the days. You need a pause between beats or they mash together. Things stop making sense. I wonder how people manage shift work, sliding days and nights around, coffee and cereal for supper, a nightcap for breakfast, despising the way the world carries on as if everyone goes to bed after a good stretch of mindless television in the evening.

Dad drops me off at Rusty in the morning. Having investigated the contents of my fridge, he presses five dollars into my hand so I'll get myself something to eat. Also, he hands me yesterday's paper.

"There might be something listed for rent. You have a damage deposit?"

"A what?" Magoo didn't ask for such a thing.

"It's usually first and last month's rent?" Now I understand what DD is in the ads. I'd hoped it indicated a dishwasher and dryer or a perk for the renter.

"Oh." I climb out, pocketing my five dollars, and wonder what food I can scrounge at work so I can save it. Sometimes Earl leaves bagels in the fridge. My stomach responds to this image with an audible growl. The driver's seat is cold and my bum has lost more of its padding of late. Everything feels a little sharper, except for my mind.

I wait for Dad's car to rumble around the corner, then I head home to get Toby, boldly parking in the driveway, because the damage is done anyway.

THE LAST TIME JUDY WAS IN THIS EARLY WAS HER FIRST WEEK AT the shelter, when she was gobsmacked by the idea of me—teenage girl—unlocking the building on my own, another practise initiated under the questionable leadership of Birdie. We've come a long way.

But she's at the front desk when I clamber in with a cage full of crow. The fact that she doesn't assist me speaks volumes. A slice of sunrise moves across her swollen eyes and sets them on fire. Her nose is Pepto-Bismol pink.

"What's this?" With some people, you can measure their level of irritation by the stillness of their face. Only her lips move.

"Magoo is going to kick me out if I can't keep him quiet." I set him down and reassemble myself. "Toby, that is."

Hello.

"You didn't think to talk to me about it first?"

Stillness. Not even a cricket to break the tension. Of course, she doesn't mean Toby.

"I'm really sorry, Judy."

"About what, precisely?"

She waits. My fingers tattoo the air.

"I shouldn't have lied."

She takes a long breath, trying to hold steady eye contact with me, something she knows I can't do. Then, mercifully, she blinks.

"In my gut, I knew something was off." She sags, pulling a crumpled tissue from her pocket. "I've been lax."

I don't dare make the mistake of picking up Toby's cage and carrying on as if this is a normal day.

"Tell me, what would you do?" she squints, the sun illuminating her whole face. "Fire the three of you?" I swallow. "That leaves me and Earl plus a couple of part-timers on the weekend. Still, we could close for a week. Regroup." She pops a throat lozenge in her mouth, considering. "Or, just pull out the weed?" That's either Rachel or me. "Well?"

"I'd..." I clear my throat, caught off guard, thinking it was rhetorical. "Um, have coffee before I did anything."

She laughs, a tad maniacally. "I've had three. Come on, we'll talk about this after."

She props the kitchen door open for me to come through with the cage. The larger one is where I left it yesterday, so I wrestle Toby inside. "Hello, hello, hello." This is, after all, the cheese room.

"How long have you been here?"

She glances at the clock.

"Couple of hours. After I talked to your dad last night I got all wound up, then I just lay there with my box of tissues."

"How did it get on the news?"

"A tip from a shelter employee."

No doubt it was Rachel. Then again, it might have been someone for the SPCA, now caring for a bona fide fighting dog.

She describes the police tape with sodden cops in the background. Waylon in the back seat of a squad car, turning his head away from the camera. Possession of an unregistered weapon with possible further charges.

"They'll be here soon," she says, using her chin to indicate the front desk.

"I'm sorry." Having just gone through the hoarding, I imagine the helpful descending on us like a zombie invasion.

"I'll talk to the media this morning," she says, lozenge a lump in her cheek, "then we'll be moving them to another location. You ought to go scrub up. You look like you slept in your clothes."

I did, of course. That's two nights with these clothes. It doesn't make a difference when your daily outfit is a floppy lab coat and a pair of rubber boots.

"What do you mean, another location?"

"They're being weaned. The mother dog needs to heal. Now, go."

It feels like a punishment, taking them away so soon. But it's standard practise. They won't be adoptable for several weeks and they're better off in a home until then. I just thought we'd have more time with them—a day or two—to get to know the quieter ones, savour their puppy smell.

WHEN I COME OUT, FRESHLY BRAIDED, HAT AT THE CORRECT ANGLE, eyes de-crusted, glasses un-smudged, Joe has arrived. Judy pours him a coffee and indicates the cream and sugar on the counter.

"I'll talk to them. You two show them the puppies. Make sure they get some footage of the mother. Try to get her to stand."

She leaves, taking her post at the front desk, and closes the door between us.

"Hey," says Joe, stirring his coffee.

"Hey," I say, pouring. The room is much larger without Judy.

"You going to be okay with all this?" he says.

Do I not look like I'm going to be okay, gripping my coffee cup in both hands to keep from tapping?

"If I say no, can I go home and hide under the covers?"

"Probably not." His eyes are very sparkly. He must have slept.

Also—I don't say anything—but I spotted his truck in the parking lot, which, I suspect, is significant, it being the first time he's driven to work.

JUDY DOES HER INTERVIEW OUTSIDE, WITH THE FRONT OF THE SHELter's giant *ARS* displayed behind her. It's a tricky angle. The sun drills the reporter in the eye. The camera guy tries to soften it with a large floppy disk while the wind toys with it. He looks unhappy. The behind-the-scenes people don't have to wear smiles or business attire. I think I might be a behind-the-scenes person. Judy might be too. I can't hear what she's saying, but she looks like a plague victim. Not that the subject of dogfighting should produce a pleasant facial expression.

The disk is lowered and the holder shakes his arms, rather dramatically. No one acknowledges his efforts. The reporter swivels in my direction and we lock eyes for a moment. Questions form like wisps of smoke above her head. But Judy says something to put a stop to that. I get the signal to ready the pups.

Rather than squeeze a camera crew into a kennel, we bring the pups into the kitchen. Toby's cage has been shifted to the boardroom, where he can look at the parking lot and greet cars, hopeful as ever.

As we herd the litter away, the mother curls on her blanket, doleful eyes watching us without objection. Peanut leads her pack, galloping ahead, detouring into a heap of dirty laundry where she snatches a filthy rag before Joe gets them back on track. There's a squeal as one of the pups finds the reporter. I can't see what is happening but I suspect a wardrobe change is in order.

Our job is to keep the mischief to a minimum while the pups play and Judy gives her spiel on the adoption process. Naturally, this does not make for an intriguing story, but Judy responds with "No comment" every time a question nibbles at the details of the dogs' arrival here. Twice, I catch the reporter looking at my hand, even though I have it contained in a pocket.

Afterwards, we lock the door, putting up a sign (sans paw-print border or interesting font) saying we'll reopen tomorrow.

"Dave's taking them," says Judy, popping another lozenge. Dave, of the city's Animal Control unit, patrolling the streets in his little truck. Sometimes, when the pound is full, we provide accommodation and Dave chauffeurs them to us. "The mother is going to be at Dr. Trainer's clinic for a while and the pups are going to the Campbells'." A long-time foster family for the shelter. "Oh, and, we need to place an ad for a new part-timer." She crunches, which does nothing to soothe a throat. Subtle, I'll give her that.

"Does that mean—"

"It means, Dot, that we need help around here."

More help or different help? She walks away, cough drop pulverized between her teeth.

THOUGH THE SHELTER IS NOT OPEN TO THE PUBLIC, WE STILL HAVE our routine with feeding, cleaning, and walking. At lunch, I find Joe in the boardroom; he's pulled a chair up to Toby and he's sharing his sandwich.

"There'll be no living with him now," I say, making Joe jump.

"Sorry." He holds out his plastic container to me and I take the remaining half of his peanut butter and jam with a nod of thanks. I'm no better than a crow.

"What are you going to do about your apartment?"

I collapse in a chair on the other side of the cage.

"Look for another place, I guess."

We chew and let Toby do all the talking. I remove my glasses and give the forehead a massage. Closing the eyes feels so good. I think of Grand and how he learned to sleep standing while wearing his leaden pack during the war. I might be able to do that.

"Your pager went off a while ago."

"Mm," I say. Maybe just a few minutes with the eyes closed. "Probably Dad." It must be awful working in a store full of beds when you haven't slept.

"Why don't you just move home, Dot?"

Reluctantly, I open my eyes and put on my glasses. He's giving the beard a good tug.

Instead of answering, I throw the question back at him, but he's got a good excuse: his family lives two hours away and his room has been turned into an office.

"All I want is," I say, straightening my hat, "a little place where I can have a dog." And a rat and a crow and two gerbils, maybe a few cats.

"Maybe you ought to move to the country."

"One day." Do I sound wistful?

"Yeah, you're needed here." His voice cracks a little, much like Toby's.

"Here?" I point at the floor.

"Here, with your...family." More chin scratching. I'm starting to wonder if he has allergies. "But, yes, here too."

"But, I can't do anything." I can't help my mother. I can't help Grand. "All I do is sit at bedsides and drink tea."

Joe shrugs. "That's enough, sometimes."

"How can it be?"

"Not to be..." He searches the ceiling for the word. "Forgotten."

"I'm not *forgetting*...anything. You haven't seen her, it's just her body now. She doesn't know I'm there. She doesn't know the world is there."

He droops in his chair, his beard a pillow for his chin.

"He knows, though," says Joe, meaning, I suspect, Dad, and not the He with a capital H.

"Here"—I point to the floor—"I can help. That's what she'd want. Where, sometimes, I save a small life."

He doesn't argue, just gazes at his toes, bent in his terrible posture.

I remember my first abuse case. I was allowed to stay longer at the shelter to help monitor him. I can't imagine that type of pain. And yet, this dog, treated like meat by a human, looked at me with complete trust. One ear was gone. I don't want to think about how. Only the fur on his chest was intact, a perfect dairy-milk-chocolate brown. Dr. Trainer made me promise not to let my tears drip on his raw skin. I couldn't get him to eat, but he'd have small slurps of water. Very gently, I'd slip my hand to his chest and feel his heart. Sometimes it would burst into a gallop. Judy said that was a wave of pain. I thought it was the memory of the flames and the betrayal. He lasted three days like that. Then his heart just stopped.

Mum put her hand to her cheeks when I told her, like a silent scream. She said he was suffering and it wasn't right for us to ask him to keep going. After, every time we had a euthanasia, she'd let me talk it out. What were the alternatives in that animal's life? Many times, it was not so simple. Many times, there was just nowhere for them to go. They didn't fit in the world of humans. Inhumane.

AFTER LUNCH, I CHECK ON THE PUPPIES, BUT THEY'RE SLEEPING IN a contented heap. So, I take a little Button time, wedging myself into his kennel for an ear scratch. He pushes his head into me as

I rub and makes a half-hearted nibble at one of the buttons on my lab coat. But he backs off when he sees me looking. I'm pondering what might be a good replacement for his fetish—maybe one of those big rubber dog toys with peanut butter and kibble jammed inside—when Judy appears at the door, grim-faced.

"Your dad is on the phone." Right, the pager buzzed at lunch and I forgot to check it.

When I pick up the receiver, his voice comes through a tiny hole in his throat. Have I infected him with my bug? This is not what he has called to say, though. His sickness is nothing.

"She's got pneumonia, Speck."

"You go," says Judy, a shameless eavesdropper.

Clearly, Dad's crying has unsettled her.

"Thanks, but I think he might be overreacting. I'll go right after work."

But she's insistent, calling it a crisis. The word makes my legs wobble, so I take a seat on the couch that's not long enough for lying down. Joe has propped himself in the door.

"Joe. You take her." Something about how she says those words, the softness of it, makes me realize assumptions have been made about us. It's not that I mind so much about Joe; he's good with dogs. He's also symmetrical. What I do mind is the assumption that someone else has to help me when I'm perfectly capable of driving myself. I say as much, leaving out the detail that Joe drives like a nearsighted old man. But Judy will have none of it, ready to arm wrestle me for my car keys if necessary.

"You're wound too tight." She looks at my trembling hand. "And Roger says you haven't slept."

JOE OPENS MY DOOR, WAITS FOR ME TO CLIMB IN, AND CLOSES IT, ever so gently.

He ejects the cassette just as it begins to wail at us. I snatch it. Radiohead.

"Mind if I...?" I say, easing it back into the slot.

He nods, reaching for the volume knob. "I'll need directions."

As we pull up to a series of amber traffic lights, Joe applying brakes as if they're made of the thinnest glass, I open the window and try to remember how the whole inhale-exhale thing goes. Pneumonia, I know the word. I know what happens. But don't people get it all the time? She's in the best place to get pneumonia, with nurses nearby.

"All right?" says Joe.

I nod because I don't want to upset a driver like him.

"It's the next light, see the sign?"

We're here too quickly, despite Joe's best efforts. He pulls into a spot and idles. No sign of Dad's car. Thom Yorke's angst fills the silence.

"I can't go in," says Joe. I feel the same way. "Exhale, Dot. She's your mother."

I reach for the door handle without opening it. Minutes pass, with Joe reminding me to breathe. Tears sting at my eyes and I don't want him to see, so I turn away.

"Okay," he says, "I know a place."

THE PLACE IS IMMUNE TO DAYTIME. TO GET IN, YOU DESCEND CEMENT stairs. Inside, the floors are dark, polished wood and the windows, high up, are milky to keep you from remembering the world out there where you should probably be doing something useful. Two barstools are occupied by the men from the balcony on *The Muppet Show* bent over small glasses.

The bartender nods at Joe and gives me an extra look. He knows I'm underage. Police will arrive and take me away in one of those vans, stuffing me into the back with the likes of Waylon.

In England, I went to the pub for Sunday roast with everyone else. Kids and dogs were welcome there. The pub owner's retriever, Sam, was always nearby when food was on the table. And I was small enough then that it was okay if I crawled underneath and sat with him.

Joe holds up two fingers: "Guinness, please."

I like that he says please, even in here.

There's a grubby laminated menu on the bar. Joe pushes it toward me, pointing to the potato skins, but I shake my head. The stomach couldn't possibly manage pub grub.

Before I can think about money, he places a ten on the bar and we watch as the bartender pulls a pint, letting it rest while the foam arrives, then pulling again. No rushing a Guinness.

We take it to the table in the corner. Joe gets a foam moustache on top of his moustache. I point. He wipes. We sit side by side and slurp. It's not my first Guinness. Mum and Dad figured if I knew what it was like, I wouldn't sneak off into the woods and gulp vodka with other teenagers. As if.

One night, Dad served stout as soup, offering it as an appetizer to Mum. She'd been in one of her *funks* for days. Her word. He led her from the bedroom by the hand, plonking her on the couch. There, he placed a bowl of stout on the coffee table, resting a spoon on a fancy napkin beside it. It was the first time she talked about San Francisco, pre-Dad—she'd slept in a public park with throngs of people. Substances were consumed, not Guinness. It's where she met her closest friends, all of them ready to change things. That's when the circles first appeared to her, the landscape overlaid with them, people dissolving into shapes, balloons lifting her above it all. Inspiration struck. The world was a code to be deciphered. She'd been painting it ever since.

"Do you want to talk?" says Joe.

His glass is half empty or half full. I can't decide.

"No, that's okay. Thanks for driving." Even though it wasn't my choice and I wanted to reach over with my left foot and push the gas pedal more than once.

He has another long sip. Wipes. Then he reaches over and lays his other hand across mine. Just like that.

"You were doing *SOS* again," he says, releasing my fingers.

I pull my hand back and settle it in my lap.

"I wish I could tell you everything will be fine," he says to his glass.

Picking up my pint, I try to catch up with him.

"Thanks. For not saying it."

Reassuring must be an impulse. And I'm not a child with a skinned knee.

"Another?" says Joe, eyeing the level of liquid.

"Better not," I say, stifling a belch.

BACK IN THE TRUCK, JOE DOESN'T PROMPT ME TO TALK. HE PUSHES the cassette in and we listen to "Fake Plastic Trees" at a good volume. Quietly, he joins in with the chorus, *It wears her out*. I think we might be friends. My throat has closed. I'm the worn-out girl. We listen to the whole A side on our way to the peach building that keeps my mother alive. In my haze, I start to wonder if he's driving slow for me.

Joe finds a spot labelled *Guest* and turns off the engine. We sit, looking at the sliding doors, a woman with a walker grimly pushing her way out.

"You don't have to come in."

He gives me the briefest of looks, but it's full of pain, like my face burns him.

"I don't think I should," he says, "but I'll stay right here."

This makes me exhale. I won't be trapped if he waits.

"I'm not sure how long I'll be."

He nods and puts his hands on the steering wheel. Sometimes our bodies do that, tell the truth. Joe's hands want to drive away, but something is overruling that. If I were a Dorothy and not a Dot, I'd hug him for that.

INSIDE, THE WALLS ARE PEACH TOO. I HAVE TO ASK FOR DIRECTIONS, as it's my first time here. She is in A Wing, I'm told. The vinyl floors make my shoes squeak. The same person who sold the shelter fluorescent lights must have installed the ones here, making sure the flicker was just right. I see a washroom sign and veer off to let out some stout.

This reflecting is getting out of hand. Sprigs of hair have broken from my braid like half-plucked feathers. I give the face a few good splashes and marvel at the puffiness around my eyes while using a dripping hand to smooth my feathers.

This is not the hospital, I tell myself.

After the accident there were tubes and lights. Mum suspended in a hammock of incoming and outgoing liquids and oxygen. She was just asleep then, a medically induced coma. It was possible to think the hushed conversations were for her benefit, unwilling to wake her until the healing took place. Time drifted off while I held her hand.

I heard the phrase "semblance of normality" murmured to Dad. The idea was if I went to Math class and Social Studies, I'd remember to be a separate person. But I held on while they detached her from devices and watched her continue to sleep.

We weren't inclined to miracles in my family, but there was anecdotal evidence in the wider world. People sometimes woke, defying odds, making doctors concede they might have been a tad pessimistic. With the help of librarians, I discovered accounts of such happenings and showed them to Dad. "That's good, Speck. There's always hope." Already, he'd lost the roundness in his cheeks.

Was it dark in her world, or was she floating in a sea of colour, a part of her paintings? Maybe she was having too much fun to come back from her weightless domain.

They moved her to another room, away from the rush of lives being saved and rebuilt. I read her *The Stone Angel* from my English class. I rubbed the smell of Ori on my sleeve and held it under her nose, hoping it might trigger a memory of time spent painting at the easel, Ori's whiskers tickling her chin as she worked. I tapped messages on her collarbone and watched her eyelids for a reply. Outside the window, the season thawed. Judy took me off the schedule and, somewhat hastily, hired the lone job applicant at the time, Rachel. But I'd show up and walk the dogs anyway, or I'd sit with the shy ones while they nibbled a bowl of food. My grades plummeted, then levelled out just above failing. A pity pass. Maybe my teachers thought the blow of missing high school graduation would be the final one, as if I'd have gone to the parties and the gowned ceremony under normal circumstances.

At Mum's bedside, Dad read her the newspaper and hummed Beatles tunes. He helped the nurses, wiping her face, even cleaning out her nose, but left when they washed her. We both did. Her bones were still hers, but her flesh was changing, adapting, leaving. The thing that makes people themselves is partly in their muscles, the way they smirk, hold their eyebrows just so when delivering a terrible joke or talking for a hairless rat.

I got to know the cafeteria, their revolving specials and the fleeting freshness of coffee. I was tempted to bring my slippers and bathrobe so I could shuffle the halls with the patients. I'd always been praised for my patience.

One night, I went down the hall to make a cup of tea in one of those undersized Styrofoam cups. Absorbed in the fire escape plans on the wall, imagining the hell of evacuating a hospital, it took me much too long to realize the kettle was unplugged. They'd dimmed the lights by the time I came out. The nurses must have thought I'd left without being prompted for once, because I heard my name come up, followed by an unfriendly grunt. Tucking back into the tea-kettle room, I listened to the rant. Working yet another night when she was supposed to have been switched to days because of the goddamn head nurse who had it in for her because she was a smidge hungover once, once (!), last year after frickin' New Years... and now she's got to give the Dead Woman a bath.

Okay, maybe she didn't say those words exactly, but trust me, it was close. Then the other voice interjected but was ignored. Not right, keeping someone in a bed here, so full of people who will actually recover. Who's it all for? This work and the expense of it? If anyone asked her it was negligence, family keeping her body alive. Couldn't they see she was gone? Didn't the doctors tell them as much?

I poured my tea down the sink and sank to the floor.

THIS IS NOT THE MINT-GREEN HOSPITAL HALLWAY. IT IS FLESHY. The patients are beyond patient; here, they are called residents. I pass a room and glimpse an apple-doll granny in a cushy chair, knitting and listening to Oprah on TV. Another has visitors gathered around the bed in full camouflage gear, as if they've just come back from stalking a deer or, possibly, they want to hide amongst the potted plants, of which there are many. Someone has decided plants are needed and planted them along the hallway and in the rooms: rubber, ivy, spider, weeping fig. I stop to rub a leaf. It's real. She'd like that, plants cleaning the air.

She's somewhere near the tip of A Wing, where the feathers thin out to a point. It gets quieter as I near her number. I stop outside and hear the hush of competing afternoon soap operas from different rooms. Someone coughs.

The first time I saw her stir from sleep, I thought the big moment was about to happen. She could feel me holding her hand and was about to cross the void between us and rejoin the conscious world. I had so much to tell her, things I'd been saving. Never mind the melting face. Her eyes opened and drifted in my direction but slid past. It was as if I was sprinting towards her, ready for the big embrace, and she just kept running past.

"Mum? Mum? Dawn?" I think I even waved. I pressed the call button. "Is she blind?" I said to the nurse. She shook her head. I understood it then. My hope should have washed away but it didn't, not until the rant from the hungover nurse.

She's "awake" when I step in now. I stop and look at the number on the door to make sure. Her hair, rarely cut, fluffed to maximum height and width, adorning every surface of our oft-vacuumed home, is missing. It's like that first glimpse of Darth Vader when Luke removes his mask. Something boils up in me. How could they remove her armour? I turn to march off and confront someone about this, nearly bumping into the nurse behind me. She has snuck up, possessing a pair of stealthy shoes. Her smile flickers.

"Where's her hair?"

"Ah."

"Did you shave her head?"

Her hand goes to her throat. I read her name tag: *Barb*. Is she a barber?

"I'm sorry, you are..."

"Dot, her daughter."

"Oh." Her mouth stays like that in a little O as thoughts whir. "Dot. You should talk to your dad about her hair. Can I get you anything?"

"Did my dad shave her head?"

"I'm not sure who shaves her head, dear." Shaves. Of course, it's an ongoing decision. "I'm sure he'll be back shortly." We're interrupted by a gasp from the bed. Barb looks beyond me, pulling her lips between her teeth. "Excuse me, dear." She bustles over to the bed and bends to check a protruding tube. "We're trying to keep her comfortable." Before leaving she pauses to place her hands on my shoulders and fix me with her gaze. "Don't be alarmed at her breathing, sweetheart. I'm just down the hall, if you need me."

I don't want her to leave. I don't want to sit in that chair. I don't want to stand in the vicinity of the body that was Mum. Her eyes rove around, right past me as if I am a mote of dust. Smaller than a dot.

"Talk to her, honey," says Barb from the doorway. "It'll help."

Barb leaves me rooted to that spot, neither in nor out of the room. Something weighs me down. It's my bladder, despite just being emptied. My mother has a bathroom right here in her room, just in case she rises from the bed, rips out her catheter, and decides to do things for herself.

There's an enormous mirror, which tilts for those in a wheelchair, I suppose. Someone has angled it up a smidge. It makes my stomach twitch to see the room off-kilter. I let out the rest of the stout and try not to reflect.

On the counter is a familiar little bag. I have a sudden flash of sitting on my parents' bed while Mum applied mascara, her mouth gaping. "Why," I asked, "why must your mouth participate?" It made her smudge and start over. Here it is, ready to keep up appearances. Does Dad do her makeup after shaving her head? I investigate. Inside is a bottle of moisturizer, the kind she trekked to a department store to buy once a year, the aforementioned mascara, a set of tweezers, and a well-worn tube of lipstick. Its end is flat, a nub, in fact. It looks dehydrated.

I venture out of the bathroom, small bag in hand, and survey the room. Dad has brought in his favourite Womble, Uncle Bulgaria—the wise leader of the other Wombles—and propped him next to the useless phone. On the wall is a framed collage, featuring artfully scissored-and-glued moments of our family outings and innings. It covers my parents' early days, the single wedding photo (not the only copy, though), my purple arrival into the world, and various small-person achievements, including Dotty on the Potty. Art must tell the truth. It was for my art class. I regretted the potty shot when my teacher announced we'd be showing our work to the class. Further bullying ensued. Ironically, I spent a lot of that school year in a bathroom stall, my feet pulled up, reading.

I note the lack of air purifying plants. If anyone could use the help of a ficus, it's Mum. She coughs as if she agrees.

"Hello," I say, sounding like Toby. I clear my throat. "It's Dot." Her face is pink, but the top of her head is blue. It tells the story of how she has been indoors for over a year. Her eyes are open, pupils gaping.

I look at the bag. I'd thought I'd apply some moisturizer, but it seems like a waste with the sheen of sweat on her forehead. But on her chin is a single dark whisker. I remember the one. She always patrolled for it with her index finger. As soon as it popped up she'd yank it out. It was, she said, like a tree trunk amongst the other hairs.

They shave her head but allow her to grow a beard? This, I can do. I lean in and get a good hold with the tweezers, clasping her chin with my other hand. Ta-da. I look around the room for things to be done. Barb passes by and gives me a reassuring wink.

"You came." Dad is in the doorway, holding a plastic grocery bag.

"You shaved her head."

He sets the bag beside the bed and touches the back of his hand to her cheek. Leaning into her ear, he says something in the same hushed tone they used when I was a child.

"It was a practicality, Speck, to make her more comfortable in the summer."

He pulls the chair closer to the bed and settles next to her, taking her hand. He tells me how he first tried giving her a haircut, small snips here and there. Each day, he'd fix what he'd done the day before. It got shorter and shorter until you could really see how it wasn't growing evenly with the scars from the accident.

"Then one day, I'm on my way here and Sinead O'Connor comes on the radio and I remembered what you said." He's looking at Mum, smiling, as if she'll chime in any moment. "That one day you were going to shave your head like her. So, that's what we did. She looks pretty rad, don't you think, Speck?"

Rad? She looks radiated, that's what I think. It's one thing to be a bright-eyed woman, belting out a rock ballad to the camera, and quite another to be bedridden for a year, shorn of the last thing you've cultivated in your appearance. But he's moving on, ignoring my twitching hands.

"Dot's here," he says. "Has she told you about her latest adventures?" He looks at me, *this is your cue to jump in,* but I don't even hop. "Risked her life to save a family of dogs. Sound familiar?" He smiles sadly and cranes sideways so she can see him from her angle, as if she's really looking at him. "I saw her on TV just now, holding a puppy in her arms." Shit, I thought they weren't showing me in those shots. I hate it when they do that. "And Judy tells me there's a boyfriend on the scene."

"Friend, Dad."

"That's precisely what I said." His tone changes to teasing. She hated it when he did that, but he was oblivious. The assumption every relationship with the opposite gender must be about sex was, what was the word she used? *Condescending.*

Mum's hand yanks out of his. We both look at her. But no, her face is slack. Dad wipes a drop of drool from the corner of her mouth, then takes her hand again.

"It looks like she'll be moving out of that flat soon." He uses air quotes with the word *flat*, knowing full well only I can see them. "But it's for the best. Any luck with that?"

"I haven't had a moment—"

"Of course, she doesn't need to worry. Her room is ready..." His words trail off because she hasn't taken a breath. Silence. No wheezing. My heart counts the beats: twenty-eight.

"Is she—" I start.

A gulping breath interrupts me.

Dad hangs his head.

"I'm afraid it will be soon, Speck," he whispers.

Before I know it, my feet have delivered me to Barb, who is standing at a wheeled cart filled with tiny cups and pills.

"What's going on, dear?" she says, reading my face.

"She's suffocating."

She frown-smiles. "It's not an easy thing to see."

"Can't you do something?"

"We're keeping her comfortable, that's all we can do now." She pats my shoulder. "Knowing you're there with her, that's better than anything we can do."

"She doesn't know that we're—"

"We can't know that, love. The best thing is to assume she does, don't you think?"

No, I don't think. I think that sounds like a nightmare. In the beginning, I wanted her to be there, fighting to get out. Now, listening to her body gasp, I want her to be unaware. Knowing I'm here with her but not saving her, that I can sit and make small talk while she struggles for air, it would break her heart.

Dad is still at her side, clutching her hand. I don't recognize either one of them. Where's my family? I can't go back in. I have to be out where there's air.

I manage to get outside without breaking into a full run, pushing past the camouflaged family at the front door.

Faint music comes from the truck. Joe sees me and climbs out, and his door flaps behind him, Thom Yorke's falsetto carried on the autumn air.

It's not so much a hug as a vertical intervention. I need reinforcement to remain standing.

"Drowning," I say.

"I'm here," he says, instead of *It's going to be okay*. The wind ruffles his shirt. He smells of shelter. "Come on. Let's get in the truck."

Until I open my eyes, I don't realize they've been closed. I see what he sees now, reflected in the truck windows. People behind us, watching. I don't turn, I let Joe take my hand and tug me forward into the cocoon.

He's placed a box of tissues on the dashboard.

"Thank you."

I know he won't ask, so I fill him in.

He nods and looks away. My sadness is spreading like a yawn.

"You should go," I say. "Just sit with me for a little while?"

I watch herds of leaves flutter past the truck, gathering under cars. The tape flips to the other side and carries on. The sky is deep blue, the perfect contrast to the reds and yellows. She would love this. Sweater weather.

"I know what I have to do," I tell Joe and climb out of the truck before he can respond.

Dad is pacing the room when I return. Seeing me, he takes a deep breath.

"Your pager is in here," he says. "Where were you?"

"With my friend." I'm growing used to the word.

"Speck, I know this is hard. Bu—"

"Light," I say, "she needs light and air and smells."

He points to the window as if I hadn't noticed it, but I shake my head and go off to find Barb.

Another nurse is at the desk, much younger. She looks at me with undisguised exasperation.

"It's not simple to move a resident like her." She rattles off the reasons.

Nothing on the list sounds difficult to me. "I work at an animal shelter," I tell her. "I'm used to all of that." Bodily fluids, distressed patients who can't speak, heavy bags of dog food...

"And it's nearly suppertime," she finishes, as if that settles it.

That's when Barb reappears, pulling the younger one aside, communicating with her eyebrows and the set of her mouth that my plan is Fine with a capital F.

Dad pushes the chair while I wheel the pole. They have her bundled and strapped in like an astronaut. Behind the building is a garden. It's another world. Raised beds so the abler residents can water and deadhead flowers, picnic tables, a fountain with an eternally urinating cherub. Who knew?

"Did you know about this?" I ask.

"I told you before we moved her," he says, "surely."

Surely, yes.

"No, not in the shade." I point. "Over there."

We roll into a beam of light. Mum's head lolls, eyes swivelling towards a tree. Her breath comes in even grunts.

"Dot, this is not..."

"Going to bring her back? I know."

I bring us each a patio chair and we sit facing her.

"If you're right," I say, "that she's underneath all of this, she'll want her last breaths to be out here."

As the sun retreats, we follow it across the garden, wheeling Mum and dragging our chairs.

She dies twice more and comes back to life. Nothing prepares you for that. Dad holds her hand while on the other side I squeeze her wrist, feeling her pulse. It's stuck on the letter E.

Barb comes out with her coat on.

"End of my shift, sweetheart. I hope you like tea." She places two cups on the picnic table nearby. Some people are born for this. How does she manage to smile and go on?

"Thank you," we say together.

"Angela is on tonight," she tells Dad. "She knows where to find you."

We watch her go, silent except for the swish of her coat. Her shadow is long, the sun sets the building aflame. I shiver.

Standing, I hand Dad his cup of tea.

He murmurs into her ear, describing the evening. "Just a few nights until All Hallows' Eve." We missed it all last year, even Guy Fawkes Night. I don't want to think about last year.

"I'll get our coats," I say.

"No, we'll go inside soon." Is he afraid I'll use this as an escape?

"Not yet, I'll be back."

On the way, I stop to look out the front. Joe's truck is still there. Has he run out of gas? From the window, I can't tell if he's inside. I should tell him to go. But I don't.

"Thanks, Speck," says Dad as I drape his coat over his shoulders. I take a seat, pulling my sleeves down over my hands. "Do you remember when neither of you would speak to me for a whole month?"

Do I? It was one of our challenges.

"I had to turn on the TV so I wouldn't go mad. I'd say things to you both, trying to get you to talk." He smiles sadly, but at the time he was livid with us for choosing silence. He didn't understand how it was anything more than a prank on him. "Like a couple of bloody mules when you decide you're doing something."

It wasn't meant to upset him. We were trying to understand what it was like. Mum thought it would help her art. At school they became concerned with my prolonged bout of laryngitis. A note was sent home: was I contagious? What we learned was the world is loud and people say things they don't mean instead of allowing time for thought, especially teenagers.

Of course, we still communicated in Morse. We got faster. Outloud laughter was permitted, as well as gestures and the occasional scribbled line.

"Then," Dad says, "just when I thought she'd never speak to me again, she started singing. It was dreadful, of course." He leans into Mum's ear. "Voice like a rusty hinge, mangling the opening lines, but you chose well." The Beatles, naturally.

"'When I'm 64,'" I remember.

He nods, tears streaming.

"Bloody daft. An absolute, certified weirdo," he says, pulling her blanket a little higher.

Her breathing is quieter for the moment, although not improved.

"Then you read nothing but poetry for a month. That was a little easier. And after that it was—"

"No meat."

"Right, that one stuck. But how did you manage your visits to Grand when you weren't speaking?"

I shrug. "He seemed to enjoy it. No one interrupted him. Shouldn't he be here? Grand?"

"Oh, Speck, can you imagine?"

Yes, utter chaos. Despite his dementia, Grand is wiry and capable of violent outbursts. Knuckles Murphy. God knows what would trigger him at a place like this. A potted plant?

"Who's that?" says Dad, squinting at the glass doors. It's dusk now, things are losing their colour. "Your boyfriend?"

The light hits him from behind, but I can tell it's Joe from the shape. "He drove me."

Dad lifts a hand, beckons, but Joe doesn't budge.

Mum gasps, we both freeze, then a whistle of air escapes.

"He's been here all this time?"

"He won't go."

"Another mule," Dad says to Mum as I head for the door.

"They told me you were out here," says Joe when I reach him. "I called Judy, she wanted to know..." He struggles to find the right words.

"I'm okay."

"And she's taking Toby home with her."

I picture Judy driving with Toby chatting away over her shoulder. What will he make of all the rabbits? Will he scream all night? Will he miss me?

"You can come out." He won't look at me. I follow his gaze to Mum's bundled form outside.

"No. I shouldn't."

"Yeah, Dad's a mess. Like me." What was I thinking to even suggest it?

"It's not that—" His eyes widen.

Dad opens the door. I'm stunned; he's left Mum on her own.

"Off to the loo," he says. "Why don't you two keep her company for a bit? She sounds a little better right now." He holds a hand out for shaking. "I'm Roger Grey, Dot's dad."

Joe just stares. Is he starstruck? It happens from time to time. Some people get funny around Dad because of the commercials. But he's just a guy who wants to sell you a decent mattress.

"M...Joe," says Joe. "Smith, sir." *Sir?* "I'm very sorry." The words rumble up his throat and out his crumpled face. Dad lets go of his hand and pulls him into a hug.

"No need to be sorry, lad. It's not your fault." He pats his back and releases him. "It's kind of you, being here for Dot. It's good to know she has a true friend."

Joe nods, wiping his cheek. Dad gives me a wink and heads down the hall.

"Come on," I say, "I can't leave her stranded."

He follows me out but doesn't come close or take a seat. I reach for her wrist and tap *hello*.

"She's been in a building for over a year."

Her face turns towards Joe, as if searching, mouth working like she'll say something profound. A groan of breath comes, spit escaping her lips.

"I'm sorry," Joe says, and when I turn he's leaving, not towards the building but on a side path, skirting the glass doors where Dad steps through, squinting into the darkening garden.

"Where'd he go?" Dad says, reaching for Mum's hand.

"Some things are too hard to see." I should have warned him better; it's been hard for me and she's my mother. But I can't think right now.

Dad nods. "Have I met him before? At the shelter?"

"Maybe."

"Dot's friend"—he leans on the word *friend* as he tells Mum— "has a beard for the birds." I'd forgotten this joke between them. She'd begged him to grow a beard big enough for a small bird to nest in, but he couldn't take more than a few days of growth. "Is he religious?"

"I don't know."

"Soft-hearted, anyway. You'd like him."

I turn my chair so I'm facing the same way as Mum. The first star is visible now. Her eyes are turned that way. Will her brain transmit that much? Even plants know about light. She liked the Oscar Wilde quote about being in a ditch but looking up at the stars.

Dad mumbles on about the first time he saw her, barefoot, chewing a pencil. She was the bookkeeper for the previous owner of the mattress store, which is probably what led to him selling it. It sounds cruel, but she's the one who made the joke. Dad didn't fire her when he got the keys. He hired Aunt Kell so Mum could focus on marketing.

He's moving backwards through their life. Her breathing has been regular for the past half hour. Maybe they have it wrong. Maybe she'll rally.

"Dad, Ori needs his meds." He doesn't want me to leave; he asks if Joe could do it, but I don't even know if he's still here. Plus, the thought of someone going through my things without me there. "No, can I borrow your car?"

He hesitates but relents, providing me with a series of directions about things that do and don't work in the car. "So just leave that door unlocked," he finishes.

"I'll be back in twenty minutes." We both know that's optimistic. "Don't worry," I say, knowing that's all he does.

Magoo II's truck is back, its right hip crowding the access to my door. I suppose the ramp needs a coat of paint or something. Maybe he's here to forcibly remove me the moment they hear the cry of a crow. God, will Toby be blamed for the family of crows that makes the rounds on garbage day?

Inside it's dark, except for the slice of light around the edges of the Styrofoam barrier. Everyone blinks painfully when I flip on the light.

Abbott and Costello stand, tiny hands pressed to the glass. Ori is a heap of blanklets. Upstairs, there's plenty of life, the TV blares a commercial, heavy footsteps pass over my head, coughing, a drain gurgles. Without a bout of exercise for Bungo, I could be back out the door in a matter of minutes. That's what I should do. What if she—

The Styrofoam squeaks. Fingers jab around the edge. It lifts enough for me to see Magoo II's face.

"Sorry, Dorothy," he says. "Just thought it'd be easier than coming around." Speechless, am I. What if I was naked down here? "Not much of a barrier, really. Don't s'pose it matters if you're leaving though."

I clear my throat.

"I'm not leaving. Yet."

"No, well. When you figure things out, I said I'd help you clear out."

"My crow, Toby, is not here"—I point to his empty cage—"and this is a bad time for me."

His face looks like it's filling with blood from all of the leaning. Not so convenient, talking through the ceiling, is it?

"Ah well, I've learned things never happen at a good time." I hate it when I detect that from older people, the *just wait until you see all the shit life has in store for you* tone. Misery seeking company.

"My mother is dying." His eyebrows lift. "Right now. She's gasping for breath. If she's lucky, she won't last the night, because she is in hell." If it all weren't true, the way his face falls would be satisfying. "So, if you don't mind"—I'm spitting the words at him now—"I'd like to do this another time."

"I...I, we didn't know. I'm so sorry. Of course, we'll figure this out later—"

"Can you put that back?" Before I lose it. The moment he started stammering my dam began to burst.

He puts it back but not without some difficulty. The Styrofoam protests and refuses to find the shape it had before. A corner snaps off and rains snow down the staircase onto my boxes. Now there's a peephole. I can't ignore his lowered voice as he explains things to Magoo. After the elder Magoo scolds him for moving his carefully cut barrier, invading my privacy. I listen to the words lash. Magoo II is reduced to a boy.

Tears fall on Ori as I pull him out from his warm cave. We may as well be in the room with the Magoos now. I dare not speak to Ori; we exchange blinks as I dribble medication into his mouth. The crickets start up.

On the drive back, I note the brilliance of stars. The sky agrees, it's not a regular night. My neck is warm with Ori snugged against my left shoulder. It's been ages since we've been for a nighttime drive. I've undone my braid so he can use my hair as a curtain when we arrive.

Dad's spot is gone, I have to park on the outskirts of the lot. It gives me a chance to scan for Joe, but I don't see his truck.

Going around the building, I follow the reverse of Joe's escape route, but my parents are not where I left them. This could mean nothing, or something. Maybe Dad was cold. Maybe the staff made him bring her back inside. I don't know what to wish for. We pause to look at Orion's Belt, bracing ourselves with it. I put my hand on Ori, *steady*. His heart taps, a tiny telegraph operator within, as my feet take us to them.

Keeping my hand on Ori's back, we pass several residents who nod various greetings. One asks if I have a sore neck. "A little," I say, checking my curtain of hair is doing its job. In Mum's room I find Dad, his upper body draped over the bed, holding both her hands.

"Oh, Speck, I thought she was gone," he says. "It was ages, more than a minute, I'm sure." He dabs at his eyes, then catches sight of Ori and calls him Jesus by mistake.

Ori blinks in surprise as I settle him on her chest.

"Dot, you're not supposed to—"

"Probably not," I say, closing the door, "but I thought you'd be outside."

Ori goes for her shoulder and tickles the side of her cheek as he smells her breath. Her eyes close. That's better. He follows the hill of her head, whiskering her baldness as he goes.

I take her wrist, feeling the pulse. Ori settles at the crook of her neck. *We're all here now*, I tap. I tell her about the sky and how the stars make me think of her. Dad sits back, watching us, his eyes drooping like an old hound's. If anyone needs a decent mattress right now, it's him. Her breath stutters and he snaps up.

Even Ori stills, while we wait. With my thumb I search for her pulse, but there's nothing. Dad leans over her face. A whisper of breath out. Then nothing. I count my heartbeats, gripping her wrist. Has she gone without saying goodbye? Anything at all. A blink?

88, I tap.

I thought she was melting before, but now everything sags, her arm heavy in my hand. I tuck her wrist into her side and watch the tension vanishing. It seems she's sinking further into the bed, like she'll disappear into a cloud.

"Dawn," Dad says.

Still, we wait, even though my own heart knows. Perhaps she's hovering above her body, deciding whether or not to return. It is both still and electric. Behind me, the door clicks and I sense movement, but I don't think to say anything until I hear a gasp. This must be Angela and, judging by the words she utters, I suspect she doesn't have a pet rat.

"It's okay," I say belatedly, "this is Ori."

"I think," Dad chokes out, "she's gone."

Angela struggles with what to do, her inner wrestle visible. So I scoop up Ori and back away from the bed while she leans over with a stethoscope. She turns to Dad and places a hand on his shoulder, utters something about peace and rest. Then she looks at me, biting her lip so she won't say anything on the subject of rats in a healthcare setting.

"Take as long as you need," she says, closing the door behind her.

"I never really believed it," Dad says, swaying like a strong wind has entered the room. I go around the bed and shore him up before he goes over. He's like a well-cooked noodle. I hug him hard.

"Speck," he says, "that's a bit tight." My aforementioned strong arms. I loosen and he pulls back to look at me. "It's just you and me now." He waits to see how his words will sit. It's a good thing, because even though my hope wasn't as strong as his, I still thought of us as a trio.

ANGELA DOES GIVE US ALL THE TIME WE NEED. THOUGH THE DOOR is shut and no one enters, life continues beyond the barrier. People cough and shuffle past. Distant laughter rings from another room. It's cruel that the world can't stop for ten minutes, or even ten seconds, to acknowledge the end of a life. After weeks of avoiding this room, I dread leaving, walking away from her, while people carry on around me. Maybe she's here in some other way.

Dad sandwiches her left hand between his two, gazing at her face like he has to memorize it. Ori stands on her chest, directly above her heart. *Out, out, brief candle!*

There's a faint knock on the door and a slightly familiar face peers through the slice of window.

"Come in," Dad says, too low to be heard.

The door creaks, but no one enters, so I go and discover a beard-less Joe. I wouldn't have known him except he's in the same clothes as earlier. His chin is hardly there at all, pasty against the angry red of his neck. He steps back from the door as if it might hurt him. So, I must open it and beckon. He shakes his head. He wants to talk to me.

"Um," I say. If I come out, the world will rush in. "She's gone, Joe."

"Oh, God," he says. I almost say *She's my mother, not yours.*

"Joe." Dad has found a stronger voice behind me. "It's all right."

So, he comes in, starting at the sight of Ori, perched on her chest.

Joe mumbles condolences, pats my arm, asks if he can do things for us, as if we've taken this time to make an itemized list. Dad squints at him, not unkindly, but in that way of trying to sweep aside a brain fog.

"He shaved," I tell Dad, helpfully. *Possibly using a wedge of broken glass.*

Dad nods, then returns his stare to Mum, straightening her covers like she might be cold. Habits don't die as easily as people.

"This is probably not the time to say this," Joe says to his toes. "But I'm worried I never will, if I don't tell you now." He dares a look at me. I'm a little dizzy, so I lean on the bed.

"Go on," says Dad.

"It was me." It's nearly a whisper, he coughs to clear his throat. "I must have been seconds behind her. It was hard to see anything. There was a bright yellow car off the road. That's what I was look-ing at." But he's looking at me now, pleading. "I just turned my wheel to pull over. I saw her at the last second...I saw her face. I can't stop seeing her."

Dad goes to him, pulls him into a hug, my mother's killer, maybe just to silence him.

Now it's me who can't breathe. He was right. This is not the time to say this.

THIRTEEN

D AWN AND IT'S GREY. I WAKE IN MY OLD ROOM. WHEN I SAY *WAKE*, it's the only evidence I've slept. I tossed so much that my pyjamas have rolled up past my knees. I would doze and have a dream, unpleasant and unsatisfying, then flip to the drier side of the pillow.

Joe could have told me, told us, long ago. Instead, Dad comforted him while I developed tinnitus.

"That poor kid," Dad said as we drove home. Not a shred of animosity in his words.

I fumble for my glasses so I can get a fix on the day. It's past eight. As I stand, my stomach moans. I cannot remember my last meal, just liquids.

In the kitchen, Dad slumps over the morning paper. Hearing me, he lifts his head and murmurs, "Tea," instead of good morning. It's a plea, not an offer. I'm glad of a task and set to it.

"Is it me," he croaks, "or does the house look different?"

"It's not you." The house has lost its hope.

I make us toast and slice some cheddar for a smidge of protein. We each take a section of the paper. Sports for Dad. Front pages for me. We don't read. We don't talk. It's just the sound of pages flipping, teeth doing their work, and the occasional slurp. This is a comfort. We will do this and then we will do our dishes and we will plod on through today until it is permissible to close our eyes against the world again.

"I have to go back, gather her things."

"I'll go with you."

"Thanks, Speck." He looks at me over the top of his paper. "Did you notice the clouds this morning?"

I nod. He nods.

The stars last night, the grey of the dawn. It's the closest thing to a goodbye from her, as if she's in the sky with a paintbrush.

"You can stay here for now," he says. It's not a question. Sometime during the night I knew it too.

THEY'VE STRIPPED THE BED DOWN TO ITS PLASTIC SELF. SHE DIED here, will it not retire now? Will the next person lie there knowing this is a deathbed? Maybe this bed sucks the life from people. I want to kick it, punch it, slash open the mattress. But I have a look in the bedside table instead, as requested. Nothing. There's a whiff of disinfectant. Either Barb or Angela must have taken the time to gather what was left into the two small bags perched on the corner chair.

Dad is gathering hugs at the nurses' station when I come out.

"You take care," he says to Barb. "Enjoy your new grandson." He gives her shoulders a goodbye squeeze. She nods, then smiles sympathetically at me. Nurses have a better sense of when and whom to hug.

DAD DROPS ME AT THE SHELTER SO I CAN BRING RUSTY HOME. JUDY must be watching from inside, because she comes out, wrapping her lab coat around her against the autumn chill.

Some people are always steady, and when there's a crack in them, it's like the planet shifts. All she does is tilt her head to one side and look at me like I'm an injured rabbit. My tinnitus kicks in as I sob on her shoulder.

No, it doesn't help when you know someone is going to die. Not a bit. I thought I had pre-mourned. But, no.

Dad idles, his window rolled down. They discuss the feasibility of me driving to the abode.

"Just give me a minute," I say, mopping snot with my sleeve. "I'll follow you." He turns off his engine and I look up at the sky, hoping gravity works on tear ducts. A dark bird glides past.

"Toby," I say, remembering.

"He's at my place...in the kitchen window with a view of the squirrels." I can picture him there, nodding vigorously, cursing, the way he does.

"Thank you."

"I'll bring him to you later," she says.

"Is Joe here?"

"No, he called in sick." She shrugs. "I kind of figured he would." I don't know what my face tells her, but she decides to add, "He was with you. Right?"

I pull my lips in.

Dad tells her instead. How Joe ran over my mother and sought me out as part of his messed-up guilt. Not his words. She rubs her forehead, listening.

"You never pressed charges?"

He shakes his head. "It wouldn't have helped anything. The police said he was doing the speed limit, no drugs or alcohol in his system, just a kid. She was in that brown coat she wore all the time..." He looks at me, but I can't talk about it. "But I think it's ruined him anyway."

RUSTY STILL SMELLS SOOTHINGLY OF PUPPY URINE. IN FRONT OF ME, Dad stops at a green light, so I give him a light honk to prod him on. At the next one, he speeds through, leaving me stranded at a red. Luckily, I know where I live.

Magoo II's truck is on the road, leaving the driveway for me, I assume. If not, I don't bloody care. The plan is to load everyone into my car, along with their paraphernalia, and Dad will grab my clothes, all of which are in the dirty laundry anyway.

"Home," I breathe as Dad comes up behind me.

"Hovel," he counters.

I give him a poke in the ribs, which surprises us both. He gives me a frown-smile. Are we not mournful? We are. Is it okay to feel other things too?

The peephole has been patched with, I think, a tea towel. Handy things.

I shift cages to the door and Dad heaves them off to the car. Together we get everyone piled in. Then I strip the bed and carry the linens out to stuff around Waldo, whose head has appeared from beneath his synthetic cave. I apologize for the recent earthquakes and turn around to find Dad ferrying Mum's paintings, still swathed in brown paper, to his car.

"Dorothy," comes a tremulous voice from beyond the Styrofoam. "Dorothy, I'd like to speak with you." Just when I thought I'd disappear without further discussion. "I'm heading outside." This is evident from the stump of his cane heading for the door.

We meet at the top of the ramp, where he transitions to a walker, for speed.

"This is my dad."

"Roger Grey." He sticks out a hand.

"Stanley McGee." Magoo squints at Dad, trying to place him. "I wanted to inquire about your mother."

"She passed last night," Dad answers for me.

"Oh dear." His hand pats his heart. "My deepest condolences. Had I known, I would not have made such harsh demands of you."

"It's all right," I say. *It's your son I'd like to kick in the shins.*

"When you get to my age, the smallest things can ruin a day."
He shakes his head. "It's been ten years since my Edith passed,
and I miss her terribly."

We both murmur our condolences.

His rheumy eyes fix on Dad.

"People have the audacity to say you should move on with
life." He coughs and glances back at the doorway, maybe expecting
Magoo II to appear. He leans closer. "One can never be the person
one was before. It's foolish to even try."

I don't know what to add. We three stand in silence, a breeze
chasing leaves around our feet. I suspect Dad is considering hugging Magoo but wondering if it might crush him.

"Well, we'll be off, then," Dad says, settling for a light pat on
Magoo's shoulder.

He waits while I start my car because we don't take engines
starting for granted in our family. He pats Rusty's hood as he
heads for his car then turns back.

"Meet you at home, I'm going to make a stop."

BUNGO LIKES THE NEW DIGS. ABBOTT AND COSTELLO ARE
higher still. It's nothing but hairy backs, with all three gawk-
ing at the sight of traffic. The front door slams and there's the
sound of clinking. I find Dad in the kitchen, clearing space in
the fridge.

"What's all this?" I say, passing him a bottle to stash next to
the milk.

"People will come over. That's what happens." He pauses and
twists the lid off a beer. "Nut-brown ale?" He gives it a slug, then
offers it my way. "Not bad. Brewed here. About bloody time." I
grab a bottle for myself before he can put it away. "I have to call
people. Your nan…"

"Right." My grandparents, across the pond, might not make the journey for the funeral at their age. "And her friends." He sighs. None of them live nearby. "We'll visit Grand together."

Instead of answering, I take a swig of beer.

DAD IS CORRECT. PEOPLE COME.

Judy arrives with lasagna and rum. "Don't worry, Dot, it's veggie."

Rachel is two minutes behind with a pack of coolers. I endure long hugs from both. Then Aunt Kell just lets herself in and goes straight to the kitchen to stash something away. Her husband, Alistair, whom I've never met before, follows. I soon find out he's a piper and the bagpipes are in the trunk, should we be so inclined. He gathers a circle of chairs in the living room and seeks out the reserve glasses from the top cupboard. Earl arrives with a bag of ice and a plastic tray of cheese, the neon pink grocery sticker proclaiming it should be consumed tonight.

Cramming the ice into the freezer, I motion for Dad to come over.

"Are you having a party?"

"No." He seems insulted at the idea. "More of a wake, Speck."

Never have I attended a wake, but I thought the idea was to have the deceased present, laid out on the dining room table, perhaps.

"Thank you for coming." Dad climbs onto a chair in the living room. "We don't have her with us." He gestures at the coffee table, as if that's where she'd be. "But we have picturesss." After his call to England, he sampled a few more nut-brown ales. Earl shuffles a little closer to the chair. Dad points at the wall. Heads swivel to take in the motley family gallery. "And that's the way we want to remember her."

"What about her paintings?" Rachel pipes up.

Dad does a slow blink.

"Brilliant, Rebecca."

"Rachel."

"Sorry."

The paintings are where Dad left them, leaned against one another on the upper landing. Alistair bangs nails into the wall for Dad, who waves off any worries about location and aesthetics. So, we end up with paintings all over: high, low, squeezed into corners, propped above my gawky school photos.

"She'd never put them up?" says Rachel, looking at a grim landscape of a burned field, ash flurrying in the foreground.

"Only on the easel, then she'd say she was done with it." I'm trying to make out the subtle bumps beneath the paint. *No touching, Dot, it's still wet*

"Are these all of them?"

"I think so."

Rachel uses the top of her bottle to rest her chin as she considers. If I could touch them, I could read them with my fingers, like Braille. *It's impolite to read someone's diary.* How about after they're gone? What then?

"This is what it's about," Rachel says quietly, probably just to herself, "making things for yourself. They're always saying that." Her eyes are all shiny when she looks at me. "I wish I'd known her."

I nod and drain the last of my warm beer to avoid speaking.

Alistair, lacking a circle of musicians, takes it upon himself to keep the record player spinning. Left to my Dad, it's either silence or "Sgt. Pepper's Lonely Hearts Club Band" on repeat. It seems no one added to the record collection after about 1980. So our wake goes from *Dark Side of the Moon* to "Dancing Queen," at which point Judy starts to mix drinks for everyone. I learn I don't like the taste of rum, but I carry it around and try to take sips, because all the beer is gone.

Dad re-enacts his proposal to my mother, using Aunt Kell as a prop. It was at the store, of all places, her in a swivel chair in the little office at the back. He'd swung her around, misjudging the spin, and it made her dizzy, so when he said the words, she actually swooned. Alistair looks a bit twitchy as Kell flops forward into Dad's arms.

I catch myself smiling and it makes me sad. Outside the street light is blurry. I know what we need.

"Bagpipes," I say, and Alistair perks up.

He warms up in the washroom next to the laundry with the door closed, as if that will make him less noticeable. I'm immediately smitten with the creak and groan of it. I want to pat the pipes, doing their best to produce a recognizable string of notes.

We follow him out into the fog, making for the highway. The grass is long and the ground bumpy beneath it. We pass two hub-caps and box of pizza. Alistair stops well short of the shoulder and we gaze up at the lone street light that has led so many cars astray.

I lean on Dad and he leans right back. He attempts to sing along, even though I don't think that's what people do with pipes. You can't really hear yourself think when you're next to them. And when he pauses between tunes, the sound goes on in your head like an operatic mosquito. Maybe that's what makes them a good instrument for the aggressively melancholy. Cars swoop along the curve, some giving us a honk. In my pocket, my fingers tap *attention*, hoping we won't cause an accident.

He saves "Amazing Grace" until last. I can't hear the others, but I see their mouths moving, at least until the bit where they're blind but now they see. It peters out after. Some bow their heads; others stare, glassy-eyed, at the offending highway. I focus on the orange glow of the light, watching the swirl of moisture flit about it like a ring of ghosts until the last groan of Grace leaks out the pipes. Alistair leads us back to the house, silently this time, and I have the sense we've done something.

Dad hugs Alistair, pipes and all, emitting a noise like an exasperated duck, and instead of a heartfelt thank you, he asks him if one of the tunes was AC/DC. Two things about this question: one, it makes Alistair taller, and two, my Dad is aware of—nay, familiar with—hard rock. Who knew?

Our drinks are where we left them. Finding mine on the end table, I claim my favourite bit of couch. Judy sinks down next to me, eyeing the level of my liquid. She pats my shoulder.

"Why didn't you call Joe?"

I tell her.

"*Murder* is a bit harsh, Dot."

"Well, she'd be here if it wasn't for him."

"How did Roger react?"

I describe the embrace, the length and squeeze of it, his concern for the "boy" after.

"Well," she sighs. "You have a right to your anger. That was a lot of lying. But what he did, it must have been hard, Dot."

"Balls," says Earl. Opposite us, in a wooden rocking chair he's been listening in, moustache flapping as he sways. "Takes balls, that does. Plus he's good with feral cats."

Judy nods and the conversation is temporarily hijacked by staffing concerns. But a good throat-clearing gets them back.

"Not balls," says Judy, "although I know he has them." She elbows me lightly then licks the side of her glass where some rum tries to slip away. "Kindness. You can see that plain enough."

"Yup," says Earl, "his skin's on inside out." A horrific image.

"Well, he's found his pack then, hasn't he?" Judy toasts the air, not waiting for a clink to drink.

"Damn straight," says Earl, lifting his glass only to find it empty. He rocks himself onto his feet and heads for the kitchen.

"This couch is going to swallow me," Judy says through a yawn.

Kell claims the rocking chair, sitting on the edge of the seat so she tilts toward me.

"Your dad," she says, sotto voce, "is sloshed." Slow wink. "Good for him. He's been a shadow of himself for the past year." Across the room, Dad has the bagpipes, but it's clear he's lost track of which bit to blow in. Alistair puts down his drink and reaches out as if they're an infant about to fall from the arms of a drunken uncle. "Don't worry about that, it wouldn't be the worst thing if those things broke. Jesus."

"It was nice of him to play."

Kell looks at me and smiles like I must be drunk.

"I saw you on television with those puppies. An awful thing. I don't know how you can work there. I'd want to bring them all home with me."

"If I had a dollar for every time I heard that one," mumbles Judy, eyes closed.

"He's proud of you," says Kell, oblivious to Judy. Instead of taking the pipes away, Alistair flips them around, but his hand covers the mouthpiece, blocking Dad from slobbering into it. "Your mum was, too."

Other than me, Aunt Kell might have been the closest Mum had to a female friend, someone she'd actually do things with, like shop or go to a show. Her other friends were what Dad called "gypsies," their string of abandoned phone numbers overflowing the pages of her address book.

"Did you go and see her? Before?"

Kell nods. "Last Saturday. They thought she was improving at the time."

"Was she bald then?"

"Dot, she's been that way for weeks. Months." Dad must have kept my lack of visiting to himself. She slides back on the chair, lets it sway away from me.

"I want to get her a wig," I say.

"A wig?"

"For the...service."

Kell examines her nails, working at a cuticle. "Is there going to be a viewing?"

"I don't know." I think of her in a box, hairless as a newborn.

"That might be something they do, you know, the people who... prepare her."

"Where would I get one?"

"I don't know, Dot." She gives her own hair a little tug as if to reassure me it's attached. "I'm sure you'll discuss it at the funeral home."

The utterance of those two words together makes me stand. I need to be away.

"You all right?" Kell says, looking at my legs.

"Fine." A multipurpose word.

UPSTAIRS, I SHUT THE BEDROOM DOOR AND OPEN A WINDOW. I'VE missed windows. Ori rests on my shoulder and we watch headlights draw curves in the black. Without my glasses everything softens, colours fatten. This is the room where she rocked me, the bed she perched on to comfort me after school.

Life is a circle. Did she say that? Am I supposed to feel better? There are a lot of feelings stirring under the numbness. Relief is one of them, and I don't know what to do with that. It's selfish and small.

Downstairs, Judy has taken up the couch, her head on the flattened arm, snoring. "Saturday Night Fever" is playing, but it's quieter.

"Thought you'd gone to bed," says Earl as I take the chair next to him, one hand on Ori to steady him as I sit.

"Hm." I didn't realize it was an option with a house full of people. "It looks like Judy has. What about you?"

"Your dad has offered his bed to anyone too drunk to drive, but I'm going to share a cab with those two when I can peel them away." He points at Kell leaning on her husband, talking to Dad about the latest in coil springs. "You know," says Earl, eyes on a painting showing a highway, "they took my licence away once."

"Why?" Ori descends my arm.

"I went straight through a red light in rush-hour traffic. Sun was in my eyes."

"Was everyone okay?"

"I didn't hit anyone, but I caused an accident. Just a fender bender. It could have been worse. A lot worse." His eyes rest on me. "Have you ever done that?"

"Run a red light?"

He nods. "Or done something you couldn't take back?"

"Probably." I give Ori a boost to the back of the chair, where he has a good view of things.

"Took me years to stop having the dreams. The worst injury was whiplash. I can still hear the screeching and the crunch of metal." He shakes his head. "But I couldn't go back and make it right. Those people had a baby in the car. This was before car seats. They hated me, Dot. I could see it coming off them like smoke. And I don't blame them one bit."

"So what did you do?"

"Slowed the hell down." He strokes his moustache. "With everything." I'd imagined Earl had always been mellow.

Rachel perches on the arm of my chair.

"I don't get why they hated you," she says, another shameless eavesdropper. "Everyone was okay."

"For what might have been," he says. "They couldn't protect their child from me." Earl and his wife never had kids.

"How long ago?" I ask.

"Oh, that baby'd be grown up long ago. I hope so, anyway."

"Alrighty, Earl, I'm calling the cab," Kell booms from across the room as if she needs to wake us all up.

"Obliged," he says, nodding.

"Keep it down, will you?" Judy's eyes are scrunched closed. "Some of us have gone to bed."

I'm the one who puts a blanket over Judy, locks the door behind everyone, and guides Dad upstairs.

FOURTEEN

"**Y**OU CAN'T BRING HIM TODAY," SAYS DAD, EYEING MY SHOULDER. "I wasn't going to." I continue my search for her favourite dress. Hangers scrape. Dad winces.

"That one," he says as I hold out a navy number with roses around the neckline.

"No way, this one was a gift from you she *pretended* to like." Floral was not her thing. It made her think of women trapped in a life of domestic servitude. Her words.

"That's not true."

"Trust me." I put it back and squeak on through the closet until I find it. A spring green with lots of fabric, a swing dress with generous pockets.

"But she hardly wore it."

"That's because she didn't want to ruin it. Ask Aunt Kell." She bought it brand new, not even on sale.

"I bloody will." He lies back on the bed with his facecloth covering his eyes.

"What about shoes?"

"Shoes?" Mostly she wore flip-flops.

"Never mind," I say. She won't be standing.

"After the appointment, we have to stop by the hospital to see your Grand." Just when I thought today couldn't get any worse. "We have to tell him."

"Coffee's ready," calls Judy from downstairs. "I've got to get going. Call you later."

"Thanks," we say in stereo. Laying the dress across the bed, I find a mark on the hem.

"He's out of jail," says Dad, taking the facecloth off and sitting up. "It was on the radio this morning." My heart pauses.

"Already?" Who would pay Waylon's bail?

"I don't know if he was bailed out. They said something about being held for twenty-four hours on the weapon charge. Still, he's got family, friends. Not everyone feels the way you do about animals."

As if this has not occurred to me. There would be no need for the shelter if the world was a safe place. Chances are, Waylon saw animals treated the same way when he was a kid. Maybe he endured tauntings and beatings too, but that doesn't make it right.

"Come on, Speck." He takes my hand, the one drumming the stain, stifling its movement, something I hated as a kid. "They can fold the fabric to hide it."

But I want to wash it. I know how this will sound, so I don't say it. Burying your mother in a dirty dress, barefoot and bald. It doesn't sound like love. So I wait for him to go to the kitchen before smuggling it to the washer.

HANGOVERS DON'T IMPROVE PEOPLE. I TAKE THE WHEEL AFTER three blocks of Dad clutching his forehead in a way that must obscure his vision. He drove us to the funeral home, but that was before the sun came out from behind the clouds.

"Did you take something?"

"Of course I bloody took something."

"Okay."

"Sorry, Speck. The sun's trying to hurt me."

We'll have to go back to the funeral home with the freshly laundered dress when it's dry, but they said it was fine. I'm not the first person to insist on unsoiled clothing for the dead. From Bob the funeral director's reaction, I'm guessing it's the least of their problems. I got the sense you could say anything to him and he would nod knowingly, and produce the appropriate brochure from an inner pocket. *Ah yes, we've used this magician many times, he does a wonderful disappearing act involving the deceased.* So, the idea of Ori attending the service was not dismissed immediately. As long as he's not out and about, he can come along.

It felt like we were in there for a full day while Bob tried to tease out Mum's wishes from the snatches of conversations we could remember. But the sun is high in the sky when we emerge.

"I didn't know she liked the woods so much," says Dad. She turned down his dream of camping our way across Canada after our one and only disastrous weekend at a provincial park.

"Not the woods, trees."

"Speck—"

"Her words."

"I hope we've got it right," he says, leaning on his window. "We didn't talk about those things."

"You heard him; the service is for the living. I think this is the street." Squinting, I read the sign just in time to switch lanes.

"You're sure a scarf wouldn't be just as good?"

"She never wore scarves," I say, and before he can say it, I add, "or hats." It's not a lack of love, or an attempt to save money, he's just oblivious to these things. Mum called him *profoundly practical*, and if she were here, she'd poke him in the ribs for it, so that's what I do.

Wanda, the wig woman, runs her business out of the house. Often, she told me on the phone, she travels to her customers. In this case, our visit to her seems like the best option. After all, a perfect fit isn't necessary.

Her street is lined with oaks, bowing their heads to provide shade to the light-sensitive. Dad risks dropping his hand from his eyes as I parallel park. I turn off the engine and we gaze up at the canopy. In our part of town, trees are still scrawny teenagers.

"This is like her painting," I say. Each branch worked in delicate strokes all the way to the clouds.

Leaves cling to the lower branches where the autumn wind hasn't whisked them off. It must be older than Dad, older than Grand. It could easily accommodate a family of crows and all their visiting relatives.

"Yes," Dad says, eyes glassy, "I remember now."

Wanda waits for us on her step, ushering us in a door with a discreet sign. This part of the house has been converted into a kind of salon. There's a chair and a large mirror where she must seat people and talk to their reflections. At the side is a long table with Styrofoam heads sporting everything from Liza Minelli to Rapunzel.

"Tea? Coffee?"

Neither of us can manage more liquid. One thing I'm learning about death is you spend a lot of time sitting down drinking beverages to make other people feel better. I suppose there's a strong possibility of dehydration with grieving. Dad takes the revolving chair while Wanda points out the types of wigs, the textures, and the way to put them on.

"Do you have anything less...tidy?" She squints at me, so I do my best to describe my mother without mentioning any eighties rock bands.

"Woolly?" she says, skeptical.

"Kind of."

"Right." She disappears into a closet and I turn to look at Dad fondling the red locks of a wig on the shelf nearest him.

"It doesn't need to be exact," he says. But all of them are glossy. Not once did her hair have a sheen, unless it was wet. He points to a long one at the end. "She was more like that when I met her."

"It's completely flat," I say. It has the look of the early seventies, a part down the middle.

"There's this one," says Wanda, re-emerging, "Someone did not follow the washing directions. I've been meaning to work with—"

"That's her." I reach for it and Wanda lets go, startled. I twirl it to see all sides. It's like Mum took it off and left it here by mistake. I look at Dad and he too is wide-eyed.

"Thank you." I'm cradling it. At home, I'll spritz it with Opium, her signature scent.

"How much?" says Dad, putting the redhead back on the shelf.

Wanda waves the question away. "I couldn't sell it in this condition—"

"It's perfect," I say. "But we need it today."

She looks at it, considering, then at me, softening.

"I won't take money for it, but I have one request."

"Anything," says Dad.

"Don't mention my name."

"Thank you," I say, removing the hair and handing her the head. "Mum's the word."

Dad gives her a squeeze. Poor woman.

She opens the door for us and we go out among the oaks again.

IN THE ELEVATOR AT THE VETERAN'S HOSPITAL, DAD MAKES ME promise to help. He could have mentioned it on the drive over here, but he has chosen instead to wait until the metal doors have shut and there are people listening into our conversation.

"I'll tell him about the pneumonia and you tell him about her death."

"What?" I say, agog.

"He's never hit you."

"Before," I say. "He's never hit me before."

But Dad is talking to himself about the other things to be done, tracking down her friends, the lawyer...his lips move as he stares at the numbers blinking above the sliding doors. I wish for an elevator mishap of some kind, but despite a bit of a wobble, it delivers us to the sixth floor.

We ring the bell and get buzzed in. A patient hovers nearby in case we leave it ajar long enough for him to dash out. Al is notorious. But he has no luck this time.

Grand is not in his room, so we carry on to the lounge and find him watching a soap opera (who knew?) with a smattering of others. Dad prods me ahead. I kneel by Grand's chair and say hello.

"Hello," he says, tilting his head like a crow. "Is it time to eat already?"

"Grand, it's Dot. Dotty?"

"That's nice," he says, eyes drifting back to the TV. The Pillsbury Doughboy giggles as a giant finger pokes his belly.

"Can we talk for a bit? Dad's getting us some tea." I point.

He cranes his neck around. "Is he?" He puts his twig hands out so I can lug him out of his chair.

"Ups-a-daisy," I hear myself say. Just being in this ward can age you by five to six decades.

"I wonder if they'll have any of those shortbreads," he says, shuffling alongside me.

We take a table in the corner with a view of the cemetery across the road, something that hadn't bothered me in the slightest before this. It was just a nice green space for people to cut through on their way to work.

Dad opens the conversation by reminding Grand he has a daughter named Dawn who was injured in an accident a year ago. Today, it seems, he knows this much. Or he pretends to. Nevertheless, he still doesn't like the look of Dad. It's easy to see that by his leaning away, head angled so he can regard Dad down the length of his nose. He shivers at the mention of the accident. I reach for his hand when I tell him. That's what people do, I think. Make sure they're sitting and then you hold onto them and say the words.

"Dead?" he says. "But she's only a girl."

"She was a grown woman," Dad says, unable to hold back his frustration, "a mother, my wife."

"Who?" says Grand, his face blank.

"Dawn." I pat his hand to pull his gaze back to me. "Your daughter, my mother, she died."

His eyes well and I'm stranded between relief and dread.

"The service is in two days," says Dad, leaning toward us, proffering a tissue. "We can make arrangements for you to come."

I shift my chair closer to Grand. In some ways, I envy his loss of time; he can have moments when he's who he always was, everyone he cares about just off in another room. But a minute later he reminds me of the downside.

"Who died?" he says.

We don't tell him a second time. Dad goes down to the cafeteria to see if he can get a packet of shortbreads, and I deliver Grand back to the TV so he can watch a soap in which people can return from the dead, because it was all just a bad dream.

My pager languishes on the bedside table now because I'm reachable by phone. When we get home with the wig there's a message from Rachel. Button dragged her out to the parking lot and she cracked her kneecap. Possibly an exaggeration, as there was no mention of medical intervention. No one has seen Joe. Have I talked to him?

I sit on my bed and try not to think about Joe. It's Thursday afternoon and I don't have anything to do. I'm not used to that.

Dad knocks and the door swings open just enough to avoid the escape of a hairless rat. Luckily, Ori is a lump under the covers.

"Going to the lawyers now."

"Okay."

"Sure you don't want to come?" Like it's an outing. I've already said no, but he's still there. "I'll pick up some food on the way back?"

"Don't. There's a year of lasagna in the fridge."

"Oh, good thing I have you," he says. "Mind putting the living room in order while I'm gone?"

I switch on the TV for company while I gather bottles and wipe up the stickiness. It's the tail end of a talk show and everyone is in pyjamas, the audience too. Did they arrive that way or was the whole crowd marched off to a change room with a fresh set of flannel PJs? The host, with glossy hair and bright lips, tells us to relax at home as the days get shorter, to let our hair down. But first, her voice drops several notes: tomorrow is Halloween. I look away before they can flash cheerful gore on the screen. Real blood I can handle, but this stuff makes me shiver. Must humans use it as entertainment?

The local news comes on, teasing the headlines. *Mild weather for trick-or-treaters tomorrow, are you Y2K ready, and...revenge in an alleged case of abuse.* Something is familiar about the figure ducking into a police car. It's the footage of Waylon's arrest. I sit down, kitchen cloth in hand, and wait out the commercials. The report flashes a series of images on screen, ending with the video of the puppies at the shelter held by someone who looks vaguely like me. Then there's a ragged woman on camera. They have to bleep out some of her words. It's Waylon's mother, livid at the vigilantes who put him in hospital. *Not this vigilante*, I think, hoping they'll detail what was done to him.

"Little *bleep*-ers grabbed him when he was getting in his car. What happened to *bleep* innocent until proven guilty?" She jabs the stub of a cigarette at the camera. "The cops best do their *bleep*-in' job. Those bleeding-heart animal *bleep*-ers did this to him. Mark my words. It ain't right."

He's in hospital in stable condition. This always makes me think of horses companionably chewing hay, of lazy flies and afternoon sunlight. But I think it means he's not going to die anytime soon. Next, an officer makes a familiar speech about not taking the law into your own hands. *Call the police.* The number is flashed on screen in case society has forgotten.

The camera goes back to the mother. She has mustered some tears angry tears, but tears nonetheless. She waves the camera-man to get away from her, lights a fresh one. What would my childhood have been like under her reign? She'd have been a vicious spanker.

I have an urge to talk to Joe. But he's not Joe, he's Morris, as he was all along. It was always on the tip of his tongue. My eyes weren't open to his holding it back. Thinking back, I made assumptions, just like everyone else.

Instead, I dial the shelter. Rachel picks up and asks if I can hold before I even say hello. I wait, trying to think of the right word for her phone manner. Curt? No, snappy. There's no hold music. I'm about to hang up when she returns with a world-weary sigh.

"Animal Rescue Shelter."

I launch straight into the latest news.

"I know," she says. "The cops were here a couple hours ago. Judy wouldn't let me call you."

"What did they want?"

"They had to follow up on any leads. His mother wants to press charges. But we were at your place, so we have lots of people who could vouch for us."

"Right." The wake.

"They don't have any suspects," she says. It was dark, the person took off, leaving Waylon out cold, that's all they'd say. "You don't think it was..." She can't see me shrug over the phone. "He's not here today. Sick again, supposedly." I don't want to get into that. "How are you?"

"Okay. Kind of numb."

"Yeah. I'd be, like, a total mess." Her voice over the phone is muffled. "Sorry, Dot, gotta go. Oh, Toby's here. Earl taught him another word." She hangs up before I can say goodbye.

I get back to it, dragging chairs to their usual homes. People left their shoes on after the bagpiping, so bits of grass and dirt are everywhere. I drag R2D2 from the closet and set to it. In spots, it sounds like I'm sucking up gravel. It's satisfying, so I carry on down the stairs and transform the front entrance, stashing Dad's sandals and coats that aren't up to the task of fall weather. Next, the crumbs in the kitchen and then all the way up the stairs to the bedrooms, leaving neat lines in the hallway, fluffing up the carpet.

Dad lets me know he's back by unplugging me.

"Jesus, Speck, you didn't have to go all out." Samosas waft from his clothes; he's forgotten about the bulging fridge again, but I'm suddenly dizzy with hunger. This might throw him over the edge, a year of her dust, gone. I watch for signs of a wobble, but he rallies. "Looks smashing, though."

He's set the table, a cardboard container at each place and a bottle of beer, cap twisted off, instead of water.

"No rum?" I say.

"God, no."

We eat without talking, the TV on in the other room so we catch bits of news. Prince Charles is in South Africa, where he'll take Harry to a Spice Girls charity concert. Then Robert Latimer's confession about the other ways he considered killing his disabled daughter. "He maintains it was an act of mercy." Dad flinches, so I leap up to turn it off, but not before we hear how she was in constant pain, how he put her in his truck and piped in the engine fumes, how she fell asleep. No more pain for her. But, I know, there will be plenty for Robert.

"Life is full of horrible choices," says Dad, staring at his last bite of food.

"How was it with the lawyer?"

"It wasn't too bad, really." He has the last glug from the bottle. "He's a good bloke."

"What's next?"

He kneads his forehead like it's made of clay.

"Phone calls, two more, I think, then the obituary. You're good with words."

"Am I?"

He turns to the kitchen's miscellaneous drawer, affectionately called Miss Drawer. She hangs onto wine corks, stray Christmas lights, dead batteries, elastic bands, old calendars, and chewed pencils. There's a pad of paper, every page used for notes between us, our comings and goings—*back for supper, dentist called, milk, bread, bananas*—much of it in her handwriting. Dad swallows and flips through until there's a blank page.

He jots down *Passed away peacefully*, then erases the last word after glancing at me. *After a long struggle with...*

"Can we say anything we want?" I wonder if they'd allow a smattering of Morse code in an obit.

"I don't know, Speck, there's a form to these things."

"But we're paying. You're paying, I mean."

"Sure." He jots down her maiden name, her Dad, predeceased by her mother.

"That doesn't tell the story."

"It's too much to get into here." He points at his scribble. "But we can talk about her life."

"People who read these are just making sure they're not dead yet," I say.

"It's people who know me, know you."

We have the paper on the table, so we can see how others have done it. Every one of them is older than her. Some are accompanied by a photo of when the person was free of creases. A freshly pressed uniform, heroically shining eyes, ready to ship off to fight the Nazis. A woman posed in a three-quarter view, pin curls framing her face.

"What photo can we include?" Evidently, a recent one is not obligatory.

Dad doesn't respond, head bent to writing—*avid painter, devoted mother, best friend*—so I go in search of the albums. I was permitted to hold the camera, even as a young child, so there are shots of my parents together, the frame slightly tilted with a pleasing blur. As the years went on, I got a firmer grip and picked my moments better. They were candid: Mum with her head in the freezer on a hot summer day, Dad Marmite-ing a slice of toast, Mum having forty (forbidden) winks, her hands covered in paint, the two of them wrestling with a strand of tangled Christmas lights. My all-time favourite was the windy day on a rare road trip. Her hair stands up, like she's in zero gravity, a lighthouse to her right. Not one dignified portrait in the lot.

I show Dad the Windy Day shot and he nods.

"She said it made her look taller."

"Sure," he says. "Why not?"

When Judy rings the doorbell, I'm deep in my closet, pulling out long-forgotten items of clothing to make space for crickets. It's not her voice I hear when Dad opens the door, but the croaking hello of Toby.

When I get downstairs Dad is wrestling the cage through the door.

"Sure you don't want a crow in your life?" he says to Judy, not joking.

"I like him well enough, but the bunnies feel differently." She lowers her voice, not sensing me behind her. "Really, she ought to be thinking of releasing him. Sooner the better, so he doesn't forget how to be wild. He can fly now."

"He can?"

They turn to me like I'm Dracula, risen.

"I let him out in the house and he made it up to the fridge. Took me an hour to get him down." She points a finger at me. "You owe me a house cleaning."

"Gladly."

"Anyway, I won't stay. I've got to get back to my critters, get things ready for the goblins tomorrow night. Don't suppose you'll be doing that here?"

"We never do," I say. When the weather cooperated, we'd head off to a beach with a pile of wood and do a bonfire for Guy Fawkes.

"Dawn hates...hated the greed."

"And the gore," I say.

One year we put a bowl of treats outside. Apples, I think. Our house was thoroughly egged.

"Right." She gives Dad a hug, then turns to me. "We can manage at the shelter without you until next week, so stay put."

FIFTEEN

ESPITE BEING FORBIDDEN TO COME TO THE SHELTER, I FIND myself here. I enter next to the laundry, inhaling the mix of chemicals and stink as one might savour the scent of a bakery.

When Button sees me he sits, back legs splaying out in that Great Dane way. One paw pats the door between us, his formal invitation. I give him a good ear rub until he drops his elbows to the floor and I can have a seat, then he does his best to perch on my lap. It hurts, but I don't mind.

"Thought I saw Rusty pull up," says Judy, stepping into the foot bath at the door.

"Sorry." Not sorry.

"The leash walks are only getting harder. There's no way we can put him up front."

"He's a pushover."

"Oh sure, inside he's a lush, but outside he's a frigging draft horse."

I wrap my arms around him and he lists like a ship going down. Together, we slide to the floor until we're completely horizontal on the concrete.

"You're not supposed to be here, Dot."

"I'm not really here," I tell Button, who gazes at me through one eye slit.

"Right, and neither is Joe," says Judy. For a moment, I wonder
if Joe sneaks into the shelter to snuggle with the dogs too. But then
I remember my new world.

"Has he quit?"

"Well, if he has, he didn't tell me."

"Have you called him?"

"Many, many times. No answer. Anyway, I'll figure something
out." She scratches at her hair, messing up one of the ponytails.

There's a greedy little pleasure in knowing things don't run as
smoothly in my absence.

"I can help."

"No, I don't want your help right now. We've had some applications come in. I just need to know what's happening with him, that's
all. You have other things to do. As do I." With that, she marches
away, then marches right back. "By the way, Button arrived in a
very small car, I'm pretty sure he'd fit in a K-car."

"*A nice Reliant automobile.*" I hum the rest of the Barenaked
Ladies song about all the things I'd do with a million dollars while
I think about fostering a giant.

As soon as Button sees Rusty's car door open, he climbs into
the back seat without any fuss. I'm pretty sure I could have taken
him without a leash. He just knew. The only issue with the ride
home is he blocks my mirror, planted as he is in the centre of the
back seat.

Not having to remove his shoes at the door, Button arrives
upstairs ahead of me. I find Dad in the living room with a newspaper
in his lap and a large, damp chin on top.

"He'd like to know if he can come up on the couch."

"Really? When you said you wanted to foster a dog, you used
the word *fragile.*"

"He is."

"Oh, all right, Button, come on then," he says, patting the cushion beside him.

"It's just for a few days."

"Right," says Dad, folding his newspaper. "Did you bring some bales of hay home with you?"

"Of course."

"And where will he sleep?"

"It looks like he enjoys the couch." He settles beside Dad, his bum on the seat, front legs on the floor, exactly like a person but a full head taller. I sit on the other side.

"We're a sorry bunch around here, Button," says Dad, looking at the walls. "I hope we don't bring you down. All we have left are splats of oil on canvas."

Her paintings are still in place, a haphazard exhibition crowding the walls. I've thought about taking them down, but I can't. All three of us sit, regarding the walls.

"Rachel was really moved by them," I say after a few minutes.

"That's nice."

"She's an art student."

"Hm."

I stroke Button's back, Dad rubs his left ear.

Hello. Hello. It's Toby calling from the kitchen.

"Christ almighty," says Dad. "I thought he'd finally nodded off."

Button's head tilts like a knob tuning a radio frequency. He follows me to the kitchen, where Toby lords over everything. His cage, propped on the counter, reaches the ceiling. Dad has covered it with a bedsheet, not an old one, but the one from his bed. I take it off and make the introductions. Button places his paws on the counter and gets his nose as close as possible. Toby curses, glaring. My heart taps. At his size, Button could do some damage. But they just eye one another.

"Well, this should go well," says Dad, leaning in the doorway. "It's only temporary."

He laughs. Temporary. Whenever something wasn't working in our house—a faucet dripping or cabinet door falling off—one of them would say the house was only temporary. It was available and affordable when they needed to buy a place, but they'd find something better. Only the big move never happened. Then I came along and it went from house to Home.

"Anyway, I have to write down what I'm going to say at the service. Any ideas?"

Button's head is well above the kitchen surfaces, so I'm trying to stash everything in the fridge before he realizes his luck.

"Poetry?"

"Right." He lets out a long breath. "I'll leave it up to you. Do you want to...say anything?" I simply look at him. Has he forgotten who I am? "Didn't think so." He shuffles off in the direction of his bedroom, Button follows as if he's been waiting for the rest of the house tour.

"I'll pick something out if you read it," I call after him.

"Okey dokey."

Outside, I spot two small superheroes kicking their way through leaves to the neighbour's walkway with a parent in tow. It's not even dark yet. As soon as they've passed, I go around and shut all the curtains on the street side of the house, then flick on the television and claim the entire length of the couch before anyone else does.

The weatherman is dressed as Cruella de Vil, with three stuffed Dalmatians hanging from his shoulders. Don't get Judy started on that movie and the inevitable trend of spotted puppies.

Apparently, it's hard to deliver a forecast with the people at the anchor desk snickering off camera. The gist of it is we're in for some wet weather. I sit through the rest, hoping for a mention of

Waylon, but all I get is a gravelly Jean Chrétien and talk of pension plans. Try as I might, I can't see Joe-Moe leaping from the shadows and attacking someone. Maybe I don't really know him, but I've seen him with timid dogs.

Someone knocks on the front door. There's a chorus of "Trick or treat!" beyond. Button barrels down the stairs and lets out some powerful woots. That's the end of the knocking. Through a crack in the curtains, I see a father laden with lumpy bags waving for the kids to move on. One of them, no higher than my belly button, is wearing a goalie mask with ketchup (I hope) smeared along the side. I shiver. What parent dresses their children as murderers then sallies off to demand candy from the neighbours? Why does no one else find this disturbing?

Button, job done successfully, ascends the stairs once more to find Dad.

It's a good time to retreat with a book of poetry and a philosophical rat. Propping myself on some pillows, I read poem after poem. The best prospect is Mary Oliver, who adores the trees. Her words put me in a meadow with wild grasshoppers and swaying grass.

I must nod off, because a slight tapping wakes me.

"Don't you think one of us should take Button out before bed?" Dad says, not opening the door.

"Good idea, but it should be two of us."

It's windless, and some of the neighbours have dared to put candles out on their steps alongside pumpkins and their hideous plastic decor. A small family ambles toward us. Then, catching sight of Button, the mother takes the hand of her miniature clown and crosses the street, even though his tail is wagging and he's not pretending to be a demented character from a horror film.

"Are you ready for tomorrow?" Dad asks.

"No. You?"

"Never. I've written down some things, but it doesn't feel like enough."

We walk a block without talking. Button selects several posts for watering. Dad has the leash, but it hangs slack, which is a surprise and a relief. I'm not sure both of us could hold him if he decided to go.

"Thanks for coming home, Speck." What can I say to that? "I know I was always trying to get you out of the house when you were a kid, but I just wanted you to have some mates." He still calls friends *mates*, even though I've explained that, on this side of the ocean, it makes people think of copulation. "The shelter is a sad place for a kid. Your friends are decades older than you. Except for Rebecca—"

"Rachel."

"Right. And your friend Joe."

"Moe."

"Right."

I can't hold it in. I haven't asked since the night she died. He'd hugged him, as if it was just...a mistake.

"My *friend*? How can you just brush it off like that? He basically killed her."

"I'm not brushing it off. Neither is he. Speck, the hell we're going through right now...just imagine if it was you—"

Dad moves just in time. Button has meticulously lined himself up, all four feet on the grass, his back end delivering a whopper of a shit directly onto the sidewalk. I reach for the bag in my pocket. Dad gags as I do my best to gather it up with both hands.

"I'm so glad you've come home," he says, once I've double-knotted the bag. "But you need to let this one go, Speck. The anger won't serve you. Trust me."

SIXTEEN

ⱺ◯ⱺ

TODAY I BURY MY MOTHER. WE SIT IN THE KITCHEN AND DRINK tea, then coffee. Button is beside Dad's chair, stoic and drooling at an untouched piece of toast. Toby dances on his perch, squawking whenever Button looks his way. Dad pats his pocket and finds the crumple of his eulogy there. It's the third time he's done that.

"You're sure he'll be all right here?" Dad says, handing Button the slice of toast.

"He can't come with us."

"It was okay for Ori," he says.

"One, Ori is not coming." He wants to sleep in. "Two, Ori weighs one hundred and fifty pounds less." Both of us look at Button, knowing that's a light estimate. "But, if you want to bring him..."

Dad winces. "It's just he might panic in a strange house."

"I think he's settled right in." Despite us tucking him in on the couch last night, he decided Dad needed company in the bed. I found them spooning this morning.

"Temporarily, anyway," says Dad, handing over his plate to be licked.

AFTER THE SERVICE, AFTER DAD CHOKES OUT HIS EULOGY AND JUDY gets up to read the Mary Oliver poem, while I clench my fists and ram my eyes shut, after all of that, we bow our heads and someone hits play on a boom box and "Stand By Me" thrums the first notes. We form a receiving line of two. People shake our hands, pat our shoulders, say words I can't hold on to. I think I nod and say things too, but it all smears together. I want to be outside.

EARL COMES TO STAND BY ME, SOFTLY, HUMMING THE TUNE, *OH darlin, darlin, stand by me, whoa stand...*He offers me his plate: white bread stuffed with mayonnaise and canned something. I shake my head, suppressing a gag.

"It'll soon be over, Dot," he says. "Just hold it together."

"You can tell."

"You look like a squirrel trapped in a bottle."

"I can't help it."

"Maybe if you tuck your hands in your pockets."

If this outfit had pockets, I wouldn't be propped next to her coffin, tapping on the lid, which, I now realize, might be disturbing. I'll never be without pockets again. Focus on something else.

In the doorway, there's a large vase of flowers. People have put some envelopes in a basket next to it, cards with scrawled condolences and pictures of birds or flowers or both. Will we sit and read them later? Do we display them on a shelf to remind us? Have they tucked in gift certificates for coffee or rum?

Across the room, Judy is with Dad, talking to a tall woman. It takes me a moment to realize it's Dr. Trainer with her hair smoothed down, wearing a dress. A dress that fits rather well. Did I shake her hand earlier? I want people to look like themselves.

Earl puts an arm around me and points to a chair.

"I'll get you some tea," he says. "Or a cigarette?"

"Tea." He heads off with his now empty plate.

There's a shuffling of people in the door to make way for a walker. It's Magoo, of all people, in a three-piece suit like a banker from an old movie. Someone points at me and he sets off, lips pressed together. I stand and offer my seat as he draws closer.

"My deepest condolences, Dorothy," he says, before sinking into the chair with a sigh. He pulls a handkerchief from his pocket and wipes the end of his nose. "It's a terrible thing, losing your mother. I wish I'd known." He folds the fabric four times, neatly, and tucks it in his pocket. His suit is full of compartments. There's a chain latched to a button, likely leading to a watch hidden from sight, and there's a whiff of mothballs. "I wasn't much older than you when my mother passed." He leans to touch my arm and fix me with his itchy eyes. "She had the voice of an angel. I like to think she's been watching out for us ever since." Not this again. If I hear another person infer she's better off in this mythical land above me, I'll—"Of course, I'd prefer she'd have lived to hold her grandson, but we can't choose. Can we?"

He tells me he's had Junior put a proper wooden cover on the stairway and my bed is where I left it. "We'll make it spick and span for you too."

"That's kind, but—"

"You needn't answer now, this is neither the time nor the place. My only request would be you find a way to keep the crow from... crowing, as it were."

Impossible.

"Thank you, Mr. MacGee."

His eyes focus on Earl's incoming plate.

"Here you go, Dot." I take the cup of tea from him and Magoo accepts a proffered date square.

Earl bends to my ear. "There's a young man outside the door. He doesn't want to come in—" Then, catching my look, "Not Joe. But he wants to talk to you."

Leaning to see around Earl, I see him pacing. It's whatsis-name, the cycling roommate.

"What does he want?"

"To talk to you." Earl shrugs, glancing behind him. "Want me to come?"

I shake my head and leave Magoo, who is concentrating on placing his handkerchief across his lap. The same one that just dabbed at his dripping nose.

"Dot?" he says as I approach. His Adam's apple is bounc-ing. Another squirrel in a bottle, by the looks of his darting eyes.

"That's me."

"I'm Mike, I'm Moe's—"

"I know."

"I'm really sorry about your mother. Can we?" He points.

We go into an identical room next door and sit facing the wall that would hold a casket.

"He wanted me to drop this off." He pulls out an envelope. "I didn't read it or anything." I take it and stare at the words *The Grey Family*. "He's been home for...days."

"Oh."

"He's barely left his room."

The room with the flying car, the flip clock, and the home-made quilt. I see it with the puppies in the closet. That's the only way the room can exist in my mind.

"Is he...sick?" I don't know how else to put it.

Mike nods, his right knee jumping up and down like it's pedalling a bike by itself. "It's bad. I had no idea about any of this, what he's been doing."

"The shelter or my mother?"

"No, yes. I mean, I knew about the car accident, but I didn't know you're her..." He stops and takes a breath. "Her daughter. Last night he told me, and he wanted to give you this." He points at the card in my lap. "But he couldn't come."

"Thank you." I don't know what else to say. This is my mother's funeral. I'm the one who needs soothing right now.

He doesn't move to leave.

"He made me promise not to call his folks, but he's been...saying things." He wobbles his legs back and forth. "And, I'm worried."

I concentrate on the carpet, the interlocking circles of burgundy and grey. In the next room, where my mother lies on a pillow of someone else's hair, there is a short burst of laughter. I use my toe to tap out the word *go* as I grip the envelope.

"Maybe you should call his family."

He nods to himself like I've confirmed something.

"Here," he says, putting a folded yellow sticky note on my knee. I recognize the number from Joe's note. "He might not pick up, but..."

He escapes while I listen to the murmurs from next door.

It's not a condolence card inside the envelope. On the front is a black-and-white photo of a donkey in a field, no florid poem, just Moe's scrawl.

I am sorry, but I can't forgive myself so I can't expect it of you.

That's it. Not even his name. The words are smudged. The donkey's head hangs, ears at half-mast. You can make out the silhouette of the photographer in the eyes, elbows jutting out to hold the camera.

In a building filled with people, you can only sit in an empty room for so long. Rachel finds me staring at the card and sits.

"Joe?"

"Moe."

"Can I see?"

It's polite of her to ask, having read it over my shoulder.

"What does he want you to forgive him for?" Before I can reply, she amends. "The accident or, like, trying to be your friend?"

"Both, I guess." I hand it to her.

"I love jackasses." She flips it over and stares at the donkey.

I'd kind of like to kick her, just a little snap in the shinbone, for donkeys everywhere. They deserve a better nickname after all the servitude.

"And will you? Forgive him?"

"It was sneaky, don't you think, not telling me who he was? He lied to all of us."

"I don't know. I wish someone was, like, looking out for me." She hands the card back. I tuck it in the envelope and stand up.

IN THE HALL, DAD IS SAYING GOODBYE TO A YOUNG COUPLE. EARLIER, he told me the woman once worked for him. Half the room is made up of people who somehow know my name. She speaks in a low voice and pats his arm while the man checks his watch. Dad embraces them both, tightly, by the looks of it. More people are wearing their coats now, as if the first exit is the accepted signal. If I don't figure something out, I'll be obligated to say goodbye to each of them. So, I turn and make for the washroom, as if there's a lower intestinal emergency afoot. Luckily, it's a single room with a locking door. A watery oasis.

The tap has a slow drip. I admire each tiny upside-down world held in a sphere before it smashes apart. I hide until the voices outside swell and fade.

DAD TIPS MINIATURE SANDWICHES AND SQUARES INTO A TUPPERWARE bin while Judy holds it steady. Catching sight of me, she winks. "Staff lunches are on me this week."

"Our fridge is jammed tight," says Dad, willing me with his eyes not to tell her it's because we haven't eaten her lasagna.

"Resourceful," I say, going back to the room where Mum is now alone except for the funeral-home staff.

Next to her casket is Bob, quietly talking to an employee wiping my smudges from the shiny veneer. Seeing me, he inclines his head and steps away.

"Miss Grey, is there anything you need?"

So much. The list is too long to name. Bob must have developed a sense about people, even people like me, because he clears his throat and beckons the employee to follow. "Please, take all the time you need." He backs out of the room, closing the doors behind him, leaving me alone with her for the first time.

I open the lid. She's nestled in shiny fabric. They've left the wig frizzy, as instructed, and tucked the dress just so. Maybe it's a tad too much blush; she glows as if she's just come in from a brisk walk. She looks more herself than she has since the accident and it makes me hurt.

Closing my eyes, I reach in and touch her hand. The wedding ring is still on her finger. Will they strip her of all that before...I can't even think the word.

Dad comes up behind me and rests his hands on my shoulders, saying nothing. I hear him sniffling, feel the tremble of his touch as we look at her for the last time.

WHEN WE'RE IN THE CAR, DAD SAYS, "WHAT ARE WE GOING TO DO NOW?"

"Wait for her ashes and then sprinkle them under—"

"Right now, I mean." He leans forward, his arms on the steering wheel, watching the flow of cars ahead. I'd argued he shouldn't drive today, but he insisted. If anything, it would help him to focus on something else.

"We should go home and see what Button has been doing."

His face brightens. "Yes, we should get straight back."

"He probably watched TV." We'd left it on for him.

Rolling ahead, we wait for a break in traffic to let us out.

"Who was the lanky guy you went off with?"

I tell him about the card and Mike's worries about Joe. Not Joe, Moe. He frowns, looking at me instead of the road.

"You can go." I point. A driver has halted to let us out. Dad squeals his tires a bit as we join the river of cars. "Mike says he hasn't left home for days."

"What's going on with him?"

"I'm guessing he's depressed." Aren't we all? Dad says nothing, which means he's gathering himself, but I cut him off. "Mum was too. You tried to hide it from me."

"It wasn't that." He looks insulted. "Not exactly. She figured you had enough on your plate. And it wasn't all the time." He glances my way and I know he's remembering the same thing as me.

It was at the end of the school year. Dad's car was in the driveway when I got home. It was 3:52 P.M. Slipping out of my shoes, I climbed the stairs with my backpack still on but stopped when I heard Dad's voice from the bedroom. I was worried I'd stumbled upon parental sex. But no, something wasn't right.

"Sleeping every day? For over a month?"

"I'm just tired. Please don't start—" Her voice was monotone. "It's just a nap, Roger."

I must have been holding my breath, because things started to go grey. I went back outside without putting on my shoes and stood there wondering what to do. When Dad opened the door he looked at me like I was an apparition.

"Speck, did you forget your shoes today?" He stared at my socks.

"No. You're home early."

"I just forgot something." His brow furrowed. "I'm heading back to the store. Want to come? We could have some supper after. McD's."

"No thanks, I'm going to the shelter."

"Right then." He patted my hat as he passed me on the stairs. "Don't forget your homework."

She was in the kitchen, opening a can of beans, a sweater over her nightgown. Without turning, she asked if I was hungry, her voice too bright. I wasn't. It was only 3:59 P.M.

"Good." She put down the can, the lid half off, angled like a bad roof. "I don't even know what I'm going to make with this."

"You don't have to make anything."

"I do, though. I'm supposed to make things." She tapped a curse word on the counter.

"There's stuff in the freezer."

She turned, her hair flat above one ear.

"I don't think there is, Dot. We're all out. Come with me, to the store? You'll help me figure it out." Her words sped up, bumping against one another like her brain had switched on but the power supply was too much.

I skipped the shelter. I waited while she got dressed, then we drove to a different store than usual. Her idea. She kept her eyes down and had me do the transaction with her debit card; she couldn't see the numbers with her sunglasses on.

The cashier gave us a look, like we might be contagious or shoplifting.

"We're vegetarians now," Mum said on the way home. "Are you up for it?"

That night, she cooked a pot of chilli, a tofu curry, and banana bread, and whirled homemade hummus in the blender... Lying in bed, I could hear the clatter of dishes above my highway noise.

The next morning, she thanked me. The colours had come back. "Never leave me, Dot."

And I promised I wouldn't.

AT THE FIRST RED LIGHT, DAD TURNS TO ME. "CALL HIM. HIS FRIEND must have been desperate, to seek you out at a funeral."

That didn't occur to me. It just felt like an invasion.

"Well, apparently he doesn't answer the phone, so where does that leave me?"

"You know where he lives. You have a car. And time." He batters me with logic until I relent. "Just let him know he's not alone. From you, that would mean something. I'll come with you, if you want."

MOE DOESN'T ANSWER THE DOORBELL. I RING THREE TIMES BEFORE realizing it doesn't work. I knock. At first I do the classic, knock, knock. No one answers. Mike must not be home. I try shave-and-a-haircut-two-bits. Nothing. One more time, louder. I could just go.

Faintly, a clink of bottles from within. So I try - - - — — — - - -.

Footsteps approach. I stand back, averting my eyes, let him decide.

"Thot?" I've never heard my name said like that. It would be nice if it didn't sound so...wet. "Got my card?"

"Yes."

He leans hard against the door's glass, forehead pressed so the skin looks pasty.

"Are you okay?"

"Fffine." He smiles, or he attempts to, but his lips seem too heavy.

I wait for him to say more or, perchance, open the door between us, but he slides out of sight and there's a telling thump.

I try the knob and discover it's unlocked. Sometimes I was with Mum when we visited Grand, before they sold his house. The smell is familiar as I push in, squeezing through the crack. He's sagged against the wall. His beard has sprouted, but the scrapes on his face are still there, like he's been scratching them. I take the bottle from him and head for the kitchen. He mumbles something, hearing the water running in the sink.

There's no way I'm moving him from where he's slumped, so I sit down opposite him amongst a pile of shoes.

"Why did you do it?" I say when his eyes flit open and find me. "Why did you come to the shelter?"

"I dunno." His lids flicker like he can only take in my image in the briefest glimmers.

"You must." Nothing, just a shift of his legs. "You must have known I'd find out who you were."

He nods and folds forward. "Knew."

In Grand's last days of freedom, he'd do this. Sometimes he'd be bloodied and bruised. I never knew why.

"Jail woulda been better," he says, eyes half open.

"What?"

"Wanted them to put me away."

"I don't—"

"Punish me."

"But it was...an accident."

He nods. "Then I, saw you on TV one day with cats. You look like her, ya know? Plus, how many teenagers are called Dot?" That must have been when Judy got a root canal a couple of months back. "Didn't mean to stay. I was gonna tell you sorry. And I hoped your mother'd..."

"Wake up?"

"Yeah." They're probably burning her body right now. I almost say it. "Every day, I meant to tell you."

I think back to Rachel introducing me before he could even think of a decent fake name.

"But?"

He shakes his head like a dog drying off after the rain. "I stopped wanting you to hate me."

He hangs to the side and retches a stream of yellow. I scramble to my feet and search the kitchen for paper towel or something. Behind me, he's mumbling apologies.

"Come on." I try pulling him up so I can clean the floor beside him.

"You don't have to," he says as I heave him to his feet.

"I know."

AFTER MOPPING THE FLOOR WITH TOILET PAPER, I FIND HIM FLOPPED on his bed, face up. Thanks to Grand, I know drunks can die this way, so I coax him to his side and prop an arm behind him like a kickstand.

"You're good," he says, his eyes closed.

Once he's asleep I find the bottles that aren't empty. Uncapping one, I take a whiff. The cheapest stuff you can get, no doubt, barring actual cleaning fluid. Before calling Dad to explain, I pour it all down the drain.

"You ought to call his family," says Dad.

"Yes," I say.

"Give me the address and I'll be over."

I lower my voice to explain why I think that might be more alarming for him than helpful. I'm not even certain I should be here, but I'm staying until Mike gets back.

Maybe to keep me on the phone, or possibly to cheer me up, Dad tells me about Button's walk and how he really does like to be vacuumed. Before hanging up, I promise to get more food on the way home.

I sit in Moe's living room and resist the urge to tidy. After an hour, I realize I know nothing about Mike. He might not come home at suppertime. What if I have to wait all night? I move to the front window and watch for a wobbly cyclist, but willing his return does nothing.

The TV has rabbit ears, but the zigzags across the screen hurt my head. In the end, I just sit with my glasses off so the lights outside blur around the room. Finally, the front door slams and Mike is there, his bike over his shoulder. He props it against the wall and yells "Hello!" to the house.

"Hello," I say. Maybe I should have waited for him to turn around.

"Fucking hell. Dot?"

"Sorry."

In the kitchen, he sees the empty bottles.

"I did that yesterday," he says. "Location, location." His eyes flit in the direction of the liquor store. Boiling the kettle, he pulls out a box of Red Rose tea and two mugs, one showing a fading picture of Peggys Cove and the other the *Bluenose*. I take a seat at the rickety kitchen table. He offers me milk from one of those tiny cartons we used to get at school recess. "Anyway, thanks for trying," he says of the emptied bottles.

"Why doesn't he want you to call his family?"

He rolls his lip up on his front teeth, considering. It turns out Moe hasn't told his family he's not in school. Mike has had to lie for him once or twice, which makes him uncomfortable about reaching out now.

"He's the first one in his family to go to university." He shrugs and takes a sip of his tea.

"How long have you known him?"

"Four years." He looks at the ceiling like it's a reliable calendar. "Before...before the accident, he was different. Always the guy who got you laughing. And calm, like unfazed, you know?"

"He's still that guy." I catch him looking at my hand, so I still my fingers.

"Yeah?" He raises his eyebrows. "Well, for the last month he's been better. But I didn't know what he was doing." Down the hall, there's movement, followed by a groan. Mike flinches and his voice lowers. "He won't make his rent next month if this keeps up."

"What about his other friends?"

"If anything, they'd take him on a bender, help him blow the rest of his money. Did you...talk to him?" He sounds hopeful.

"He wasn't making a lot of sense, then he got sick."

He stares hard at me and lowers his voice.

"Did he tell you about the other night, the police?" I shake my head and wait for him to choose his words. "They wanted to talk to him about the guy that got beaten up?" I nod, waiting. "They asked if he might have had something to do with it."

"And?"

"And he said he was here that night. All night. And I backed him up."

"He wasn't?" I say, my heart coming to a complete stop.

"No, I wasn't," says Moe, making us both jump. His face is puffy and colourless except for the scratches. He shuffles into the kitchen like one of Grand's fellow residents and fills a glass with water. "I followed him to his car." He keeps his back to us. "I thought I'd killed him. I wanted to."

"Fuck's sakes, Moe, then it would be all over for you," says Mike.

"I know," he says, his voice flat.

"But you didn't," I say, "kill him."

His shoulders drop an inch. When he speaks his voice is hoarse.

"Better than killing a good person by accident. In my head, it made sense. Swap one for another."

"Were you drunk?" I'm imagining him bleary-eyed behind the wheel.

"Not then." He gives a short laugh. "Ever since then, though."

Mike stares at me, shaking his head. Moe picks up a bottle of vodka and tips it, finding it empty. Then the cans of beer and the rum.

"Tea?" Mike pushes his chair back and goes to press the button on the kettle. I'd like to tell Moe to get in the shower, wash off the stink, try using a better razor.

"You should go, Dot," Moe says. Now that some of the alcohol has fizzled out of his system, he won't look at me. Can't.

I don't budge. It's not just next month's rent at stake. Mike must know it: Moe has every intention of running out of money because he doesn't think he'll need it anymore.

Moe stares out the window at a decrepit shed surrounded by heaps of wet leaves. No one says anything; it's only the kettle. I can't stand it much longer, but I can't go until I've said what I came to say.

"You have to call your family, Moe. They'd never forgive themselves if they lost you. Give them that much." I know this too well. "Until someone is gone, you can't know the...aching...for all the things you didn't say." He doesn't turn, but his shoulders hunch forward, shaking slightly. I stand and zip my coat. Mike nods a silent thanks. I'm at the door when I add, "And, I don't hate you."

Then I go.

BY THE TIME I GET HOME, I'M ON OVERLOAD, EXHAUSTION CREEPING into my muscles. Dad wants to know where the dog food is.

"Shit," I say.

"It's fine, I made us each a burger." Button wags. "It was getting late."

"I'm going to bed."

"It's not even eight," says the Sleep King.

"Really?" It's dark, and that's all I really need.

"Don't worry, I fed them all." He glances at the ceiling, indicating my brood above. "I'm not sure of the exact amounts..." Will I find Waldo outnumbered? Will the crickets have taken him down?

"Not burgers all around?" I say, because, who knows? His only experience is feeding me, and even then, he offers me things I can't stomach.

"Hello," croaks Toby from the kitchen.

"Just sit for a sec, Speck." He pats the cushion next to him, leading Button to stretch out completely, so I take the chair and let out a generous yawn. "I've been thinking," he says. "Your friend Moe, he needs to talk to someone, a professional."

"Maybe he has."

But Dad carries on as if I've said nothing. "I'm not a therapist, but I've done a lot of reading on what keeps people awake at night." He flashes his commercial smile, a line from one of the TV spots. "There were times—and I never shared this with you—she said things about herself. She'd go dark, you know? There was nothing I could say to change it, and she refused to see anyone." He takes a long breath, stroking Button. "I think it's that she didn't want to leave you. I think that's what stopped her. At least that's what I think. It could have been chocolate." He tries a smile. "Anyway, Speck, I don't want you to get pulled in."

"You're the one who told me to talk to him."

"I know. But you can't take this on by yourself."

I consider telling him about Moe beating up Waylon, but it would worry him too much. He'd get the wrong idea. What if he decided to report him? I feel like if I fell over right now, I'd leave one of those cartoon person-shaped holes in the floor, so I just nod and climb the stairs to my room.

SEVENTEEN

S UNDAY TRAFFIC WHISPERING ALONG THE HIGHWAY WAKES ME.
Downstairs, it's just Toby, Dad's bedsheet still over his cage. I leave
him that way, knowing he'll have things to say as soon as I take it off.
Every day he's more impatient, lifting both wings when he caws at
the birds outside the window. The noise doesn't bother me as much
as it does Dad, who keeps his bright orange earplugs at the ready.

Quietly, I assemble a cup of tea and settle amongst her paint-
ings in the living room. Here are the last years of her waking life.
For weeks, she'd be at it all day and keep going into the night.
Obsession is how art is born. At least, that's what I used to think.

They're hung according to shape and space, not chronology.
Finding the first of them, I pull it off the wall so I can run my
fingers along the bumps, feeling her dots and dashes. I grab a pen
and paper, jotting down words. I have to guess at the line breaks.

Tiny breath shaking
Fists blooming flowers
Sightless eyes gaping

The canvas is a spring day. Not the obvious sort. Blotches of
hardened snow in the corners, leaves struggling from the soil in
the foreground. Tulips? The colours are cool, the grass yellowed
from hiding under a white blanket for months. Weak sun filters
through a spring flurry, the dots translucent. I find the last line.

For warmth in blinding white.

By the time Dad comes downstairs I'm on the third one.

"Did you ever read them?" I say, instead of good morning.

"You know I didn't. One, I never learned it like you. Two, she hid them as soon as she was done."

"They're poems," I say.

The third one is the mouth of a cave, a campfire, untended, with various objects strewn around as if the campers ran off suddenly. It's just one line.

No shelter wide enough.

"Well, there's nothing stopping you now, I suppose," he says through a yawn. "The paint's dry."

It's a full half hour before Button follows Dad downstairs. He props his bum on the couch and yawns.

"Eggs?" says Dad, not asking me.

I listen to his kitchen clatter as I move onto the fifth, a city park with blankets draped everywhere. A single line again.

Dreaming it awake.

Bubbles this time, coming from a caravan to the side. The colours are much richer.

Dad brings out a cereal bowl containing scrambled eggs and holds it while Button eats. I give him a look and he shrugs, knowing this little scene will be used as evidence against him, should I be accused of overdoing things with animals.

"She never knew her mother." I'm looking at the spring day painting. Were hers the *sightless eyes*?

"An awful thing," says Dad, taking the bowl back to the kitchen. "To die in childbirth."

They'd eloped because her family wouldn't allow the marriage—her being decades younger than him. She must have been in her second trimester by then. Scandalous at the time. Dad wedges himself onto the couch and Button leans in, seeking a cuddle.

"Her family tried to take the baby away, but he wouldn't have it."

Knuckles Murphy, changing diapers, brushing hair, showing little Dawn how to use a potty. Grand as father and mother. Mourning. Angry. Teaching his little girl how to survive but not how to live.

I stare at the painting Rachel liked, the burned field with all the ash. There's hardly any colour, a wash of grey tones punctuated by a looming tree, blackened but standing. It takes a while to find the code, hidden along the ridges of the tree's branch.

No one comes back from this place.

It's probably somewhere in France. The soldiers who returned were altered.

Dad reads over my shoulder. "I don't know what do with them," he says between slurps. "They hurt."

"Yes, except for that one."

I think it's our house, tall, like a milk carton, windows aglow. It's not perfectly straight, the walls bend as if swaying, alive. It's a candle. It's not just the highway; roads swoop all around it, some yellow, some red. Light flares into the sky until you can't be sure what comes from below and what are the stars. Unlike the other canvases, she's taken extra care with the dots, all of them perfect circles. There are no other houses on the street, just us, with life coming near, but not touching. An island in a river of light. The message is small, embedded in a garden we've never had.

Temporary bliss.

"I think she was finding her style in that one," Dad says. I can only nod, because this one makes my eyes leak. "If she had more time, she'd have been a—"

Shrieks from the kitchen cut off the rest of his words. Dad winces as I go see what the fuss is about. The sheet is still over the cage, but there's a gap just wide enough for Toby to see out. Mourning doves have settled in soft lumps on the sunlit ground, flaunting their freedom. I slide the sheet over the back so the window view is doubly covered. There's no pleasing both of them. Toby wants his view and Dad wants his quiet. In the fridge, I find some cheese and break off a bit to appease him.

Dad has his hands over his eyes when I go back into the living room.

"I could move him to my bedroom," I say. Where it is, the cage dominates the kitchen counter. He doesn't speak right away. He sighs and reaches a hand out to stroke Button.

"He can't stay, Speck. This cannot go on." I sputter he's not ready, but Dad is firm. "He is. Judy said so."

"Yeah, well—"

"The vet did too." She may have hinted at it.

"I'm worried about releasing him in November."

"Then take him to the woman who does wildlife rehab. He's not a pet, Dot. The longer you keep him caged, the harder it will be for him to go back to his proper life. No one is happy in a cage." Spoken as if he, the Sleep King, is an expert.

"I know."

"I want *you* to stay for as long as you like. But I can't live like this. It's too disruptive."

The phone rings, and Button groans as Dad leans to reach for it. I can't hear the other side of the conversation, but I watch his face as he listens and gets heavier.

"Well," he says, "it's not up to me." He holds out the receiver with his disapproving face.

"I know I said you shouldn't worry about the shelter," says Judy, "but it's happened again, Dot."

THE KITCHEN IS CROWDED WITH CRATES AND PITEOUS MEWLING. Judy tells me this hoarder was in the city. She's busy at the sink, scrubbing her hands.

"It's just you and me?"

"I tried Earl. The bugger isn't picking up. I vaguely remember him talking about going away..." No lipstick this morning. Rachel and the weekend crew come in later, but they'll be dealing with the ones already here, and this kind of thing isn't really for the volunteers and part-timers.

"When did you get here?"

"Couple hours ago. But they called last night, you know, just to make sure I wouldn't sleep."

"We should be able to handle this." I count a dozen cages.

"You haven't seen the office yet."

In the office, sound is muted by the industrial carpeting so you can make a phone call or have a moment to think. That's why Judy has the trembling ones in here, inside their crates. All of them are thin; some have open sores. They don't come near their cage doors to see me.

At the far end is a heap of fur, not moving. You'd have a hard time identifying it as a cat. I've learned to read stillness. Inching the door open, I reach in and place my hand on protruding ribs.

"Best wash your hands," says Judy, taking a seat at her desk.

"This one's gone."

"I don't know how much more I can take." Her voice shakes.

"What do you mean?"

"We should be getting ahead of this stuff." She points at the stack of cages. "It shouldn't get to this point."

Two hoarding cases back to back, the litter of pups, gaps in staffing. She's just worn out.

"I'll feed the ones in the kitchen."

"Thanks, Dot." I know she doesn't just mean the feeding.

"Did you try Moe?" She squints at me like I've spoken Russian. "If his roommate's there, he'll pick up."

"No, it's okay. We can manage." She waves away the idea like it's a bad smell in the room.

"Just call him? If you get his roommate, say I'll be there in ten minutes." Her gaze drifts to the stack of cages. "I'll be back in twenty." My estimate is a tad optimistic, but there'll be no traffic on the bridge today. I have her full attention now; she's watching my hand, not my face, as if she can read the message there. Finally, she shrugs and says fine.

WHEN I ARRIVE, HE'S AT THE DOOR. THERE'S A WHIFF OF SOURNESS when he climbs in, but he's not drunk. He's in a ball cap, worn and faded from the sun, advertising a company that makes farm equipment. He tugs it down lower once he's in the car.

"Why?" He says, not looking at me as be buckles up.

"If I have to go on, so do you."

"I'm sorr—"

"Not now." I'm glad to be driving, to have traffic lights and pedestrians and left turns to negotiate. Another day to climb through. He's silent, looking out his window. "Have the police come back?"

"No." It seems to wake him. "Why?"

"Nothing...I saw his mother on the news after and she was really wound up. I think her words were *fucking bleeding heart animal lovers.*"

"Yeah." He looks out his side window. "She's right."

"Did it feel good? Beating him up?"

"Yeah, it did." He lets out a long breath. "Not after, though."

"Good."

JUDY'S EYES WIDEN AT HIS APPEARANCE. SHE CALLS HIM *JOE,* THEN looks at me. I suppose she only saw him in his blushing, bearded form. In a matter of a week, he's lost both colour and volume.

"I've been sick," he tells her. "Sorry for missing work."

"Good that you're here now." She avoids his eyes. "I can handle these ones with Dot's help. You can take care of the ones in the kitchen. Get them set up with clean bedding, fresh trays, note if they have sores or fleas..." She counts it off on her fingers. "You'll probably have to improvise."

He nods and staggers off. Judy stares after him.

"I don't want to talk about it." I don't want to lie to her again. It wouldn't take much for her to figure out what happened with Waylon.

"Fine. But I need people who show up for work."

"It's just...he needs this right now."

She gives me an appraising look. "Right, well, we'll be putting down the ones on the end." She glances at the cages neighbouring the one who's already passed.

"We're not waiting for Dr. Trainer?" So that's why she wanted me here. Her time as an emergency tech makes her pride herself on getting a vein the first time, but she needs someone who knows how to restrain.

First, it's the one with the rattling chest, then a small female whose eyes are gummed shut. All of them are too weak to protest as she slides the needle in. I barely restrain; it's more a matter of uncurling them, talking into their ears while I hold them.

"I. Fucking. Hate. This," Judy says, pushing a strand of hair from her eye. She goes to the bathroom sink and washes her hands while talking over her shoulder. "Some places have outlawed euthanasia. Did you know that?"

"No." I want to live in a place like that.

"This shouldn't be the solution." She collapses into her office chair. "Sorry."

"I know." Haven't I always been the one to argue the To Die list?

"No, I mean I shouldn't complain...to you." She gives a sad smile. "How's Button?"

I tell her how Dad—who said we'd never get a dog—is bagging Button's giant turds on walks, despite his gag reflex, that he's talking about bringing in a line of specialty dog beds for giant breeds. As if a lanky dog isn't perfectly happy on the queen mattress with the nice sheets and the fluffy duvet.

Judy doesn't hide her smugness. "Guess I can sign off on that adoption, then."

WHEN THE VET HAS COME AND GONE, I FIND MOE ON THE BACK step. He's biting his nails. Not a good plan when you think of what his hands have been doing for the past few hours.

"Ready to go?" I say, not taking a seat beside him. For the past few hours, we've managed to work together without speaking.

"You don't have to drive me home."

"I know."

I plant my feet and wait for him to get up. One thing about Mum's naps, she always got up for me. I'd just sit on the bed and say nothing.

The back door creaks open and a dog bursts through with Rachel tethered behind, cursing. He makes for the garbage and leaps, nabbing a blackened banana peel. "Drop it, drop it, drop it." After tossing it in the air a few times and nearly hitting her, he does.

"Dot," she says, noticing me, "you're leaving?"

"I'm not even here."

"Right." She nods. Judy has probably made that clear. "How about you, Joe? Shit. I mean Moe."

"He's going to help me with something." I catch his look, but he doesn't argue.

Rachel doesn't move, despite being tugged by the dog.

"You guys don't have to, but my show is next weekend, my performance piece with the nest? We're supposed to invite family and friends." From her back pocket, she pulls out a crumpled flyer. I've never seen her blush before. I wonder if she'll dress as a bird, and if so, what kind.

"How could I miss that?"

"That's great," she says, smiling, finally giving in to the dog's energy.

MOE DOESN'T ASK WHERE WE'RE GOING. HE SEEMS RESIGNED TO whatever I have in store. When we get there, I shout hello to the house. Cawing and screeching comes from the kitchen. Button, seeing Moe, lets out a mighty woof and gallops for the door. It hurts, being whipped by a tail at that height.

"Jesus," says Moe, smiling as he's knocked off balance.

"He's a Great Newfoundlander," yells Dad from upstairs.

Dad is in the same spot as when I left. One side of his hair looks crumpled, as if he's snuck in forty winks. He pulls out his earplugs.

"Helping out at the shelter?" He's slightly too cheerful. Maybe I should have called ahead and mentioned about Moe.

"Did what I could," says Moe, leaning awkwardly on Button's back.

"It seems there's no end to it. Dot's been working there for what?"

"Six years."

"And the place is always full to bursting."

"Good that it's there, I guess," says Moe, not looking at Dad. He's taking in the art gallery, trying not to ask. It feels as if the walls are inching in, like the scene in *Star Wars* when they get trapped in the garbage compactor and Luke gets pulled down by a flailing tentacle.

"Hello," croaks Toby, indignant at being excluded.

"Hello," says Moe, already turning for the source. Button trails us into the kitchen where Toby does a jig along his branch to get nearer.

"Can he come out?"

I shoo Button and close the kitchen door, watching as Toby hops straight to Moe's arm.

"Make him eat some lasagna," Dad calls through the door.

An excellent thought. It's now dominating the freezer. But he shakes his head, no. It probably takes a while to fire up the old digestive system after what he's done to it.

"Looking good, buddy," Moe tilts his head so Toby can run his beak through his hair, knocking off his ball cap with one swift motion. Then he pecks at his face. "No beard, sorry."

"Are you going to grow it again?"

He considers before answering. "No."

"You might need a better razor, then."

"You're funny," he says. But he's not laughing.

"Am I?" The skin has scabbed over, but it still looks raw to me. "What was with that, anyway? The lumberjack look?"

He shrugs.

"Shaving meant looking in the mirror, you know?"

Do I? Even now, with a very large mirror in the bathroom, I only look when necessary, like to get Button's fur out of my eye.

Moe gives Toby a careful tour of the kitchen, pausing to let him flick the lights on and off.

"He can fly now," I say. "According to Judy." I've seen it too, his clumsy landings on the smooth surfaces around the kitchen.

"That's great." Moe addresses this to Toby, who responds with a splat of turd on the kitchen floor. "Isn't it great?"

"I guess so." On top of the fridge there's a spray bottle and some paper towel because Button drools at meals, great slimy pools of it that have to be dealt with before socks find it. It does the trick with crow poo, too.

"So, you can release him." Toby has flapped himself to the top of the counter and is exploring his cage from the outside.

"What if he's not ready?" I say. "He can talk now. He likes cheese. He's practically human. And winter is coming." It sounds ominous when said aloud. I tap the word *ice* on the counter. "He's used to indoor life." Toby hops to the windowsill and curses at a song sparrow swaying on a branch.

"Birds are resilient," says Moe. Why did I think he might be on my side? "His family might still be there. Where you found him. They have territories—"

"They're wild."

Moe shrugs like it's up to me, he's done. I'm sapping his strength.

Dad has made it clear Toby can't stay. Judy's on his side. I can't go back to Magoo's, and Moe isn't offering to take him in as I'd hoped. It just feels rushed to me. Healing takes a long time. How can he be ready for the cold world?

I could take him to the wildlife rehab place, but she might just release him, and how would she know where to take him? He should have a chance to find his family.

It's a heavy sky, much like the day I scooped him from the curb, excepting that all the leaves have shrivelled and blown away. A mother huddles in her coat watching her toddler. The little girl climbs a slide, booted feet slipping as she talks a blue streak about castles.

While I scan the sky, Moe carries the cage to the base of the tree. What are the chances they'll show?

I open the cage door and sit back on my heels. Toby fluffs himself and swallows. He lifts his right foot, getting used to the weight of his new bracelet. It's bright orange, and I've painted blue dots on it. On the inside, it has the shelter phone number. I hope it won't smudge.

We say nothing, just watch him angling his head to take in his surroundings.

"You coming out?" Moe offers his arm as a bridge. Toby reaches out a foot, toes splayed, and takes sliding steps up to Moe's shoulder. Pulling a few peanuts from my pocket, I scatter them on the ground.

"Can I pet the boyd?" says a tiny voice behind us.

"Charlotte!" calls her mother.

"Better not," I say. "He might peck you."

"Charlotte, it's time to go."

The little girl switches focus to the peanuts on the ground and starts gathering them. This is too much for Toby, so he takes a hasty leap into the air. He scrambles over to get the one remaining nut, and cracking it open savagely, he gobbles it up. This is so delightful, she tosses her handful into the air with a giggle before her mother tugs her away, all apologies.

We settle on a bench and watch Toby claim the rest of his feast. The air starts to mist.

"Have you seen him fly?" asks Moe.

Out of peanuts, Toby strides around, jabbing at the ground.

"Just in the kitchen."

Toby stiffens and lets out a series of croaks. In the distance, there's an echo. We cock our heads to the sound, watch the flutter of movement approach through the grey. They land in the tree above and speak to one another in throaty coos and clicks. Toby answers and flaps his wings as if to test them, then he's in the air, landing sloppily at the top of the slide. One of the others lands on the ground and I toss a handful of peanuts. One at a time, they come, until there are five strutting about, eyeing Toby.

"Is this them?" Moe asks, as if I've had a formal introduction.

"Might be."

"Good spot to find a meal," says Moe, looking at the overflowing garbage.

Toby bobs his head and moves from one foot to the other like a teenager at his first school dance. Finally, he lifts off and lands at the edge of the gathering. They're busy with peanuts but eye his approach. Toby ambles about, like he's not interested. *Ho-hum.* Just a browsing shopper, hands clasped behind his back.

Done with their snack, their attention turns to him. One crow, maybe a smidge larger than the others, approaches, the others parting to allow him or her through. Toby ceases strolling and spreads his wings, bowing his head. I think Moe gasps. I don't know what is communicated, but after much consideration between the two, Toby hops over to us and says, "Hello." I reach into my pocket and grab the last of the peanuts.

"Ah, he's their meal ticket," Moe says in a hushed voice.

The mist turns into drips, Moe's hair sags. The murder lifts off, landing in the branches above, Toby among them. I keep my eye on his movement. Except for his bracelet, he's one of them. We must be small to him now. How easy it is for them to move about the world; how sad our lives must seem, stuck to the ground. Who would choose that over the sky?

He can't stay with me. He's wild.

It's not like he's a cuddly, comforting presence. But it's the timing of his arrival, like there's some fragment of the universe speaking through him and I have to listen. Moe reaches across the bench and stills my hand with a light tap. I've been spelling *sky* over and over.

"I forgive you." I say it just loud enough that Moe can hear. Maybe it's not one hundred percent true, but I'm getting there. He doesn't respond, and I'm about to say it again when I see him wipe at his eyes. "Can you forgive yourself?"

"Never."

"Then you don't need my hatred."

Slumping forward, he places his face in his hands.

"I can't...I can't live with mine, though, Dot."

This makes me feel cold. The drinking isn't just to numb his thoughts; it's a slow death. How long would it take him? Weeks?

"Here's how you will have my hate. Chuck away your life because you can't handle feeling it."

"I'm not—"

"Even broken animals fight for what they have left. You owe her that much."

We sit there until the rain soaks through our clothes, until Toby and his family are on a distant telephone wire, until Moe stands and nods at me once and I can gather the empty cage and go home.

EIGHTEEN

◝◠◟

WHEN EVERYTHING IS STACKED, DAD GETS ON HIS TIPTOES AND coaxes the woolly walls down. I stand in the doorway, looking at what was my abode for—I count on my fingers—four months and a day. It's not an apartment or a flat or a studio. It's an unfinished basement with dodgy plumbing.

"Ready?"

"What about the bed?" I think of Magoo II's offer of the truck.

Dad puts an arm around my shoulders and squeezes, as if I've asked the cutest of questions.

"We'll leave it. God, you're skinny."

The last thing is the Womble towel on the door. As I fold it, Dad hums the theme song. *Underground, overground, Wombling free...*I know he misses her, but he seems to stand a little straighter each day. Maybe it's just to make himself slightly taller than Button.

I drop the key in Magoo's mailbox and get in the back seat of the car. Button has the passenger side, the seat slid back to accommodate his legs. He's got his paw slung over the open window like a furry arm. It's not really warm enough, but lacking power windows, we can't be bothered to wind it back up.

Everything I had in the abode fits in Dad's trunk. It's a good thing, as there was a sizeable puddle of oil under Rusty this morning.

It dipped below freezing for the first time this season. Together, we pushed him out of the way so Dad could get out of the driveway.

"After I drop you, we'll head to the store." By *we* he means himself and Button, who, he hopes, will happily snooze at the back of the store. Perhaps he'll become a fixture there and star in a TV spot or two. Dad's words. "You've got a ride back?"

"I'll be okay."

Dad drops me in the exact spot I found Toby, pulling over long enough for me to climb out. It's been nearly a week since his release. Every day I come by and hope for a glimpse of him. I watch Dad drive off, Button's ears fluttering in the wind.

I have a book and some peanuts. Last night I dreamed Toby was waiting for me and I can't get past it. He wanted to come home, he was pecking the message into the trunk of the tree, leaving gashes in the wood. I didn't tell Dad. He would have said it wasn't Toby. He would have said it meant something else.

He's not here and the bark of the tree doesn't contain an anguished plea to return home. I circle it several times, feeling along the rough ridges, thinking of her paintings, her thoughts buried under oil. I ring the tree in peanuts and think of how she made our house stand apart from everything, but there was a garden there. Was she going to plant the garden? Was I?

The trees are skeletal now. I can see the tops of them for several blocks. Fingers pointing to the sky. The bench is warm from the afternoon sun. It won't last long, though; we're well into the bleak part of fall. I might have an hour before it dips too low. Then the temperature will plunge. I'll warm up by walking to the shelter, where I might beg a ride home or attempt a journey by bus.

They come just before the sun leaves. Four land in the branches nearby to size me up, gauge my danger level. I squint at their legs, searching for an orange polka-dot bracelet. Three caws are shouted across the sky, answered by three more caws. Food or treasure? Maybe it's the same thing. They land in a confusion of wings and I try to stay still. Instead, I rap the bench with my knuckle six times. Louder, with a pause of several seconds. Maybe he's not here. Another one glides across the sky, landing a little late to the party. That makes five, just like the other day. But no Toby. Six, I repeat. Pause, six, pounding the bench. Did he go back to his old ways and get in trouble with a car? Did the murder do away with him? Were the nights too cold? It was too soon. He needed shelter. Maybe he wasn't wild anymore. Or maybe he's gone solo. Maybe he doesn't need the others, an extroverted crow that can talk to humans. But that could get him in trouble too.

My long-forgotten pager breaks into song. I pull it out: Rachel, probably a reminder about tonight. It's habit to carry it around, but I don't really need it now Mum's gone and I see Dad every day. How was I to know I'd be without wheels tonight when I said yes to Rachel?

Without warning, he drops in, making me jump. He grabs the pager with his toes and takes it a few feet away before letting it fall. The orange has already dulled, but my dots are bright. I knock *six*, gently this time.

"Hello," he says, and I burst into sobs. Great, horrible things that should scare him away. But he just fiddles with his prize, tossing it around for the others to see while I hug myself and attempt to regain control. I want to name this emotion, as it's new. Not despair or anger or gutting loneliness. It is something close to joy, adjacent to it. Joy's frail landlord who needs a walker sometimes.

At last, I say hello too and find one more peanut squeezed in the recesses of my pocket. I hold it out for him. He comes, taking it, rather gently for a wild thing, and places it at his feet. He regards me in his way, head sideways, the wind carving waves in his feathers. There I am, reflected in his dark eye, an alien lump on a bench.

"Watch out for her, please. I think she might be up there some-where." Even though I shouldn't believe in things like that, it's just a feeling.

But I swear, he blinks *88* before popping the peanut in his beak and rejoining his family.

WHEN I LET MYSELF IN, JUDY IS IN THE OFFICE. IT'S PAST CLOSING time, but she's at her desk, lit by the computer screen. Her smile fades when I get closer.

"Your eyes are puffy."

Always critiquing the state of my face.

"Crying," I say, unnecessarily. My mother just died, for crying out loud. "But I'm fine."

"Well, I'm glad you're here." Her smile is soft. "Maybe you can give this a proofread." She gets up from her chair and waves for me to come around.

On screen is a document titled *No-Kill Shelter Proposal,* and below it she's detailed a plan with large dots separating each point: a neuter plan for feral cats, converting local pet stores to adoption centres, adding outdoor dog kennel spaces to the shelter, imple-menting a mental health awareness program to help spot signs of hoarding and abuse. I scroll through several pages, glancing at her expectant face from time to time.

"You want the staff to be trained vet techs?" I say. It would eliminate me.

"Well, maybe not all. But you can't be a shelter worker for-ever." Can't I? I stare at the cursor on the page. It blinks like a tiny heartbeat awaiting her closing sentence.

"Dr. Trainer offered me a part-time job a while back."

"I know." She shrugs. "She fessed up. It would be perfect when you're a student."

"I—"

"You'll always have a place here. If you want it."

"So, this," I say, pointing at the screen, "you'll have to get the board to approve it."

"If something doesn't change, I'm out of here. I'll start my own thing." Judging by her expression, she's given this a lot of thought.

No more To Die lists. No more freezer people.

"It'll cost money."

"Fundraising, grants, sponsorship...people will help, Dot." She smirks. "There are some good ones out there."

"So...what can I do?"

She takes a deep breath. "Sign your name. We'll all quit if things don't change. Without us, there's no shelter."

She pauses, awaiting my answer, but I'm crying again.

"What about the Waylons of the world?"

She blows out her cheeks, shaking her head. "All I know is for every Waylon, there's a Dot and an Earl and a Moe. Hell, even a Rachel."

"And a Dawn." My voice comes out all wrong. I don't even wipe the tears away. Judy nods at me, but she looks all wavy.

"It's okay, let it out," she says, passing me the box of tissues. "It's about time."

JUDY DRIVES ME TO RACHEL'S PERFORMANCE. WITH A LITTLE COAX-ing, I convince her to come in too, though she grumbles about parking downtown on a weekend.

"You sure you're up to this?" she says, wrapping her coat around her neck as we lean into the wind.

"No," I say. But when you say you're going to show up, you show up.

The art school spans a number of old buildings, all of them creaky-floored with draughty windows. A small sandwich board bears Rachel's name. We descend a staircase into a room lit with shimmering blue lights so it feels like we're in water or sky or both. From three wires, a nest is suspended from the ceiling. People walk around it, murmuring and touching the cluster of objects. Woven through netting and straw are plastic bottles, fishing rope, cigarette butts, a kitchen faucet, a bicycle tire, small bones, and a dog collar. I stop at the collar and finger the tag. A name is still visible, though smoothed by its time in the sea.

Someone claps and asks us to stand back so the artist can begin.

Music starts softly, expanding so I can feel it in my chest. It's a cello, or maybe a whale. It's keening, thrumming the air when Rachel steps in, her feet bare. She's not dressed as a bird, but her hair has been back-brushed, braided, knotted, and wired into its own elaborate creation, small things nestled inside. Her skin has been rubbed with blues and greys. She's in her gauzy clothes. Her moves are slow, as if she has to fight a current to get where she's headed. Ever so gently, she climbs in and I think we all stop breathing, waiting for the nest to crash from the ceiling. She pushes off with her toes as she sinks into it, slowly disappearing amongst the tangle of objects. Piano enters the music and we watch the nest sway, seemingly in perfect time with the swelling notes. I'm rocked along with it and transported. It feels like we're in a womb, imperfect and messy.

I want to know what it all means.

"It can mean something different to everyone," Mum once said, "when done well, that is." I held the tape for her. The brown paper was thick; she needed both hands to wrap the canvas.

"Do you name them?" I asked.

"Only in here," she touched the base of her neck. "If a gallery takes them, it will just be a description of what's there, or maybe a number." I handed her a strip of tape and watched her smooth out each bubble.

"But why not give them a name?"

She stopped and ran her hands through her hair, pulling the curls into a halo of frizz.

"Then they'd only have to glance at it. I can't just give them the key. My soul's in here." She smiled to make light of her words, pressing the paper into a neat triangle before reaching out for the next piece of tape.

"Can you tell me?"

Silence, while she finished taping both ends.

"It's better if you find it yourself, Dot."

I don't know how long it goes on, the swaying of the nest and the music. The room is full of people now. I'm guessing it's all the students and their families. Sniffling is coming from the far corner. My eyes are leaking again too, the dam shattered.

The moment the nest stills, the lights go out. In the darkness, someone takes my hand and I don't try to pull away. It is warm, folding around the chill of my fingers. The music ends, and in the hush that follows I hear breath around the room.

When the light comes back, Rachel is gone and Moe is there, still cradling my hand, and we manage to share a smile in the applause that follows.

AUTHOR'S NOTE

THIS BOOK IS SET IN 1997 BECAUSE, THANKFULLY, SHELTERS HAVE improved substantially in the past two decades. In a perfect world we'd have no need for such places, but I'm glad they exist and I'm doubly grateful for the people who care for the vulnerable and the voiceless.

Dot's story was inspired by my time as an employee at an animal shelter in the nineties, but it's a work of fiction. None of these characters (human or otherwise) bear any resemblance to anyone I knew then.

I refer to the code of *88* in Dot's story which means *love and kisses.* In the 1800s telegraph operators created a list of shortened codes, sort of emojis of the time, for frequent phrases. Phillips Code is still used by some hobbyists today.

ACKNOWLEDGEMENTS

Thank you:

To my editor, Penelope Jackson, for just the right mix of queries and cuts and affection for the characters. It was a joy to sculpt this with you.

To my first readers. Carol Bruneau, mentor and friend, who should have said no because she has plenty of her own stories to cultivate. A fresh read on a manuscript with a professional critique is worth a lot of crickets. And Sarah Sawler, for their honesty about the character of Rachel and for sharing with me that as a child their grandfather used to tap Morse code on the wall at bedtime. I thought I was making it up, but it turns out reality is just as interesting as fiction.

To my parents, Frank and Jen Eppell (to whom the book is dedicated), for their love of animals. Our house was full of all creatures great and small. I was a lucky kid.

To Whitney Moran and the whole team at Nimbus Publishing, for saying yes to this quirky book and for letting dogs roam their offices.

To Kevin Doucette, for talking to me about what the police do when someone waves a gun around.

To Cathy Spence, for consulting on medical matters once again. Her training as a nurse began shortly after our calamitous backpacking trip thirty years ago. Our first-aid kit was used so often that she figured she ought to go professional.

To Chris Davison, for all the cups of tea and listening to my mutterings about fictional people and animals.

To Dylan, for putting up with a weird mother who translates dog body language into complete sentences, song lyrics, and bad poetry, unbidden.

To Jersey May the basset hound, for her soothing snores, spotted belly, and popcorn feet. She is the unpaid mental-health therapist of our household.

NICOLA DAVISON'S first novel, *In the Wake*, won the 2019 Margaret and John Savage First Book Award, the Miramichi Reader's Very Best Book Award for Fiction and was a finalist for the Dartmouth Book Award. A graduate of Dalhousie University and the Alistair MacLeod Mentorship Program, she's an active member of the Writers' Federation of Nova Scotia and can be spotted at most events toting a cumbersome camera. Her meandering path to writing this novel included time working at an animal shelter, several veterinary clinics, and a dog daycare. Now a professional photographer, she lives in Dartmouth with her husband, son, and a stubborn but delightful basset hound who is terrified of cats. She has no idea how to use Morse code. She's not even that good at texting.

nicoladavison.ca